Also by Kerry Hotaling

What They Endured, What They Wrought:
Comparing Regimental Casualties at the Battle of Gettysburg

When you visit the Gettysburg battlefield, you are surrounded by numerous regimental monuments. These were erected in the 1880's and 90's, by survivors of the battle to honor their fallen brethren. This book is a history of some of these regiments and how they fared at the battle. It is the story of the ten highest regiments in the killed in action and percentage loss category. It can be used by the first time visitor or the seasoned Gettysburg sojourner.

What readers have said about
What they Endured, What They Wrought

"...amazing in the details as to what each regiment went through...This is a must read for all Gettysburg enthusiasts." –W. Stewart

"... a great job of bringing into perspective what the soldiers endured while fighting at Gettysburg. Between the great writing style and the inclusion of maps, the book brings the battle to life. A great book for anyone interested in the Battle of Gettysburg or the Civil War in general. Highly recommended." —M. Weiss

"...gave a clearer understanding of the battle from the hottest spots on the battlefield. Not only did it show the damage to the hardest hit units, but the damage they inflicted." —L. Canto

THE YANKEES HAD SOMETHING TO DO WITH IT

KERRY HOTALING

TO: STUART

WELCOME TO CURLING

REGARDS

[signature]

2015

Christopher Matthews Publishing

www.christophermatthewspub.com

Boston, Massachusetts

The Yankees Had Something To Do With It

Editor: Kevin Hotaling, Ryan Evans and Jeremy Soldevilla
Cover design: Neil Noah
Maps: Nikki Walkowicz
Cover illustration: *Battle of Gettysburg,* 1898, by Paul Philippteaux, Library of Congress
Typeface: Georgia, Rosewood Std.

ISBN 978-1-938985-68-3
ebook ISBN 978-1-938985-69-0

Published by
CHRISTOPHER MATTHEWS PUBLISHING
http://christophermatthewspub.com
Boston

Printed in the United States of America

Acknowledgements

Writing a book is a solitary art. Bringing a book to print is the work of many. I have many people to thank for their efforts in making this book better. To the many readers who offered their suggestions I offer my thanks. They include John, Dan, Tom, Kevin and Gerry. Also, thanks to one reader who is a descendent of John Burns, the civilian from Gettysburg who fought beside the Union army on July 1. It was a pleasure to have Tom Burns as a reader for this book.

A special thanks to my editor who did not get to read the book for enjoyment, but to point out errors with a fresh eye. My son, Kevin, undertook this job and I owe him special thanks, along with a cigar and a beer. Tremendous job. Now you may read the book for pleasure and get to enjoy the story.

Another special thanks to my map maker, Nikki Walkowicz. She redrew many maps until I was satisfied and did it without complaint. By the time she was finished, she stated she could draw the Gettysburg map from memory. Her maps add immeasurably to the book. Nikki, you have my deepest gratitude.

The three maps depicting the battle on July 1 are based on similar maps from the book by Bradley Gottfried entitled *The Maps of Gettysburg*. This is one of my favorite books on the battle and an excellent source for anyone wishing to know more about the battle. I sent copies of my hand-drawn maps to Mr. Gottfried. He has given me permission to use these maps in this book. He has encouraged me in the writing of this book and wished me well. I thank him for his cooperation.

The last kudo goes to my publisher, Christopher Matthews Publishing and its editor, Jeremy Soldevilla, who read the whole manuscript and said they would be thrilled to publish my book. On their website is this quote from Richard Bach, "A professional writer is an amateur who didn't quit". This is so very true. I have the numerous rejection letters to prove this point. Thank you so much for taking a chance on this unknown author.

I am an early riser, so most of this book was written between the hours of 4 and 8 a.m. on Saturday and Sunday, while my family slept. I thank them for being late sleepers. Being a book on Gettysburg, it was not work, but a labor of love.

To paraphrase Michael and Jeff Shaara, this is a book of fiction. It does not intend to tell the whole history of the battle of Gettysburg. There are many books that cover the historical aspects of Gettysburg. All the characters found in this book are historical people who were at Gettysburg. This book presents the battle of Gettysburg in a story form. It is my hope you will be drawn into the story and get a sense of what these men experienced and the decisions they made as the battle unfolded before them. All the dialogue is of course fictional, but it is based on the post battle writings of all involved.

If this is your first venture with any Gettysburg book, perhaps you will be inspired to visit Gettysburg. It is well worth the journey.

I would be remiss if I did not mention two books that have come before this and are excellent stories in their own right. The first is *The Killer Angels,* by Michael Shaara. A portion of this book covers General Buford's fight on the morning of July 1 northwest of Gettysburg and I had to be careful not to duplicate the fine efforts of Mr. Shaara. The second book is *Cain at Gettysburg,* by Ralph Peters. General Meade's meeting with General Hooker on the morning of June 28 is well written. Reading these two books along with my story will give one many facets of the battle seen through the eyes of the participants.

Lastly, I would like to express my thanks to my wife Carol. She slept as I wrote and has been supportive of my writing. It's just beyond the next bend!

Kerry Hotaling

Contents

FOREWORD

IN APRIL 1863, General Joseph Hooker, commander of the Army of the Potomac, moved four corps to the northwest along the Rappahannock River. His intention was to cross the river at three different fords and get behind the army of Northern Virginia, encamped on the high ground west of the town of Fredericksburg. Hooker would then march these four corps east on different roads, until they arrived in the rear of General Lee's army. Hooker's plan was to trap Lee's army against the Rappahannock River and hopefully help expedite the end of the Civil War.

Hooker's plan began well as his four corps crossed the river from April 27 to April 29 and proceeded to a town known as Chancellorsville. On April 30, a fifth corps arrived to bolster troop strength to 75,000 men. On May 1, Hooker sent orders to his five corps commanders to proceed east to Fredericksburg. None of these four got close to Fredericksburg. General Lee learned of Hooker's flank movement and sent approximately 26,000 troops west to block Hooker's advance. This small force thwarted Hooker's advance and he ordered his troops to retreat to Chancellorsville and occupy the entrenchments around the town they had left in the morning.

On May 2, Lee divided his forces yet again and sent General Stonewall Jackson, with approximately 13,000 men, to march around the Army of the Potomac and attack them in the rear. This attack surprised Hooker's army and they ended up fighting on the defensive against a smaller force until they retreated north across the Rappahannock River by May 4th.

Hooker attempted to lay the blame for the defeat at the feet of some of his subordinates, which incensed his corps commanders. Here is where this story begins.

General Joseph Hooker—Commander of the Army of the Potomac. He was promoted to this position in January 1863 after the defeat of the army at Fredericksburg. After the battle, Hooker led a revolt against his former commander, General Ambrose Burnside that was successful in having him removed from his position. Joseph Hooker was the replacement and became the new man at the top. He graduated from West Point in 1837, twenty-ninth out of fifty cadets. He saw action in the Mexican War and was awarded three brevet promotions to the rank of lieutenant colonel for his gallantry. In August 1861, he was appointed a brigadier general in the Army of the Potomac after the Civil War broke out. He was a division commander at Second Bull Run and became a corps commander at Antietam.

General Daniel Butterfield—Chief of Staff of Army of the Potomac. Graduated from Union College in 1849. He joined the New York Militia and when the Civil War broke out was a colonel in the Twelfth New York Militia. Through political connections was commissioned a brigadier general in September 1861. When Hooker was named commander, he appointed Butterfield as his Chief of Staff.

General John Reynolds—Major General in command of the First Corps. He graduated from West Point in 1837, twenty-sixth out of fifty cadets. Fought in the Mexican War and received two brevet promotions to the rank of captain. During the Civil War was appointed brigadier general in August 1861. He led troops during the Seven Days' Battle, Second Bull Run and was promoted to commander of the First Corps in September 1862. He was secretly engaged to a young woman named Kate Hewitt. He was a Protestant and she was a Catholic, so they kept the engagement secret from their families. They would not announce their intentions until this war was over.

General Abner Doubleday—Major General commanding the Third Division of the First Corps. He graduated from West Point in 1842, twenty-fourth out of fifty-six cadets. He fought in the Mexican War. He was second in command at Fort Sumter in April 1861 when Confederate forces fired on the fort in Charleston Harbor. He saw action at Second Bull Run and Antietam. He was promoted to commander of the Third Division in January 1863. His division saw little action at Chancellorsville, so Doubleday had not had a chance to lead his men in combat.

General Darius Couch—Major General in command of the Second Corps. He graduated from West Point in 1846, thirteenth out of fifty-nine cadets. He fought in the Mexican War. He resigned his commission in 1855 and began life as a private citizen, working in various business ventures. When the Civil War broke out he was appointed a colonel in command of the Seventh Massachusetts Infantry. In August he was promoted to a brigade commander and by the spring of 1862 was in charge of a division. Promoted to Major General in July of 1862, he was the most senior officer in the Army of the Potomac behind Hooker. He led the Second Corps into combat at Fredericksburg and Chancellorsville.

General Winfield Scott Hancock—Major General in command of the First Division, Second Corps. He graduated from West Point in 1844, eighteenth out of twenty five cadets. He fought in the Mexican War. During the Peninsula Campaign in 1862, he led a brigade into combat and was noted for his work by General McClellan in a telegraph that stated"Hancock was Superb today." This led to the nickname of Hancock the Superb. He was promoted to Major General in November 1862 and led a division at Fredericksburg and Chancellorsville.

General Dan Sickles—Major general in command of the Third Corps. A New York City lawyer with a somewhat checkered background. He was voted to Congress in 1856. He shot the lover of his wife, Philip Barton Key (son of Francis Scott Key, author of The Star Spangled Banner) in broad daylight on a street in Washington, D.C. His attorneys sought his innocence using a plea of "temporary insanity." He was found not guilty, but found his political career suffered.

When the war broke out he raised an entire brigade from New York and was commissioned a Brigadier General after the first battle of Bull Run in 1861. In November 1862, he was promoted to Major General and led a division at Fredericksburg. He was appointed commander of the Third Corps in February 1863, by his friend General Hooker.

General George Meade—Major general in command of the Fifth Corps. He graduated from West Point in 1832 in the upper third of his class. He was an engineer who designed and helped build lighthouses on the coast, which still stand today. He was a devoted family man, with a wife and seven children. He commanded a brigade during the peninsular campaign and at Second Bull Run. At the battle of Antietam, he was in command of a division, but was promoted to command of the First Corps when General Joseph Hooker was wounded and unable to continue during the battle. He led a division at Fredericksburg, the only Union army division to penetrate the Confederate line. He led the Fifth Corps at Chancellorsville.

General John Sedgwick—Major General commanding the Sixth Corps. He graduated from West Point in 1837. He saw action in the Mexican War where he was promoted three times for valor. He saw action in the peninsular campaign and was promoted to Major General in July 1862. He led a division at Antietam and Fredericksburg. In February 1863 was put in charge of the Sixth Corps. He was loved by his men, who dubbed him"Uncle John".

General Oliver Howard—Major General in command of the Eleventh Corps. Graduated from Bowdoin College intending to be a teacher. Was offered an appointment to West Point, which he accepted. He graduated in 1854, fourth in his class. A deeply religious man, he began studying theology to enter the ministry. When the war broke out he devoted his energies to the cause of the Union. He was a lieutenant when the Civil War broke out in 1861. By September he was promoted to Brigadier General and put in command of a brigade, which he led during the peninsular campaign. He led another brigade at Antietam, in General Sedgwick's division. When Sedgwick was injured, Howard took control of the division. He led this division at Fredericksburg. In April 1863 was given command of the Eleventh Corps. Only thirty-two years, he was the youngest Major General in the Army of the Potomac. His corps was routed at Chancellorsville by General Jackson.

General Henry Slocum—Major General in command of the Twelfth Corps. He graduated from West Point in 1852, seventh out of a class of forty-three cadets. He left the army in 1857 to begin a career in law. After Fort Sumter, he rejoined the army as a colonel with the 27th New York Volunteers. In October 1861 was given command of a brigade. In May 1862 was put in charge of the First Division of the Sixth Corps. In July 1862 was promoted to Major General and after Antietam was made commander of the Twelfth Corps. He led this corps at Fredericksburg and Chancellorsville.

General Gouverneur Warren—Brigadier General who was chief topographical engineer. He graduated from West Point in 1850, second in a class of forty-four cadets. When the war broke out, Warren was a mathematics instructor at West Point. He raised a regiment and was named colonel of the 5th New York Infantry. He commanded the regiment through the siege of Yorktown then he led a brigade through the Seven Days Battles. He was promoted to Brigadier General on September 1862. He led a brigade at Fredericksburg. In February 1863, General Hooker named Warren his chief topographical engineer.

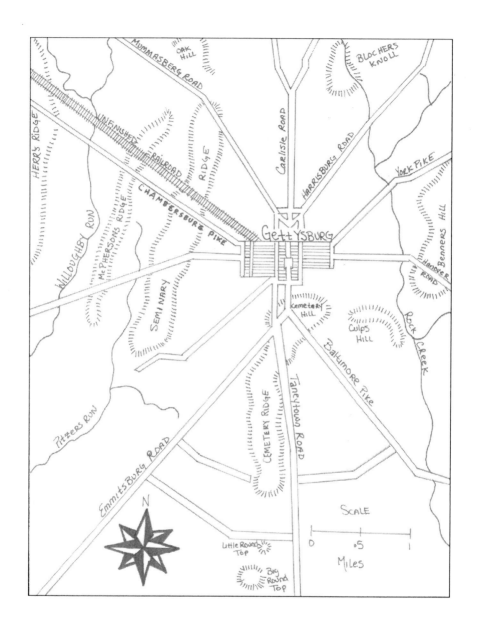

PART I
A GENERAL REVOLT

CHAPTER 1

May 1863

THE PLAN HAD BEEN BRILLIANT. General Hooker had surprised Lee with his wide flanking movement. Fighting Joe Hooker had successfully moved to the west, crossed the Rappahannock and Rapidan rivers at three separate fords, and had the Rebel army trapped. What had gone wrong? General Slocum, in command of the Twelfth Corps in the Army of the Potomac, pondered this question as he rode. The recent defeat at Chancellorsville had been unfathomable. The flanking movement, which had surprised the Rebel forces, was somehow squandered and what started as a promising campaign had been turned into yet another bitter defeat at the hands of General Lee.

Hooker had lost his nerve. Hooker was in over his head. Hooker was drunk. This was the gossip going around the army. Yes, this was Hooker's first engagement as commander of the army. The responsibility was vastly greater than being a division or corps commander, But why did it seem the Rebel forces had the better man at the top?

Slocum was riding with a few of his staff to the Fifth Corps to speak with their commander, George Meade. Slocum had talked with other generals and the consensus seemed almost unanimous. Hooker had to go. How quickly the tables had turned. Four months earlier, after another debacle by the Union army at Fredericksburg, General Hooker had been at the center of a movement to have General Burnside replaced as commander of the Army of the Potomac. Hooker had succeeded, maybe more than he anticipated, for he became the next general to command the army and try to muster a victory against General Lee.

The riders reached the outer pickets of the camp. A sentry spoke,"Good morning, General. What is your business?"

"I am General Slocum of the Twelfth corps. I wish to speak with your commanding officer, General Meade."

As he and his staff were lead to Meade's tent, Slocum wondered how this meeting would go. Meade was known for his quick temper. This meeting might unleash it, but it was too late to turn back. Slocum had the backing of other corps commanders and now he would present the argument to Meade.

"Henry, what brings you around?" spoke General Meade as he came out of the tent.

"Walk with me, George. We need to talk."

"Would you care to come into the tent to speak on matters?"

"No! We need to be away from prying ears. We have matters of utmost importance to discuss."

General Meade had a notion the topic to be discussed involved General Hooker. He may have been fighting Joe Hooker before the recent battle, but in the eyes of George Meade and other generals, the nickname did not apply anymore. Meade had heard all the scuttlebutt and gossip. It permeated the air, as thick as the smell of coffee around the campfires. The President and General Halleck had arrived at Falmouth, army headquarters, to have a conference with General Hooker. Could it be the commanding general was in danger of being removed and replaced?

They walked to a spot away from their aides. Slocum spoke first."George, I'm here at the behest of others to tell you there is a movement to oust Hooker and to have you put in command of the army."

"Henry, this is damned preposterous! I'm outranked by many of the corps commanders. You're senior to me in rank. As much as we disdain that damned Hooker, we are soldiers . . ."

Slocum cut him off,"I have the backing of Darius and Uncle John, both senior to you. I myself would back you. We're ready to present your name to Halleck as the man we want to lead this army. Word is John Reynolds is ready to back you. Hooker has made a mess of things, and with his recent address to the men . . . Well, you heard how he tried to deflect blame from himself for the debacle, instead pinning the defeat on Howard, Sedgwick and Stoneman! The man is despicable and has no business leading this army anymore."

Yes, Meade had heard of Hooker's rants, and he could not disagree with Slocum's assessment. However, being considered for command was news to Meade. General Darius Couch of the Second Corps was a fine old soldier. He was the ranking general, and if anyone was to take command it should be Couch. Uncle John—General John Sedgwick of the Sixth Corps. Here was a general who was beloved by his men. And Henry of the Twelfth Corps, all senior to Meade and all willing to be subordinate to him.

"Damn it all to Hell, Henry, what makes you all think I'm capable or willing to take on the responsibility of command? I've been in command of a corps for one engagement. This does not give me the experience others have to lead an army."

"You proved your mettle at Fredericksburg. Yours was the only division to garner any success. You broke through that tough Rebel line and even though you were forced back, everyone saw what you did. We had Lee flanked at Chancellorsville and could have crushed him if Hooker had not lost his nerve and called off the attack."

Meade had similar thoughts. His corps had been one portion of the flanking march and had got in behind the Rebel army. He was leading his corps easterly on River Road on May 1, being the northerly wing of a three-pronged attack against the rear of the Rebel army. But Fighting Joe Hooker froze and was turned into Timid Joe Hooker. He called off the attack when the middle prong ran into resistance. Damn that man. Slocum was not saying anything about Hooker that could not be heard in any corps headquarters. A majority of the generals had lost faith in Hooker.

"What about that damned rascal Sickles, is he in on this?" Meade blurted out.

"No. We're staying away from Sickles. He is firmly entrenched in Hooker's camp. Hooker promoted him to corps command. I do believe he takes delight in the camp girls Hooker has staying near his headquarters. They are calling them Hooker's girls."

Before he could continue, Meade cut him off."We're not the French rabble. We are soldiers in the United States Army. We took an oath upon leaving West Point and those that wear the blue uniform mean to uphold that oath. That damn Sickles bought his way into the army and his promotions are nothing more than political pandering. I'm not sure we should be going around telling Mr. Lincoln who should be running his army." He felt he could not take part in this plot. It went against all he believed."Henry, I mean no disrespect here. I'm in agreement with many others who have lost faith in that damned Hooker. I cannot accept your plan to nominate me to be head of this army. It is the job of others to decide who will be in charge of the Army of the Potomac!"

There, he had said it and he felt a weight lift off his shoulders. He wanted no part in this insubordination. This was an army. There had to be discipline. It was imperative that he and the other generals uphold this discipline.

Slocum stared at the ground for a moment. Then looking up and out toward the horizon, he said,"I'm sorry you feel this way. We need a firm and confident hand to lead this army. With your background in engineering many of us thought you would be a wise choice. We will not pursue this any further without your blessing. We all feel Hooker needs to go. No one has any confidence to follow him into battle. Take care of yourself, George."

"You too, Henry. I just want to get this damned war over and get back to my family."

ৎ৵৵৺৻ঌ

Later that day, Meade was alone in his tent. Many thoughts whirled through his brain. Hooker was a problem, but he, George Meade, would not take part in any attempt to have Hooker replaced. It was just not how he did things. Meade was an engineer. He was happiest building lighthouses on the coast. He was a family man and missed his family. He took up a pen and wrote home to his wife. He wrote of his encounter with General Slocum and explained he would not join in any movement against Hooker.

George then put down words to show his disgust for General Hooker . . ."I see the papers attribute Hooker's withdrawal to the weak councils of his corps commanders. This is a base calumny. These last operations have shaken the confidence of the army in Hooker's judgment, particularly among the superior officers." He wrote of camp life and then asked how things at home were going. Home. His heart was there. He was certain no one missed their home and family more than he did. Meade signed the letter and prepared it for delivery.

CHAPTER 2

GENERAL COUCH COULD NOT BELIEVE what he heard. Lincoln and Halleck had left Falmouth and returned to Washington, leaving Hooker in command of the army. Hooker was not going to be replaced. This was a travesty. The news from General Slocum did not brighten his disposition. George Meade had refused the offer to have his name forwarded for command of the army. His head was pounding from the stress. This much he was certain of, he would not serve under General Hooker. The man was not fit to lead this army. That son of a bitch was nothing but a braggart and a shameless self-promoter. He showed his true colors by deflecting blame for the defeat away from himself and onto others. This was intolerable. As Couch saw it, the defeat was squarely on Hooker's shoulders. He lost his nerve and called off the attacks on May 1. The other corps commanders, with the exception of General Sickles, felt as Couch did. They spoke of it with each other. But what could he do? The president and General Halleck had spent the day at headquarters and for some unknown reason to him, had left with Hooker still in command.

He went for a walk. He would pound the dirt with his boots, hoping to alleviate some of the pounding in his head. Walking helped him think. Perhaps it was the blood moving around, but he always found walking to be helpful. He could smell bacon cooking and coffee brewing. These were the smells of camp life amongst the army. He would remember these smells long after the war. The men had not failed. Their spirits seemed strong. No, he repeated to himself, the men had not failed. But their commander had failed them. The battle had been a dreadful performance at the top. Couch could not let these soldiers continue to be lead by that son of a bitch named Joe Hooker!

A plan was formulating in his head. It may be ruinous to his career, but it may be the only way to let those at the top see how dire the situation was.

He was a veteran of the Mexican War. That was a war. The army had excellent commanders at the top and their strategies defeated the Mexican army on their own soil. He was proud to have been a small part of that war. But this war was being directed by politicians. Commanding generals were being changed quicker than shoes on a cavalry horse. How is an army supposed to succeed if strategies and generals are thrown out and replaced by seemingly more incompetent fellows? None of this was taught at West Point.

He would draft a letter to the President and spell out his plan and damn the consequences. The army deserved better than Joe Hooker as their commander. He would ask to be relieved of his command in the Army of the Potomac, for he was unwilling to serve any longer under General Hooker. There were good division commanders in the Second Corps ready to replace him as corps commander. He thought of Winfield Hancock. McClellan had dubbed him"Hancock the Superb". It was said he could walk into a camp in civilian clothes, start giving orders and the army would obey without questioning him. This was a trait very few possessed. Hancock was ready to lead the Second Corps, Couch thought.

As he continued his walk, it felt right. The army was more important than himself. If he was to be sacrificed, so be it. He got back to the headquarters tent and asked for a cup of coffee.

"After you bring the coffee, I wish not to be disturbed," he told his aide."I have important correspondence to attend to."

"Yes, sir," the aide replied. He delivered the coffee and left the tent.

Chancellorsville

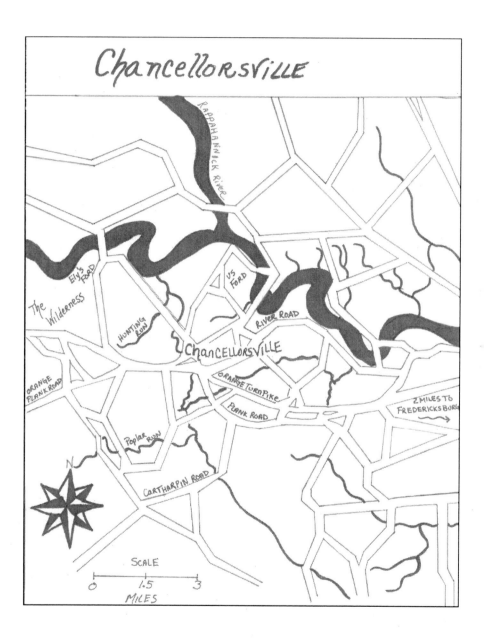

CHAPTER 3

GOVERNOR ANDREW CURTIN OF PENNSYLVANIA arrived in Falmouth to hear for himself about the defeat at Chancellorsville. He knew both General Meade and General Reynolds. They were from his home state and each commanded a corps in the recent campaign. He wanted to hear their views of the battle first hand. Rumors were running rampant in Washington. It was good to get away. This would be a fact-finding mission. How was the morale of the men? What did the officers think of General Hooker?

He was in the First Corps camp and lead to headquarters. General Reynolds met him outside of his tent."Welcome governor. I hope the trip down was pleasant. What brings you to the front?"

"John, good to see you are well. I am here to see for myself how things stand. The papers talk of another rout of the army. How is your corps?"

"The corps is in very good shape. We saw very little action, so casualties were extremely light. We did not even cross the Rappahannock River until May 2. Our orders were to put the river on our right and extend our line south. We were guarding the right of the army. Hooker did not want the rebels to get around us," Reynolds hesitated."There are harsh words being spoken about Hooker. Come into the tent and we can talk more. May I offer you anything?"

"Coffee would be welcome," said the Governor.

They entered the tent and sat down. Coffee was bought in and the two were left alone.

The Governor started the conversation."Rumors are abundant in Washington, which I am sure you can imagine. The papers say Hooker will be replaced. There is even talk of bringing McClellan back for a third time. What is going on John?"

"The officers have lost total confidence in Hooker's ability to command. Sickles, who owes his corps command to Hooker, is the only general who will stand with him. From what I have heard, Hooker seemed to have lost his nerve and called off an attack on May 1." He did not live up to the name he was dubbed, Fighting Joe Hooker, thought Reynolds. What was it about squaring off against Lee that seemed to unnerve the generals that led the Army of the Potomac? First, there was McDowell, then McClellan, Pope, McClellan again, Burnside and now Hooker. Was there anyone capable of leading this army?

The governor interrupted his thoughts,"John, I have heard many of these reports. I am here to see how true they are. It seems Hooker is on the hot seat in Washington and from what you are saying, here in Falmouth also. What can you tell me of the campaign and the May 1 attack?"

"Come over to the table. You will understand the campaign better seeing the lay of the land." Reynolds led the governor to a map sitting on a table. Fredericksburg was toward the right side of the map. The Rappahannock River meandered from the northwest to the southeast. The Rapidan River flowed into the Rappahannock from the west, north of the town of Chancellorsville. The governor studied the map as Reynolds continued.

"Hooker left three corps across the river from Fredericksburg to keep Lee and his army in place. He then marched west with four corps, attempting to get behind the Rebel army, without being observed. This part of the plan succeeded. On May 1, there was to be a three-pronged attack from the west that would have surrounded the Rebel army. The attack ran into some opposition from the Rebel army on the Orange Turnpike, but nothing that should have deterred the overall advance. For some unknown reason, Fighting Joe" (he couldn't mask the sarcasm in his voice)"called off the attack and ordered all four corps back into a defensive position. This did not sit well with the corps commanders. They voiced their opposition to this move, but Hooker would not relent. General Meade was part of that attack and he has some harsh words about Hooker calling it off. I have spoken with him and I suggest you do the same."

Curtin stared at the map as he listened. He saw the soundness of the plan. The Rebel army would have been caught in a vice. What would have caused Hooker to call off the attack? He needed to speak with others before he returned to Washington.

"I intend to do that, John." The governor paused a moment. He was not sure how his next suggestion would be taken, but it seemed the right time to ask."Are you aware there are those who are proposing that you be offered command of the army?"

Reynolds looked sternly at Curtin and spoke,"I will not accept any talk of being offered command. It seems to me that Washington interferes too much with the commander in the field. Cover Washington, cover Harpers Ferry, yet seek and attack the Rebel army. It is no way to fight a war. I mean no disrespect governor, but the demands from Washington seem to handcuff anyone put in command. If you are looking for someone to replace Hooker, George Meade would be my recommendation."

This statement caught the governor off guard. There were many corps commanders with seniority over General Meade, yet here was Reynolds putting his name forward to be considered for command. He would think on this.

"The coffee was good. I would like to visit with George. Would you direct me to his headquarters?" asked the governor.

"I will have an aide take you there."

ॐ੪)(୪ॐ

As he rode to Fifth Corps headquarters, Governor Curtin went over all he had heard from General Reynolds. Things seemed more dire than he had thought. Perhaps the talk around Washington was not that far off the mark. Fighting Joe Hooker had been spooked enough to call off a well-planned attack. He would hear what General Meade had to say. George was another Pennsylvania man. George had been in command of the Fifth Corps at Chancellorsville and from what Reynolds had told him, was leading the northern prong of the attack on May 1. George had been in the front and would be able to speak of the attack first hand. It would be good for the governor to get an account from a source, who was both in the fight and whom was a trusted General from his own state, Pennsylvania.

They were stopped briefly by guards as they entered the camp. Official words were exchanged. They were given a rider who would lead them to General Meade's tent. They came to a halt outside of the headquarters tent. In a moment, General Meade stepped out.

"Governor, it is good to see you. What brings you out here?" George asked.

"It's a beautiful time of the year to get out for a ride in the country. Washington can be a bit stifling at times. I am out on a fact-finding tour. Is there a place we can talk candidly?"

"We will speak in my tent. May I offer you anything?"

"Something cold to wet these parched lips would do just fine."

Curtin dismounted, shook the general's hand and they went into the tent. Inside were a desk and chair, a table with maps and a cot. Cold drinks were delivered and the two were left alone.

Meade spoke first,"I am sure this is not just a joy ride in the country. What facts are you looking for?" He was direct. It was the engineer in him. Let's get to the problem and see what can be done about it.

"I am seeking to find what went wrong at Chancellorsville. Washinton is drowning in rumors. Everyone has an opinion and most of these opinions are formed from here say. I had to get out before the water filled my lungs. I have spoken with General Reynolds. He tells me you were with the flanking movement and were in position to attack the rear of the Rebel army."

Curtin did not want to give away too much of what he knew. He would let Meade speak and compare notes later."What can you tell me of the battle?"

"Governor, I would like to speak off the record. We are just two friends speaking and getting some things off our chest. Agreed?"

Curtin thought a moment. He needed to hear what Meade had to say, but could he keep his word once back in Washington. There were no secrets in that city. Ears were everywhere. Confidences were compromised daily.

"We will speak off the record, George." As Curtin spoke these words, his mind was already in doubt.

"That damned Hooker lost his nerve. He called off a well-planned attack for reasons that confound all who were there."

His temper was rising. He did not know if he would be able to keep it in check. Ah hell, they were speaking off the record. It would be good to get it off his chest.

"General Hooker has disappointed all his friends by failing to show his fighting qualities at the pinch. I think this last operation has shaken the confidence of the army in Hooker's judgment, particularly among the superior officers. Fighting Joe Hooker my ass!" His temper would not be held in check."We had flanked the enemy and were in position to attack his rear. Then, for some inexplicable reason, that bastard Hooker ordered us to stop the attack and retreat to the breastworks we had left that morning. Here was that damned Rebel army caught in a vice and the commanding general just quit. He just quit on his army. It is for this reason the officers have lost confidence in Hooker's ability to lead. I pleaded with him in the field to continue with the attack. I have talked with other corps commanders who told me they did likewise. But Hooker would not change his mind. He ordered us back and put us on the defensive. Come over to the map and I will show you a plan gone to hell."

They walked over to the table. On the table was a well-used map, with dirt smudges, lines showing where it had been folded and what appeared to be some small blood stains. It showed all the signs of having recently been used in the field. Curtin looked at the map and decided it was similar to the one he had seen in Reynolds tent. Now he would hear from a commander who was in the field on May 1. He studied the map as Meade began speaking.

"Here is Chancellorsville to the west of Fredericksburg," said Meade as he pointed to the town on the map."The plan was to march west along three different roads and get to Salem Heights by nightfall on May 1. This would put our forces behind Lee's army, which was dug in on the high ground west of Fredericksburg." Meade pointed to Salem Heights."From this position we would have four corps behind the enemy with the other three corps across the river. Lee would have to attack us or retreat to the south, leaving his entrenchments."

Curtin studied the map as Meade spoke. It appeared to be a solid plan. Why had it gone wrong, he wondered.

Meade continued,"My corps was to march north and east along River Road, proceeding to Bank's Ford, where we would hook up with the rest of the army. They would hook up with our right flank and extend the line south. Slocum's march would take him south and then east along the Orange Plank Road, until it joined the Orange Turnpike."

As Meade spoke, he was pointing out the different roads, so the governor could follow along."General Sykes, of my corps, led his division down the Orange Turnpike, followed by the second corps. He was to meet Slocum at the intersection with Orange Plank Road and proceed east to Salem Heights. We were told by the Bureau of Military Intelligence that

Jackson was still on the heights above Fredericksburg and we should not encounter any forces greater than a rear guard. With three corps, we should have reached Salem Heights by nightfall with scant resistance."

Curtin looked over the map. Salem Heights was to the west of Fredericksburg and appeared to be an excellent point to rendezvous forces and launch an attack. He would allow Meade to continue.

"The woods were thick governor. The locals call them The Wilderness. In some spots we had to march two abreast. Noise was muffled and visibility was poor. We were marching easterly on River Road when sounds of artillery and musketry were heard to the south. We figured General Sykes or General Slocum had encountered some of the enemy's rear guard. We did not even have a sniff of any enemy troops, so we continued towards Banks Ford."

Meade paused for a moment. He rubbed his forehead with his left hand, wondering how much he should tell the governor. This talk was off the record, but how much should he divulge?

Politicians talked and in Washington, ears that were not meant to hear were everywhere. Meade would not say anything here today that he had not already said to Hooker.

Meade continued."I received an order to stop the advance and return my corps to the breastworks around Chancellorsville. I was confused by this order and sent a rider to confirm it."

"I can understand your confusion. Were there any enemy forces in your area?" asked the governor.

"None at all," Meade replied."We could still hear fighting to our south, but the thickness of the woods muffled the sound. We were unaware how heavy any fighting was in that sector. It was my belief we should not be halted by a defending rear guard. When I received word conforming Hooker's orders to retreat, I sent out orders to my two divisional commanders to about face and return to Chancellorsville. There were some damned unhappy generals in my tent that night, wondering what the hell was going on."

"George, did you find out about the fighting in the south?"

"It seems we were given faulty intelligence. General Sykes ran into a well-entrenched division on Orange Turnpike. It was not just a small rear guard. He had to halt his march and get his men into battle formation. He was engaged for nearly two hours and found he was in danger of being cut off as the enemy forces were overlapping his lines both north and south. He sent word back to Hooker of his predicament."

Meade pointed out the position on the map. He waited for the governor to give any sign of acknowledgement. Curtin looked at the map and nodded. Meade continued.

"General Slocum ran into Jackson's corps, which was supposed to be on the heights above Fredericksburg. And to Slocum's surprise, Jackson was advancing and attempting to advance beyond Slocum's right. From everything I can gather, this was the moment Hooker sent out orders to retreat."

"Damn it, governor, everyone tells me we could have fought and held our position. General Sykes may have been hard pressed for a while, but the Second Corps was on the march to his front. Sykes told me he could have held until reinforcements arrived."

Meade took a heavy breath. He looked over the map. He pointed to the defensive positions the army fell back to around Chancellorsville. The initiative had been lost on May 1.

"We sat idle for most of the next day, wondering what Hooker would do. I rode over to see the general and expressed to him we should continue on the offensive and not sit around. We still had four corps in position, prepared for a fight, with two additional corps arriving that day. The commanding general would not move."

The governor spoke."What did the other corps commanders think? Were you able to speak with them before Jackson's attack?"

"We were in close enough proximity to be in contact with each other. Couch and Slocum were in favor of a renewed offensive. We sat and we waited, spending most of the day killing mosquitoes. Fighting Joe Hooker became Immobile Joe Hooker. Stonewall Jackson marched around the army, attacked the right, collapsing our flank and creating havoc."

This still impressed Meade. Jackson had marched his corps around the Union army seemingly undetected. Toward sunset, his corps attacked the unsuspecting Eleventh Corps, a majority of who were eating dinner. The Eleventh were routed, and only darkness saved the Union army.

"One damned Confederate corps caused Hooker to lose his nerve. He ordered the army to retreat behind the Rappahannock River. Imagine pulling up stakes of five corps, roughly 65,000 men and getting them safely across a river, with an enemy in close pursuit, an enemy scenting victory."

Meade paused. He wanted to gather his thoughts. He needed the right words and emphasis to make the governor understand exactly what was being said in the camps. He looked Curtin square in the eye.

"The officers have lost all confidence in that son of a bitch Hooker!"

The words hung heavy in the air and echoed around the tent. They had come from deep inside, from a place that stored rage, a place that needed to be aired out, even for a trained, disciplined general.

Curtin felt the rage. His eyes, locked with those of Meade, could see the anger. He was disturbed. Here was the army, defeated once again and the commanding general lacked the support or confidence of his corps commanders. He had spoken to both Reynolds and Meade. It was quite clear that Hooker was in trouble. A commanding general in trouble was not good for the health of an army.

"George, I thank you for your forthrightness. It was probably good to get it out. Washington is rife with anti-Hooker sentiments now. I have come out here to get the tone from the generals. What I have heard alarms me." Curtin knew this talk was off the record, but certain people in Washington needed to hear this information. He hoped his reports would stay with these people, but his confidence in this prospect was far from certain. However, the news of the officers losing confidence in Hooker had to reach the high command. The situation seemed worse than he had anticipated, but Curtin had spoken with those who had been there. It seemed to him the defeat was squarely on the shoulders of Hooker.

"How is the morale of the army?" asked Curtin.

"The morale seems fine. My commanders have been around the camps and they tell me the men are in good spirits." Meade thought of the aftermath of the debacle at Fredericksburg last December. The army was in bad shape. Morale was non-existent and the men were madder than hornets. Their anger was directed mostly at their leaders. It had been a disaster and the men were the ones who always had to pay the price. Fredericksburg was a senseless slaughter.

"The army is in much better straits than four months ago, governor. They will be ready for the next fight. The officers will do their duty, but I hope it will be under a new commander."

"Thanks for the drink, George. I guess it is time to head back to Washington. I will think on what you have told me. Stay well and keep your head down."

"Yes, sir. I have much to do when this all ends." Meade wanted to say more, but kept these thoughts inside. He wished to be back home with his wife and family. This war had dragged on for two years and there seemed to be no end in sight. Would the country survive, or was the young republic doomed? If the Union was to be split, what would the future hold? These thoughts entered his mind as the war marched on, and the youth of the country were being cut down.

CHAPTER 4

GENERAL DAN BUTTERFIELD HAD JUST LEFT General Hooker's tent. Hooker was in a foul mood and his chief of staff, Butterfield, could understand why. The commander of the Second Corps, General Darius Couch, had sent in his resignation papers to Washington, stating he would no longer serve under General Hooker. Couch had asked to be relieved. The resignation had reached Hooker, and he was being asked from Washington what was going on.

Butterfield had been called to Hooker's tent. He was not prepared for Hooker's angry diatribe. This would not play well in Washington. Hooker was already on the hot seat. Yes, Lincoln and Halleck had come to Falmouth on May 7 to confer with the general, and when they had left, Hooker was still in command, but rumors were circulating. It was bad enough that the New York Herald had called for Hooker's dismissal after the battle with Dan Sickles, from New York, to be his replacement. Butterfield had ordered any future copies of the Herald being delivered to the army to be burned. He was doing what he could to protect Hooker.

Butterfield owed his position to Hooker. When Hooker was named as commanding general, he asked Butterfield to be his chief of staff. Butterfield accepted the appointment. It seemed only fair in his mind after the injustice Burnside had heaped on him. Butterfield was the Fifth Corps commander during the battle of Fredericksburg, and it was his understanding this was a permanent position. Burnside had other notions and replaced him with George Meade after the battle. Meade was a West Pointer and was only senior to him in rank by eight days. Butterfield was now chief of staff and George Meade would have to obey his orders. It was good to have political connections.

Now Hooker was in trouble, which meant Butterfield was also in trouble. If Hooker was replaced, Butterfield's future was uncertain. He had attained a high position, which was not bad for one who had not attended the Point. There was a definite rift between those who had graduated from West Point and those who were politically appointed generals. Butterfield had sensed it and had even lost his corps command due to it.

His assignment from Hooker was short and terse. He was to ride to the Second Corps and tell General Couch that his resignation would not be recognized by Hooker. He was certain Couch would not be happy, but Hooker was in no mood for a revolt by his senior generals. If he could end it here by keeping Couch in command, it would send a powerful message to the other corps commanders that Hooker was still in charge. Butterfield would deliver his order to Couch to help protect his commander and his own job.

~ひ⚭CS~

Butterfield had just left and Darius Couch was alone with his thoughts. It seemed Hooker would not accept his resignation. Hooker was attempting to assert his authority, and at the same time, send a message to the other corps commanders that insubordination would not be tolerated. Couch did not think this was a possibility. Now what was he to do? He would walk over and meet with Hancock. The walk would give him time to think. First Division headquarters was not far away. He told his aides to stay at corps headquarters in case any orders were delivered. The army had been inert since the battle. He did not think any orders would be coming down today.

His senses were filled with the aroma of flowers in bloom. The month of May was a time of rebirth and renewal. Of course, there were the smells of the campfires and food being cooked. It was a perfect time to be out and about.

He was led to General Hancock's tent. He thanked the troops for the escort. Hancock came out to meet him.

"Sir, it is good to see you. Coffee?" asked Hancock.

"Yes, I would like a cup. No cream or sugar, just coffee," Couch responded.

Hancock ordered two coffees to be brought to his tent. They went in and sat down. The flaps were open to let in the spring air.

"What brings you here, General? Orders from the high exalted one?" Hancock said with just a bit of sarcasm. Hancock knew Couch was no supporter of the commanding general.

"Win, I fear the army is in trouble with Hooker at the helm. He is so completely full of himself and he has surrounded himself with similar rapscallions. Butterfield as his chief of staff? Sickles as a corps commander? These are political generals who have no business being in the positions they are in. They say the right things to the press and their political connections, but when it comes to fighting . . . Well, you were at Chancellorsville; I don't have to tell you of their abysmal performance."

The coffee was delivered. Hancock said thanks and told the aides they were relieved. Couch took a sip and felt the warmth pass into his body. Coffee in the field seemed to have its own unique taste.

Hancock took a sip and put the coffee down."General, I am in complete agreement with you about Hooker and the bastards he has put in positions of authority. Hell, Sickles got away with cold-blooded murder. An insanity defense? Right. If he is insane, why in the hell is he in charge of a corps? Can you answer me that one?"

"Good point, Win. Perhaps you could raise this question with Halleck!" Couch chuckled."Perhaps you could be an attorney after this war ends."

"It does not take an attorney to see that common sense has gone out the window. Hooker wanted people around him that would not challenge him. He wanted people who he could drink and carouse with. Those damned girls Hooker has bought in are all the talk. It seems a commanding general has immunity from any form of common sense or decent behavior."

"I am in complete agreement with you, Win. This is the reason I am here. You have been a division commander, and a damned fine one, for eight months. You have led your division superbly for three campaigns. I believe you are ready for corps command. It may be on the horizon." Couch paused for a moment. Hancock did not know of his initial resignation letter. He would hear of it now."Win, I sent in my letter of resignation to Halleck, stating I would not serve under Hooker."

Hancock was momentarily stunned, but recovered to respond before Couch could go on."I am sorry to cut in, sir, but I would rather Hooker be replaced. Hell, Sickles should be sent packing before you go anywhere. You fought in Mexico and have earned your stars. You are needed to help fight this war."

"Now, hear me out, Win. Some of the other corps commanders were ready to sign a petition to have Hooker replaced by George Meade, but Meade would have no part of it. The corps commanders, with the exception of Sickles, are adamant about Hooker needing to go. With Meade out of the picture, no one is willing to step forward, so the movement to have Hooker replaced has died. I cannot let it die. Some action needs to be taken. You are more than ready to take over the Second Corps. My resignation was a notification to Washington that Hooker has to go. My reputation is not important here. The army needs a quality commander and Hooker has failed in all categories."

Hancock interrupted,"They may let you resign and Hooker may put one of his political cronies in charge of the Second Corps. We could be in worse shape."

"I strongly urged Halleck to put you in charge of the Second Corps. That was part of my resignation agreement. However, Hooker has rejected my attempted resignation. He sent Butterfield to me personally to let me know he would not allow it to happen. Hooker still wants to throw his weight around. But I will not be deterred. The army and the country are more important than me. I am here to tell you that I will resend my resignation, Hooker be damned. If I have to be sacrificed to have him replaced, it will be worth it."

Hancock sat and stared at his corps commander. He knew Hooker was in trouble, but was unaware of the movement to have him replaced. He felt a sense of admiration for Couch. Here was a man of honor sitting in front of him, a man whose principles were more important than reputation. It seemed to Hancock that Couch's reputation would not suffer, but would be greatly enhanced by those generals who valued honor and loyalty.

Hancock went to his footlocker and pulled out a flask containing whiskey."General, we shall drink to your service and to better days for the army." He offered the flask to Couch. He nodded his head and then took a long drink. He handed the flask back to Hancock, who threw down some whiskey.

Hancock spoke."You know, General, we may have won this war by now if General Lee had stayed with the Union. He is the best either side has. How much bloodshed could have been spared, we'll never know. He has lost his mansion in Arlington. I am wondering if we have anyone who can beat him." He shook his head. Who was capable of matching Lee? Grant was having some success out West, but he was not fighting against Lee. John Reynolds came to mind.

"I wouldn't mind having Reynolds put in charge. There is one fine general."

Couch responded."I have spoken to John about this. He feels there is too much interference from Washington. Hell of a way to fight a war. John will not accept command of the army unless it is on his terms. Washington will not comply. So Reynolds will stay a corps commander. He probably has the finest corps in the army, with those boys from the Northwest. Rugged frontiersmen all!"

"We have a hell of a corps ourselves, General. I would pit the second against the first any day."

"Well, Win, you'll have a chance to show what the second can do when you assume command. I am serious about this resignation. I will keep submitting it until I get reassigned. Halleck can't keep ignoring my request. He will be forced to overrule Hooker and this corps will be yours. You are more than ready for corps command!"

They sat in silence, lost in their own thoughts. A warm breeze came through the tent. Hancock had great admiration for General Couch and he was honored to have served under him. Couch would leave and Hancock would take over the corps. It would be his first command at that level. He felt sure he was ready.

Couch got up first." I enjoyed the drink. You'll make a fine corps commander. We just cemented it with whiskey. I must take my leave and get back to headquarters. Good luck, and may God go with you."

They shook hands and walked outside the tent. Hancock watched Couch until he grew small on the horizon. Damn, he thought, there goes one of the honorable ones.

CHAPTER 5

DAN BUTTERFIELD WAS OFF to see his friend Dan Sickles. He was in need of some strong drink and a dash of Sickles' philosophical spin. It had been a rough couple of days at headquarters since Hooker's return from Washington on the thirteenth. Hooker went to the capital at the request of President Lincoln. They were to discuss plans for a new offensive. While in Washington, Hooker heard some alarming news from an acquaintance of Governor Andrew Curtin. The governor had been to the White House and told the president of his trip to Falmouth and the loss of confidence in Hooker by most of his corps commanders. The news had stunned Hooker.

Meade and Reynolds, thought Butterfield. Both Pennsylvania men. They were consorting with their governor to put Hooker in a bad light, perhaps to have him replaced. It had been less than six months since Meade had taken over Butterfield's corps. Was Meade seeking to become commander of the army? If Meade took over, he would certainly name his own chief of staff. Imagine being ousted by the same person twice in the same year.

When Hooker had returned from the capital, his first order of business had been a meeting with Meade. Butterfield was thinking about that meeting while riding. It had heated up very quickly. Meade tried to defend himself by stating his words with Curtin had been in confidence. Did he really think his governor would keep his words in confidence? Meade had intentionally spoken these words to plant the seed for Hooker's demise. This would open the path for his ascension to commander of the army. Butterfield saw it all very clearly in his mind.

The meeting got even more heated. Hooker and Meade were both letting it fly and not holding back. Butterfield thought Meade should be written up for insubordination. An army commander should never allow the type of exchange that he had just witnessed. Hooker was too much in ill temper to make any decisions.

If all of this was not bad enough, there was one other item that could be Hooker's undoing. While in Washington, Hooker had demanded Lincoln bring the disgruntled corps commanders to the White House to hear their account of the battle. What was Hooker thinking? This was pure madness. Even their friend and ally Salmon Chase had sent a telegram telling Hooker this was a bad idea. Chase stated each general would have the luxury of hindsight and could offer the president their view of how the battle should have been fought. Each general would tell of their plan that would have won the battle. It is always easier to fight and win after the battle. But during the fight, decisions were made based on information one had at the moment. After the conflict, it was easy to sit back, have a drink and dissect command decisions. Then one could state what should have been done.

Hooker would not be persuaded. The President would meet with these generals and Butterfield saw nothing good that would come from it. He had been doing damage control with Hooker ever since the battle. Now the opposition would have their say with Lincoln. Events were spinning out of control. He had a bad feeling how this would turn out. He needed a drink. He was getting closer to where the Third Corps was camped. He would be led to headquarters and Dan Sickles. Sickles would have plenty to drink.

CHAPTER 6

MEADE WAS WITH REYNOLDS. His meeting with Hooker had not gone well. He had come completely unglued and was certain he would be brought up on charges. As much as he loathed the commander, Meade knew he had crossed a line that generals dared not cross. Perhaps he might be demoted to brigade commander and not end up at the wrong end of a court-martial.

Reynolds interrupted his thoughts, "Things may not be as bad as you think. It sounds like you both got into it pretty good. Just two hard headed generals having a difference of opinion."

"I went too far. I was madder than hell at Curtin for betraying a confidence, and now I was standing in front of this . . . this bastard of a commander who was yelling at me for being insubordinate. It was too much; I snapped and the dam broke."

"You have many more friends at this time than Hooker does. I don't think Hooker will do anything rash. He's in enough trouble. I've received a telegram from the president; He wishes to hear my account of the battle. I'm certainly not going to hold my feelings back about Hooker being the sole cause of our defeat; especially since he publicly blamed the defeat on Sedgwick, Slocum and Stoneman."

Meade spoke,"I received a telegram also, but didn't wish to mention it yet. Thought it was an invitation to my court-martial." He chuckled to himself in relief.

Reynolds shook his head and smiled,"I don't think you're going to any court-martial. I've spoken to other commanders, and they, too, have been beckoned to the White House. Evidently, the president wants to hear many views. Perhaps after we have our say there will be some change at the top. You know, most of us have lost faith in Hooker. I would hate to see this army head into another battle with Hooker in command."

"I'm in full agreement. You'd make a damn fine man at the top John, but I've heard you have no interest."

"I won't command this army until Washington cuts all their interference. Can't fight a war with politicians ordering you here and there as they see fit."

"How about Sedgwick? The word is he is loved by his men. Can you imagine that? I must've slept through that class at West Point."

Reynolds thought of Sedgwick. He was a fine corps commander, but Reynolds did not think he would fare as well at the top. His love of practical jokes would not play well as an army commander. Reynolds had reservations about Sedgwick being promoted, but it was not in his nature to speak poorly about other generals, except for Hooker.

"Uncle John is certainly loved by his men," said Reynolds. "I'm not sure he is ready to be at the top just yet. I've heard there is talk of putting you in charge. You'd have my blessing."

Meade put his hand up. "Not a chance. I've been a corps commander for one battle, damn it. That does not qualify me for army command. There are many with far more experience at corps command. They also outrank me. Would they be willing to see me vault over them? I just don't see it in the cards."

"From what I'm hearing, it's those same generals who outrank you that are willing to have you at the top. Word got to me that you were approached by some of these generals and you turned them down. Something about you not wishing to take part in any insubordination. I guess you forgot to heed your own advice when conversing with Hooker." Reynolds attempted, but could not hold the laugh inside.

Meade couldn't help but laugh. "Nice shot!"

The laughter was cathartic for Meade. Inner tensions were loosened. Maybe Reynolds was right. Lincoln would hear accounts from different generals about Chancellorsville. Couch, Slocum, Sedgwick and Howard had all spoken ill of Hooker since the battle. If they held true to their convictions and continued with their anti-Hooker sentiments before Lincoln . . . well, maybe Lincoln would have no choice but to replace Hooker. But who would get the nod? The one most capable, John Reynolds, did not seem interested. Would Meade be willing to take command? He thought of the honor, but also the weight. Would his name be mentioned to Lincoln during the upcoming meetings? He was sure the president would be seeking opinions about whom the generals might consider for command. He thought of his duty as a soldier and realized if selected, he would do his duty as best he could. It was all he could do, all he had ever done during this war.

Many soldiers would soon be mustered out. Two-year enlistments and nine-month volunteers would be leaving the army in May and June."John, I'm losing thirteen regiments to expiring enlistments. Hell of a way to run a war. I don't get to go home!"

"We're all losing units, George. I'm losing a brigade of nine-month volunteers and another brigade is seeing three of its four regiments leave. There will be some reorganization. It is a hell of a way to fight a war, as you say. I can understand the two-year terms. When they signed up in 1861, no one foresaw the war would still be raging when their terms expired. We all believed one great fight would put down the rebellion. I don't understand signing men for nine-month enlistments. Just about the time they're trained and arriving at camp, it's time to muster them out. We might get one good fight out of them."

"I can't understand nine-month enlistments either. Well, we don't make policy, we just fight with the damned hand they deal us. They want nine-month enlistments, so they must have a good reason for it."

"And we're to put together an army with whatever reasons they come up with. Again, hell of a way to fight a war," added Reynolds."It won't be easy planning any new campaign. Regiments will be leaving, new ones will arrive from wherever and corps will be realigned. Perhaps that is why there is no talk of any new movements. I wonder what Mr. Lee has planned."

Meade thought for a moment. It had been eerily quiet. The army is most often awash in rumors, but recently this was not the case. There was some talk that casualties in the Rebel army had been high at Chancellorsville. Stonewall Jackson had even been shot. There was no word of his condition

He spoke,"You know John, we may have put a hurting on Lee and his army. No telling the shape they're in. Could be they are sitting across the river licking their wounds instead of moving. I've got to get back to my corps. Thanks for the talk."

"Keep your spirits up, I don't think a court-martial is in your future," said Reynolds."We'll have our chat with Mr. Lincoln and see where it leads."

CHAPTER 7

GENERAL BUTTERFIELD PERCHED on a rock by a gently moving stream. Water tumbled over several rocks into a small pool. The sound was soothing. It took him back to his youth in Utica, New York, and time spent fishing. He took a puff from a cigar, held it in his mouth and blew the smoke out slowly. It had a relaxing effect. He had left headquarters for some solace. Things were not going well. Lincoln had met with the disgruntled generals. His contacts had informed him they all laid the blame for the defeat at Chancellorsville squarely on Hooker. He had lost his nerve, they had said.

Damn it, he thought, Sykes had reported he was in trouble on May 1. The Rebel army was overlapping both ends of his line. Slocum had sent back reports that Jackson's corps was slipping around him and attempting to outflank him. Hooker had ordered them all back on May 1, so the army could regroup. The intelligence he had received concerning the whereabouts of the Rebel army had been quite faulty. Hooker had to amend plans while fighting. Howard was ordered to face his men west, but he did a poor job of this, leaving his flank exposed. Jackson chewed up that exposed flank on May 2 and collapsed the right wing of the army. Hooker was making plans to bolster up his defensive positions when a shell exploded nearby, knocking him down. Suffering from a concussion, he was taken from the field. What did all this have to do with a loss of nerve? Hooker was responding to the reports he was receiving from his field generals. He was protecting the army on May 1 when he ordered the retreat. And now these generals had turned on him, saying he lacked nerve and was fully responsible for the defeat at Chancellorsville. Damn hypocrites!

Butterfield felt the blood rush to his head. The rage was increasing as he thought on matters. He took another puff from his cigar. It helped the anger settle a bit.

General Couch was another sore spot. After Hooker had refused his request for a transfer, Couch continued with his undermining ways and wrote another official request. This one was granted. Was this type of subterfuge taught at West Point? Hell, Butterfield would have fired them all and promoted men who supported their commander. Hooker had been warned by many that allowing Lincoln to speak with these generals would be a recipe for disaster. How right they were.

Well, can't change what has been done. The question he pondered was whether the damage would be harmful. There was silence from Washington on the matter.

He took one last puff on the cigar. With his forefinger, he flicked it into the moving water and watched it ride the current downstream.

CHAPTER 8

HANCOCK RECEIVED THE NEWS on May 22nd that he was to assume command of the Second Corps. Couch had followed through with his conviction to get transferred away from Hooker. This time, his superiors, even Hooker, accepted the transfer. Couch was true to his word. This was a trait Hancock respected highly. Hancock was certain this did not play well at headquarters. There would be some colorful language spewing from Hooker's mouth.

It was too bad Hooker was staying and Couch was leaving. Hancock would have preferred an opposite outcome. Couch had handled the Second Corps magnificently at Chancellorsville; setting up a defensive perimeter around the Chancellor House to hold off the enemy army so the Union forces could retreat across the Rappahannock River. Couch had saved Hooker's ass. Hancock was not sure how the army would fare in the next fight with Hooker still at the helm.

His first order of business was to name the new First Division commander, his recent command. If he wished to keep the appointment within his corps, he had three viable candidates to choose from, Brigadier General John Caldwell, Brigadier General Samuel Zook and Colonel John Brooke. With Brooke being only a colonel, he was quickly dismissed in Hancock's mind. Caldwell and Brooke both had some stains on their records leading men in battle. Neither of them had gone to West Point, so they were learning on the job. This could account for these blemishes.

Caldwell had earned his star in April 1862, making him senior to Zook. Caldwell had fought well at Chancellorsville, carrying out Hancock's orders and making necessary adjustments in his sector of the fighting. Perhaps his apprenticeship was over and he was now ready for higher command. Caldwell would be in a hard spot, for Hancock knew the other brigadiers would inform him of any poor decisions made by Caldwell. It was natural to make comparisons to the previous commander. Human nature was also part of this equation. One or two of the brigade commanders would have their nose bent out of shape that Caldwell was promoted over them, feeling they were more qualified. They damn well better get over it, Hancock thought! As corps commander, he could keep an eye on Caldwell and move in to adjust battle lines if necessary.

He would appoint John Caldwell as commander of the First Division of the Second Corps of the Army of the Potomac. The order would be written and sent forward up the chain of command. As usual, Hancock acted quickly and decisively. He was not one to labor long over matters.

There was still no word from headquarters concerning any movement for the army. He was not sure what Hooker was planning. He would not care to be in Hooker's shoes now. Hooker had bungled the last battle. In his after battle reports he blamed some of his commanders for the defeat, when they knew the fault lay with Hooker. Couch had been openly insubordinate stating in his letter for reassignment his distaste for Hooker. How would this army fight in any new campaign with all this controversy swirling through the air? Hancock shook his head as he pondered this.

There were other concerns on the horizon. His corps would be losing nine regiments of soldiers as enlistments ran out for two-year volunteers and nine-month enlistees. Hell of a way to run an army, he said to himself. This was equivalent to two brigades that would need replacing. It is hard to maintain the effectiveness of an army when whole regiments of battle-hardened veterans get to muster out at the same time. Every raw recruit is anxious to get into battle and kill some Southern boys, but until one stands toe to toe with other soldiers and faces enemy fire from both infantry and artillery, will anyone be able to know how combat will affect them? Hancock hated to lose this much experience. He didn't make policy, so this was beyond his control. He would train his troops and have them ready for the rigors and demands of battle.

ஒ௸ௐ௸௭

The month of May came to a close. The opposing armies were encamped along the Rappahannock River. The Army of the Potomac was on the northerly side, while the Army of Northern Virginia was on the southerly side. Neither army seemed anxious to move.

There was turmoil among the Union commanders. It was still uncertain if Hooker would lead them in the next campaign. He did not have their confidence, and there was no sign from Washington that he would be replaced.

The war had been dragging on for two years. It was becoming increasingly unpopular in the North. Their army had suffered many defeats in Virginia and their young men were dying in droves. Peace movements were arising. There was open talk of making peace with the South. This would split the country. The young republic was in trouble.

Chapter 9

June 1863

IT WAS JUNE SECOND. John Reynolds was riding away from the White House, after a meeting with the president. Lincoln had summoned Reynolds to the house on Pennsylvania Avenue. He thought of how tired Mr. Lincoln looked. The war seemed to be aging this man considerably. He had been in office a little over two years, but his face had the appearance of being twenty years older. Reynolds had the weight of a corps upon his shoulders, while the president was burdened with the weight of holding the country together. Reynolds could only imagine how heavy this burden was.

Lincoln had come right out and asked Reynolds if he would be willing to replace Hooker as commander of the Army of the Potomac. Reynolds had explained the conditions under which he would command. The strings to Washington needed to be cut. He wanted no interference from the president or the secretary of war. He felt the war could not be won if Washington were calling the shots.

His conditions did not sit well with the president. Reynolds was undeterred. He would only command under his terms. He emphasized to Lincoln the failings of General Hooker and the need for him to be relieved. He mentioned Meade's name as an acceptable replacement. Many of the corps commanders would back Meade. Lincoln had a rather odd response to this. Reynolds remembered Lincoln saying something about a gun misfiring. How had Lincoln put it;"I am not willing to throw away a gun because it misfired once. I would pick the lock and give it another try." Was he contemplating leaving Hooker in charge? Time would tell.

He looked in the distance and saw the unfinished Capitol building. The dome was under construction. Unfinished business, just as this war! Which would be finished first? He had no answers.

The young democracy was struggling to succeed. In the history of mankind, the reign of democracies was short-lived. Kings, monarchs and emperors were more often the power brokers over countries. Greece and Rome had dabbled in democratic forms of government and neither survived very long with this form of rule. Rome was ruled much longer by emperors than as a democratic republic. Could a democratic form of government survive, he wondered.

There was talk in the North of putting an end to this war and negotiating a peace with the rebellious states. *Our grandfathers, who fought to form this country and throw off the yoke of a king, must be rolling over in their graves.* He could not understand the desire to destroy what the revolutionary generation had started. In his eyes, the Southern states had ripped up the constitution and were willing to discard this chance for democracy. Upon leaving West Point, he had sworn an oath to uphold the constitution and defend the country from enemies, both foreign and domestic. The enemy was domestic. Many of his classmates had broken that oath and were fighting for the enemy. It was beyond him!

The North held the edge in manufacturing, raw materials and manpower. How were they losing this war? There were successes out west, and it was being reported that Sam Grant had the city of Vicksburg under siege. If Vicksburg fell, the Union army would have control of the Mississippi River, dividing the Southern states and slowing the flow of goods from states west of the river. But there was still Lee to contend with. No one could defeat him. The Army of the Potomac had fought against him time and again and lost. Commanders changed after each battle, but the outcome remained the same.

The steadiness of the ride turned his mind to thoughts of Kate. Kate Hewitt was his fiancé. They had met when he returned from his duty out west. As is the case with matters of the heart, there were issues. She was Catholic, he was Protestant. Marriage outside of one's religion was not an acceptable practice. It could enrage family members and people of the community. They could face being ostracized. It could have detrimental consequences on his military career. Yet, they fell for each other and decided they would marry after the war. Neither one informed their family members.

It could wait until the war ended. He had survived two years and was now in charge of a corps. Corps commanders tended to be away from the thickest fighting, staying well behind the lines, keeping an eye on the progress of the fighting. It was from this position they could send aides riding out with orders for their division commanders. He was not apt to be killed as a corps commander.

∽•🙰ʘʖ🙱•∽

Lincoln was retaining Hooker. The word was getting around Washington. Lincoln had heard from various corps commanders and their disgust for Hooker was evident, but no one was willing to replace him.

He had indirectly offered the command to Slocum, Sedgwick, Hancock and Meade. They had refused, yet they all felt Hooker had to go. He had brought Reynolds to the White House for a face-to-face meeting. Reynolds would only take the position if certain conditions were met. He wanted to put an end to all civilian control over the army. Lincoln could not accept these terms. Julius Caesar riding triumphantly into Rome came to mind. Lincoln would not let this young government be usurped by the military. They were still under his command.

Hooker was a problem, but no one was willing to be put in his shoes. Lincoln had only one option. He would have to write a direct order that would appoint a new commander.

CHAPTER 10

THE SKIES SOUTHWEST of the Rappahannock River were being filled with large clouds of dust. Troops were moving. It was apparent to the Union forces there was movement by the enemy to the west.

General John Sedgwick was commander of the Sixth Corps. His corps was positioned to the east of the Union line. They were the left wing of the army, facing south across the Rappahannock. He received orders from Hooker to cross the river with his corps and perform a reconnaissance in force. If enemy troops were moving to the west, Hooker saw a chance to exploit a perceived weakness in their rear. Sedgwick sent his Second Division across the river and soon found they were up against stiff resistance. Lee may have been moving, but he left plenty of firepower in this sector.

His orders were explicit. He was to perform a reconnaissance in force, not bring on a general engagement with a heavily entrenched force. He wrote a dispatch to Hooker."I cannot move 200 yards without bringing on a general fight. Before bringing over the rest of my corps, I await orders."

He called for an aide."Take this dispatch to General Hooker and present it to him with my compliments. Wait for his reply before you return."

"Yes, sir," the aide replied. He saluted Sedgwick and rode off.

What was Lee up to? It was evident from the dust Lee was moving vast portions of his army to the west. Sedgwick thought of the position of his corps. They were the furthest corps to the east. He felt his flank would not be in danger. Yes, there was a large Rebel force across the river, but they were dug in facing east. They did not appear to be making any move to his left.

Sedgwick thought of the possibilities. Lee had many options. He could attempt a wide flanking movement and attack the right flank of Hooker's army. He could attempt another invasion of Maryland as he had done the previous September. He could try to swing around the Union army and threaten Washington. What was Lee planning, he wondered?

Sedgwick would ride over and discuss these options with John Reynolds after he heard from Hooker. Reynolds' corps was encamped nearby at White Oak Church. It was a short ride of four miles. That is, unless Hooker ordered him to attack. He would await his answer.

Sedgwick was a competent commander. The army had been his life since his graduation from West Point in 1837. When given orders, he saw that they were carried out, but he had some odd quirks that left his peers doubting his ability to command an army. The men under his command loved and respected him. They dubbed him"Uncle John". He smiled when he thought of this nickname. A commander was supposed to be feared, not loved. He was quite comfortable as a corps commander and did not seek any higher position. He had been indirectly approached to head the army, but turned it down. He was not too happy with Hooker and wished him gone. However, Hooker was still in charge, and now the Rebel army was on the move. It was no time to change the man at the top.

After a while his aide came back."Sir, General Hooker sends you these orders with his compliments."

Sedgwick took the orders."Thank you. Tend to your horse and then get yourself something cold to drink. You are dismissed."

He read the orders. Hooker did not care to bring on an engagement. He wrote that one division was sufficient to be deployed across the river, keeping pressure on the enemy forces. Hooker was also ordering General Wadsworth to move his division from the First Corps, to a position of support for the Sixth Corps. They would be under his command while in this position. Sedgwick was to keep an eye on the enemy's right flank. He would write out orders to his division commanders, and then ride over to see Reynolds.

❧⬩⊰⊱⬩☙

Reynolds and Sedgwick exchanged pleasantries. They talked of the weather, which had been hot. The heat arrived sooner here in Virginia than their homes in the north. They still had trouble adapting to it. Sedgwick was from Connecticut, Reynolds from Pennsylvania.

"Too soon for heat of this magnitude," said Sedgwick."I'm still not used to seeing heat like this until July, and it's only June 5. Looks like another hot summer in Virginia."

Pennsylvania had weather similar to Virginia. Reynolds was more accustomed to it, so he left the comment alone."Hooker has dispatched Wadsworth's Division to your sector. He will be temporarily under your command. What is happening down there?"

"We've all seen the clouds of dust moving west. It is quite apparent Lee is moving numerous troops in that direction. Hooker ordered my corps to cross the river and make a reconnaissance in force. Thought we could surprise Lee and hit him in the rear."

"Lee is too crafty to be surprised."

"Crafty and brilliant. During the Mexican War, he was in charge of finding routes for Scott's army from the coast to Mexico City. He outwitted Santa Anna the whole campaign. I was there. Lee never hit the Mexicans head on, he found routes around them, hitting them in their flanks or coming upon them from behind. It was brilliant strategy and he was moving in unfamiliar country."

"What's not to admire," said Reynolds."He's the best on either side. He has continually confounded this army with his tactics." What would cause such a man to leave the army and take up arms against his own country, a country he had sworn to protect and defend? Reynolds admired Lee's fighting skill, but he would never understand his willingness to break the oath. As was his custom, he would keep his personal opinions to himself.

"He's up to his crafty old self," said Sedgwick."I sent one division across the river and encountered a well entrenched body of the enemy. It was too strong to be just a rear guard. I informed Hooker of the enemy's disposition and asked for further instructions. I did not wish to bring on an engagement with that strong a force without orders."

This was classic Sedgwick, thought Reynolds. He would follow orders, exactly as they were written, but he had trouble executing any type of independent command. This was one of the quirks Reynolds had seen in this man. Sedgwick was certainly loved and respected by his men, but he was best suited for carrying out orders from above.

"Could you detect the size of the force to your front?" asked Reynolds.

"I estimated it to be a division. As I said before, they were entrenched too firmly to be a rear guard. They were not pulling up stakes and moving anytime soon. Do you have any ideas on what Lee is doing?"

"None whatsoever," Reynolds replied emphatically."I am sure whatever we think he will do is more than likely the opposite of what he will actually do. The man continues to astound and go against military logic. He may be attempting to march around our flank and attack our right wing. This strategy worked last month."

"Lee loves the flank attack. He seems to know where our weakest flank is and then he brings hell down on that position. But he may wish for Hooker to think this, watch as the right wing entrenches on some good ground, then circle around and attack the rear."

"Or threaten Washington," added Reynolds."He could move behind the mountains, screening his position. He could attack Winchester and then Harper's Ferry. From there he could move east through one of the gaps and surprise us anywhere. An invasion of Maryland is not out of the picture. An invasion would cause panic in Washington and Baltimore. He has many options."

"And he knows he has the advantage squaring off once again against Hooker!" Sedgwick did not hold back his disdain.

Reynolds felt the same way. Lee would use Hooker's timidity against him and plan a campaign that would exploit all of Hooker's failings as a commander. Lee seemed to have the ability to understand his foe and to out-general him. He had demonstrated this ability time and again against different commanders of the Army of the Potomac. Reynolds stared into the distance.

Sedgwick interrupted his thoughts,"It seems we're stuck with Hooker. We've been sitting around for a month and no change has been made. If Hooker was going to be replaced, I would've expected it before now. With the enemy army on the move, it wouldn't be fair to appoint a new commander. He would have to respond to whatever threat Lee has in mind. A new commander would be forced to be reactive. Anyone taking over now would be put in a bad position."

"You make a good argument, John," said Reynolds."We'll cast our lot with Hooker and hope for a better outcome."

CHAPTER 11

THE STAFF MEETING WAS OVER. Dan Butterfield left headquarters heading for his tent. The past week had started on a high note, but was quickly spiraling out of control. On June 9, the cavalry had surprised Jeb Stuart at Brandy Station. *Neither side claimed victory,* thought Butterfield, *but we punched Stuart in the mouth. Our cavalry, considered inferior during the early stages of the war, was now on equal footing with Stuart.* Training and improved leadership were significant factors for this turnaround.

Hooker had appointed General Pleasanton to command the cavalry after their disappointing showing at Chancellorsville under their previous commander General Stoneman. Hooker had made it clear Stoneman's poor performance was one of the causes for the defeat. Butterfield agreed with Hooker's assessment. In his mind, Hooker acted quickly by replacing Stoneman. The results were paying dividends. Fighting Joe Hooker was alive and well.

Butterfield reached his tent. He needed a stiff drink to settle himself. He found his flask, took off the top and put it up to his mouth. The bourbon was smooth. He felt the warmth as it made its way to his stomach. He put the top on and returned the flask. One drink was enough. He sat down and thought on the recent events.

The attempted coup by his corps commanders seemed to have run its course. Hooker was still in charge. *Damn them all,* he thought. Lee was moving, and a new campaign was underway. There was no way Lincoln would replace Hooker at this critical time. However, the recent events made him wonder.

After the encouraging news of the Brandy Station skirmish, Hooker was receiving no support from Washington for any of his plans or requests. He had desired to cross the Rappahannock and to attack Richmond. He felt this would alarm the leaders in Richmond, and they would order Lee back to defend their capital. Any intentions Lee had of moving north would be waylaid. This plan had been quickly halted by both Lincoln and Halleck. They ordered Hooker not to cross the river, but to keep his army between Lee and Washington. If Richmond was vulnerable, why not capture it, he thought. It might put an end to this war. Butterfield hated the interference from Washington.

Hooker had followed orders and put the army in motion on June 10. Reynolds was named commander of the left wing, which was marching northwest toward Bealton Station on the Orange and Alexandria RR. Under his command were the First, Third, Fifth and Eleventh Corps. The Second, Sixth and Twelfth Corps were moving in a northerly direction toward the town of Dumfries. Lee's intentions were still unclear, but Hooker would follow orders and shield Washington.

Hooker had requested reinforcements from Harpers Ferry and the troops garrisoned around Washington. This request had also been denied. With enlistments soon to expire, the army would have roughly 89,000 troops by July 1. How could he fight Lee with so few forces? Why did Halleck and Lincoln not understand this? Butterfield sensed there were still forces working to have Hooker relieved. These forces were blocking all of Hooker's requests. Perhaps it was their intention to act in this manner so Hooker would resign.

The latest news was the most disastrous. The town of Winchester had been attacked and captured by Lee's forces on June 14. Losses for the Union forces were astonishingly high. How had Lee moved a corps that far north without detection? Hooker was stunned by the news. He had called his staff together to inform them of the defeat. This was the meeting Butterfield had attended earlier.

He sat in his tent pondering the recent developments. With Winchester in his possession, Lee could set his sights on Harpers Ferry. The small force defending this town would be hard-pressed to hold it. The Army of the Potomac was too far away to render assistance in time. The Shenandoah Valley would once again be under Lee's control. Then what? Hooker would have to respond to Lee's movements. Butterfield shook his head. The army would have to cover many miles to be put in position to intercept Lee. The men would be tired from the long marches in this heat. Lee could swoop down from the mountain passes and attack the army that would be stretched out and most likely in some untenable position. It would be hard to force march the army and to have them in a well-entrenched defensive position.

Those damned mountain passes, he thought. They were called gaps here in Virginia. Lee had hidden his intentions by moving his army behind the mountains. He had placed his cavalry at the gaps in solid defensive positions. General Pleasanton could not penetrate any of these gaps, therefore he could not report on the whereabouts of Lee's army. Pleasanton had done well at Brandy Station, but now he was failing Hooker. The cavalry were the eyes of the army, and the eyes were now blinded. Pleasanton had informed headquarters the gaps were too strongly defended to penetrate. This had incensed Hooker. He ordered Pleasanton to find out where the enemy was, even if it meant he had to lose men in the process.

Butterfield stood up, walked across the tent and retrieved his flask. He needed another drink. Lee had a head start and now the advantage of position. He could attack Hooker's army at a place where it was the weakest. It could turn into another Chancellorsville. Another defeat and Hooker would be gone. Butterfield's tenure as Chief of Staff would be over. The new commander would name his own staff and Butterfield knew he was not high on anyone's list to be considered for a staff position. He put the flask to his lips and took another drink.

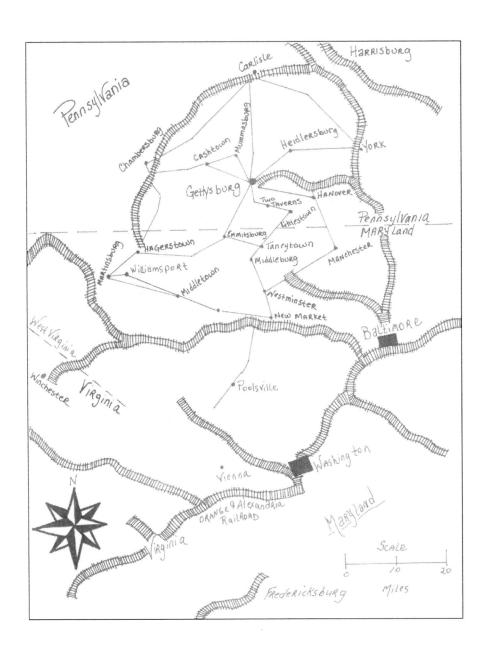

Pennsylvania

Harrisburg

Carlisle

Chambersburg

Cashtown

Mummasburg

Heidlersburg

York

Gettysburg

Two Taverns

Hanover

Littlestown

Pennsylvania
Maryland

Emmitsburg

Tanrytown

Manchester

Martinsburg

Hagerstown

Williamsport

Middletown

Middleburg

Westminster

West Virginia

New Market

Baltimore

Virginia

Winchester

Poolsville

N

Vienna

Washington

Orange & Alexandria Railroad

Maryland

Virginia

Scale

0   10   20

Miles

Fredericksburg

60

CHAPTER 12

GENERAL MEADE WAS IN HIS TENT attempting to write a letter to his wife. It was June 19th. The Fifth Corps was positioned just east of Aldie Gap in the Bull Run Mountains, supporting Pleasanton's cavalry. His men had endured hard marches through the heat in reaching this spot. They had covered roughly 62 miles in 6 days. The men were tired. He had been ordered to send one of his divisions forward on June 20th to support a probe by cavalry units. He ordered General Barnes to be ready to march at 3 a.m.. The rain was a steady drone on the outside of his tent. It did not seem to be letting up. Rain was a relief from the heat, but with the rain came mud. Barnes' division would be marching through the mud, while the rest of his corps could rest in their tents for the day. He had no further orders to move at this time.

The news of Lee's army moving into Pennsylvania had angered Meade. Now Lee had become an invader. Lee had turned down command of the Union army in 1861, for he could not lead the army intent on invading his home state of Virginia. Lee had defended Virginia with a fierce tenacity. Meade could not agree with Lee's reasoning for leaving the army, but he certainly respected his fighting ability! Sure, Lee had led his army into Maryland the previous autumn, but Maryland was a border state with many Southern sympathizers. Pennsylvania was a different matter. It was a Northern state, and now Lee had become a commander of an invading army. This war had changed many people.

Meade was angry at the ineptness of Hooker and his staff. How had they let Lee move his entire army from south of the Rappahannock River into the state of Pennsylvania undetected?His family was in Pennsylvania. Would they be in danger?

As far as Meade knew, the Army of the Potomac was still south of the Potomac River. They had marched hard for 6 days to get to this position, but it seemed they were still many miles away from Lee's army. More hard marches were sure to follow. That bastard Hooker had his army marching all over northern Virginia. Now it was apparent he did not know where Lee was, yet he was marching his army here and there. Did Hooker have any plans? Why was he still in charge? These thoughts put Meade in a sullen mood and the rain beating down on his tent did not help.

꙰ ꙮ ꙰

Lee continued to move his army into Pennsylvania. By June 23rd, Ewell had his entire corps within Pennsylvania. June 26th found all but three divisions inside the state. On the same day, General Early marched his division into Gettysburg, demanding supplies. They tangled with a local militia west of town, but dispatched of them quickly, capturing 175 men. The next day, they moved onward toward York. They did not leave a favorable impression on the local population. A Gettysburg professor after his first encounter with Confederate soldiers wrote they were like"so many savages from the wilds of the Rocky Mountains." The outraged *Lancaster Daily Express* printed this description of the Confederate Army:"If highway robberies, profanity, vulgarity, filthiness and general meanness are the requisite qualifications for constituting a high-toned gentleman, then indeed may the Southern soldiers claim the appellation."

By June 27th Lee had his whole army in Pennsylvania. The citizens of the state were in a panic.

Hooker started moving his army across the Potomac into Maryland on June 25th. He put Reynolds in command of the left wing, which now consisted of the First, Third and Eleventh Corps. General Buford's cavalry division was assigned to Reynolds' command to shield the infantry and perform reconnaissance duties. The Army of the Potomac would endure long marches through Maryland to catch Lee in Pennsylvania. They still did not know of Lee's intentions. There were reports of his army in York, Carlisle and on the outskirts of Harrisburg.

Hooker was falling out of favor in Washington. He had lost the whereabouts of Lee's army, which had first captured Winchester and was now marching across Pennsylvania. He was demanding reinforcements, but this demand was turned down. He was tired of fighting with his superiors. On June 27th, he wrote to Lincoln."I earnestly request that I may at once be relieved from the position I occupy."

In the previous few days, Lincoln had become increasingly dissatisfied with Hooker. He was disobeying orders and he was demanding more troops that could not be spared from other commands. Now he had asked to be relieved. Lincoln would oblige him. Lincoln remembered one name all the commanders had favored and that was George Meade. That night, General Order No. 194 was drawn up. It relieved Hooker and placed George Meade as commander of the Army of the Potomac.

PART II
A CHANGE OF COMMAND

CHAPTER 13

JOHN REYNOLDS PUT ON HIS BEST DRESS UNIFORM. He wished to look his best, while at the same time showing his respect for the newly appointed commander of the Army of the Potomac, General George Meade. Reynolds approved the change, but wondered at its timing. The army was on the move in pursuit of Lee. One did not stop midstream to change horses pulling a wagon through fast water.

Reynolds had marched his corps from Middleton to Frederick, a distance of ten miles, during the day. He had received marching orders for the First Corps around nine that morning, his first order from the new commanding general. Tired as he was after the day's march, he cleaned himself up and was now riding over to headquarters. He wanted to congratulate Meade in person. He wondered how the meeting between Meade and Hooker had gone. This was not the time or place for another heated exchange.

Then there was Dan Butterfield. Reynolds knew of the animosity between Meade and Butterfield, which was made even worse when Meade was appointed as commander of the Fifth Corps earlier in the year. This appointment was made at the expense of the outgoing Fifth Corps commander, Dan Butterfield. Would Meade keep him on as chief of staff? Butterfield would know the disposition of all the troops and might need to be retained. Two bulls circling in the same field!

Reynolds arrived at headquarters and waited outside. Butterfield came out first. He saw Reynolds, paused for a moment, then glared at him. He walked off in disgust. The body language told Reynolds all he needed to know. Butterfield was none too happy.

Meade appeared from within the tent. Reynolds came to attention and brought his right arm up in a sharp salute."My compliments to the new commanding general of the Army of the Potomac."

Meade gave a quick return salute, and stood there shaking his head."I don't recall sending out any orders for an inspection of the troops. What's with the formal attire?"

"Just paying my respects in proper military attire. After all, you are now the commanding general." A smile came across his face.

Meade snapped back,"I'm just holding onto this damned job until we chase Lee out of Pennsylvania. Then I'll tell Halleck to appoint you as my replacement. You're the one who should be holding this job. You're far more qualified than I am!"

Meade put out his hand. Reynolds recognized the gesture, put out his hand and they exchanged a firm handshake.

"Thanks for coming by," said Meade."It's been a hell of a day. A courier from Washington woke me at 3 a.m.. I was certain I was court-martialed. Couldn't be so lucky. Instead, I've been ordered to take command and fight Lee."

"Who better to fight Lee in Pennsylvania than a Pennsylvania man?" chided Reynolds.

"You're also from Pennsylvania."

"Yes, but every good general needs a great wing commander. I'll protect your left and find some good ground to fight on." Reynolds paused for a moment, before changing subjects."Mr. Butterfield didn't look too happy."

"He's not, and it appears I am stuck with him as chief of staff. Williams, Warren and Humphries turned down my offer to be chief of staff. They feel their present jobs are too important with an upcoming fight looming on the horizon. They suggest I keep Dan in his present capacity, to afford some continuity with current intelligence and troop movements. After Hooker left, I found no written orders. I asked Butterfield about this. He shrugged and told me Hooker kept all the plans in his head. Nothing is written down and that son of a bitch Butterfield tells me he hasn't a clue what Hooker was planning!" Meade felt his temper rising.

Reynolds interjected,"Take a deep breath. What do you know?"

Meade turned to an aide."Reynolds and I are heading off to that stand of trees. We'll keep in sight in case any important orders come in." He turned to Reynolds and said with an edge,"I've got to stay close to headquarters. Don't want to miss any dispatches from Washington."

They walked so to be out of earshot. Meade wanted to keep this confidential.

Meade stared at the horizon."Lee is scattered across Pennsylvania, about 100,000 strong. Ewell's corps is on the Susquehanna River across from Harrisburg. Longstreet has his corps in Chambersburg and Hill is encamped between Chambersburg and Cashtown. That is a broad front. My orders are to keep this army between Lee and the Baltimore/Washington region. If Lee is to make a move on either, I am to block his way and give him battle. Butterfield can't tell me with any certainty where all our corps are located. I have ordered them to make haste and get to Frederick. I need to gather the army and then send it forward in an orderly manner to follow Halleck's instructions. Can I turn this over to you and go back to being the Fifth Corps commander?"

Reynolds smiled."I'll command your left wing. Hell, I've got Sickles to contend with, unless you wish to order him closer to your position."

"Not on your life. I've got Butterfield, you get Sickles! I don't need all the headaches."

They both laughed at this.

As he spoke, Meade put his hand on Reynolds shoulder,"I'll need you to find some good ground to fight on. At this point I will have to concentrate the army quickly when Lee makes a move. My initial plan is to fight defensively until I get a handle on where and how strong my army is. I'll keep you in charge of the left wing with the three corps you have been assigned by Hooker. I want you to march to Emmitsburg, keeping the South Mountain range on your left. See if there is any good ground in that area to defend. Keep me informed."

Reynolds responded,"I've got Buford riding ahead of me. He's the best we've got in the cavalry. He'll report on any movement by Lee's army. I've got to get back and get the men ready to march. I know you have enough to do without me hanging around. Let's see what we can do to Lee on our own soil."

Reynolds stepped back and saluted. Meade returned the salute. They walked back to headquarters where Reynolds horse was tied. He mounted, grabbed the reins and turning toward Meade, nodded his head in a show of quiet confidence. Then he rode off.

∽ഇ൦ര⊱

Dan Butterfield was livid. Of all people, it had to be Meade that replaced Hooker. Dan despised Meade and he felt certain it was a mutual feeling. He was old enough to know this is how it is between certain people. There's no explaining it. Reynolds added to his mood by showing up at headquarters in a clean dress uniform. Evidently much had happened behind the scenes to ensure the demise of Hooker. Butterfield was being retained as chief of staff. He couldn't figure out why. He wondered if Sickles would be relieved of his Third Corps command.

What made him really hot under the collar were some of the items in the written order from Halleck to Meade. Halleck put Meade in charge of the garrison at Harpers Ferry. Hell, Hooker had been asking for this for the past two weeks, but Halleck kept answering with an emphatic"no!". Troops from other commands were too important where they were to be added to Hooker's army. Sure, don't allow Hooker to strengthen his army, but the order for George Meade to replace Hooker included this little caveat. Butterfield could not walk fast enough to lose his rage. Where was the justice? He didn't know where or when, but he would someday repay this injustice to his friend Joe Hooker.

∽ഇ൦ര⊱

What a day it had been. Meade was awoken from a sound sleep at 3 a.m. as commander of the Fifth Corps. Before the cobwebs had time to clear in his head, he found he had been appointed as commander of the Army of the Potomac. He remembered the words Colonel Hardie, the messenger from Halleck, had spoken."I have come to bring you trouble." It certainly was trouble. Meade's head was the next one on the chopping block.

The meeting with Hooker had been cordial. Hooker spent most of the time complaining about Halleck and giving his reasons for resigning. To Meade, Hooker seemed relieved.

They spent some time discussing the whereabouts of the army. The seven corps were scattered all over Maryland. Hooker had pointed out their approximate locations on the map. Meade noted their positions and felt the anger start to well up inside. He had to keep it in check. His engineering background could discern no rhyme or reason for the location of the army. As he listened to Hooker, he began to understand there was no concrete plan in place. Meade knew he had much work to do.

His first order that morning had been for the army to march to Frederick. He knew it was Sunday and the army generally rested, especially after the long marches the troops had endured this past week, but he felt it necessary to get in position to intercept Lee. All but two corps had made it to Frederick by nightfall. The Second and Sixth Corps had been too far away to reach their ordered destination.

An aide came in with some coffee. Meade thanked him. The day had been so busy he couldn't recall if he had eaten anything. There was too much work to do to worry about food, he thought. His day had started at 3 a.m., eighteen hours ago. He should be tired, but the day was filled with issues that needed his immediate attention. There was too much adrenaline pumping through him to be tired.

He took a sip of coffee and recalled some of the day's events. He had met with General Warren, his chief engineer, and gave him instructions to find good ground to fight on. Warren was a fellow engineer who was held in high esteem by his peers. Meade could trust his judgment. At this point Meade was not sure if he would be waging an offensive or defensive operation against Lee. Included in his orders from Halleck to assume command of the army were instructions to keep between Lee and the cities of Washington and Baltimore. He reached for the orders on his desk. He wanted to read a certain section again. He looked down the page and found where he wanted to start;

Your army is free to act as you may deem proper under the circumstances as they arise. You will, however, keep in view the important fact that the Army of the Potomac is the covering army of Washington, as well as the army of operation against the invading forces of the rebels. You will therefore maneuver and fight in such a manner as to cover the Capital and also Baltimore, as far as circumstances will admit. Should General Lee move upon either of these places, it is expected that you will either anticipate him or arrive with him, so as to give him battle.

So, according to his instructions, he was free to act, within certain parameters, as spelled out by Halleck. These must be the restraints Reynolds had mentioned as the reason he could not accept command of the army.

Meade looked at the last line. He was supposed to"anticipate" Lee's movements. He was an engineer, not a clairvoyant. He had not been asked to take command, he had been ordered to. He would follow his orders and carry out his duties as best he could.

Reynolds. He's the man who should be in charge. He had come over in his dress uniform to pay his respects. Meade smiled as he thought of this simple act. Reynolds had the attributes to make a fine leader, but he would also be an outstanding subordinate.

Sedgwick had also come by to offer his congratulations. This was so like Uncle John. His Sixth Corps had marched hard all day and were encamped nine miles south of Frederick. After the day's march, Sedgwick rode the additional nine miles, just to shake Meade's hand and to offer his support. Their backing was important to Meade, for both Sedgwick and Reynolds were senior to him in rank.

Meade was stuck with Butterfield as his Chief of Staff. He had asked three different people to take the job, but each had turned him down. They all spoke of the importance of their own jobs in the upcoming battle with Lee and felt it was not the right time to assume a new job with new responsibilities. Meade could find no fault with their reasoning. As long as Butterfield carried out his orders, they would survive each other.

His marching orders for the next day had been spelled out and his adjutant, General Seth Williams, would write them up and have them delivered in short order. For the men, the morning would come early, as marches were to start at 4:00 a.m.. Meade's plan was to fan out from Frederick in a northerly direction. The left wing would march to Emmitsburg. Two corps would march in the center towards Taneytown and two corps would head toward New Windsor and make up the right wing of his army. The marches would be longer than he would wish, but it was no time to follow the army manual for marching. Lee was on Northern soil, and he had to close with all possible speed on him.

CHAPTER 14

June 29th

HANCOCK IMPATIENTLY AWAITED ORDERS. The pre-dawn chattering of the birds had woken him from his sleep. His aides told him there were still no marching orders for the day. It didn't make sense. Yesterday his corps had marched 20 miles to end up a few miles south of Frederick. His orders had been to get his corps to Frederick without delay. He had pushed his corps hard through the heat and humidity, but could not reach Frederick. Now, it was 7 a.m. and he had no orders. He knew Meade was still getting settled in his new job, but it seemed inconceivable the army would halt for a day while Lee was marching around Pennsylvania. If he heard nothing soon, he would send a rider to Frederick, find headquarters and see what was transpiring.

Hancock had finished his breakfast an hour ago and was on his second cup of coffee. His men were awake, fed and doing what troops do when there was nothing to do. Hurry up and wait. This was a soldier's mantra. A large portion of time was spent doing nothing.

There was drill, picket duty and marching, but there were large chunks of time spent doing nothing in camps. No one could fill in hours of nothingness better than an enlisted man in the army. Combat was a welcome relief from the boredom.

"Rider coming in, sir."

Hancock turned and saw a rider being led to his tent. Now he would have orders. His impatient energy could be transferred into action. The rider got off his horse and was led to Hancock.

"Sir, your orders with General Meade's compliments," the rider said while saluting.

Hancock returned the salute and took the orders. He opened them and started reading. A look of disbelief came over his face.

"Damn it, son, do you know what these orders say?" Meade asked quite agitated.

"No, sir. I received them last night and was told to get them to you immediately. I couldn't find your corps in the dark, so I stopped for a quick rest and fell asleep."

Hancock exploded in rage at the rider,"You fell asleep with orders you were to deliver immediately. Son of a bitch, eight hours later is not immediately. These orders call for me to have my corps marching by 4 a.m.. Do you know what goddamn time it is, son!"

The rider knew he was in trouble. He tried to minimize the damage,"Sir, I was out looking for your position until 2 a.m. . . . . "

Hancock cut him off."Your job was to deliver these orders to me last night. Where in hell does it say you get to take a bloody nap? I am now three hours behind schedule." He turned to an aide and barked an order,"Get this man over to the kitchen, with explicit orders he is to be cleaning pots and pans until hell freezes over! Get this bastard out of my sight."

Hancock started barking orders to his aides. This young rider had ruined his morning. Now he had to make up for lost time. His orders were to march towards Taneytown. He went over and looked at the map. Hell, he thought as he studied the map, Taneytown is about 36 miles away and he was already three hours late. Less than one month as a corps commander and he might become known as"Hancock the Tardy." He would not let this happen. He would drive the men hard until they reached their destination.

He rode over to see John Gibbon, his Second Division commander. Hancock had decided Gibbon's division would lead the corps. John was a hard driving man and would obey orders given to him. He was the right man to be in the front.

He arrived at Gibbon's tent. Gibbon had heard the news his corps commander was in camp to see him. Hancock rode up. Gibbon saluted him. Hancock halted his horse and returned a quick salute.

"John, I've just received our marching orders three hours late. The damn courier had some bullshit story about not being able to find us. We're to march to Taneytown, which is about 36 miles north of here. I'm having your division lead the corps, for I can count on you to set the pace so we get there. Strike your tents and get on the road quickly. I've sent riders to the other division commanders to fall in behind you. I came here myself, so you would grasp the urgency of this order."

"Yes, sir. We'll begin the march by 8, less than an hour from now. I'll see you in Taneytown tonight."

They exchanged salutes. Hancock turned his horse and rode away. He admired Gibbon and knew he would follow through. It would be a long day.

৯‑৪০৫৪৩‑৶

Mid-afternoon

Headquarters was moved to Middleburg. Meade was in the headquarters tent with Adjutant General Seth Williams and a few aides. A drenching rainstorm had just ended. It was the second such downpour of the day; very heavy, but short in duration. It broke the humidity, but the roads would now be muddy. He hoped the marches would not be adversely affected.

Dispatches and intelligence reports were coming in continually. Each one needed his attention. Meade would respond and then go back to studying the maps with Williams. They were discussing different scenarios Lee might attempt and counter moves the Army of the Potomac could undertake. The problem confronting Meade was a problem generals had faced through the ages. What was the enemy planning and what would be the best strategy to counter that plan? Meade looked at the map. His army was too far away from the last known position of the invading army. Two days of hard marching would close the gap, but at what cost? Would the men be too exhausted to fight effectively? He would need to address this issue.

An aide entered the tent with a dispatch.

"Sir, this just arrived from General Slocum," said the aide.

Meade took the dispatch, read it, then looked up at Williams shaking his head."It's a good thing the chief of staff isn't here. It seems his friend Sickles is not making good time on his march. Slocum writes he was held up for four hours on the road between Middleburg and Frederick, awaiting the slow moving Third Corps to pass by. He could not resume his march until 10:30 and fears he will not reach his destination by nightfall."

They both looked at the map, tracing routes with their fingers. Williams raised his eyebrows and said,"Sickles should have been by that point early this morning. At the latest, he should have been through there by 8 a.m.."

Meade agreed with his adjutant."I want you to write a harsh reprimand to that S.O.B. Sickles. Don't sugarcoat it. Let him know the slow movement of his corps is unacceptable to this command."

Williams went to the desk and wrote to Sickles as ordered. When he finished, he showed it to Meade for approval. Meade read it and stated,"It'll do fine, maybe not as harsh as I would like it, but it lets him know of my displeasure." He paused for a moment and rubbed his chin. He looked at Williams and said,"I'd like to replace him, but now is not the time. Reynolds will keep him in line."

Another dispatch arrived. It was handed to Meade. He read it and said,"New intelligence on Lee's army from Colonel Sharpe. It seems there are no more than 80,000 troops and 275 pieces of artillery. These figures were derived while Lee passed through Hagerstown. This will even the odds. I'll forward this information to Halleck. Don't want to start off on the wrong foot with him." He turned to Williams,"I'd like more coffee. How about you?"

"Yeah, I'll have some."

An aide went for coffee.

Looking back at the map, Meade pointed to the town of Gettysburg."Here is the perfect place to gather an army. Ten roads converge on the town. The trouble is Lee is closer, and if he hears we are marching toward him, he can join his forces quicker than we can."

Williams listened intently to his commander and then added,"This could give him an opportunity to attack our army piecemeal. He could take one or two corps out before we gather. I suggest we consider a defensive strategy and see if Lee takes the bait. He cannot stay in Pennsylvania too long for fear of getting cut off from supplies and an escape route back to Virginia. I think his desire is to attack our army with the hope of defeating us and giving more impetus to the peace movements."

Meade agreed with this assessment by Williams. Lee did not have the time to dig in with his army. He could not afford to sit in one spot and await an attack. The Union army would not be forced to attack. They could surround him and wait him out with a siege.

Looking at the map, Meade said,"If we are to adopt a defensive strategy we need to find good ground. Have we any word from General Warren or his staff?"

"Nothing as of yet. He's thorough and he won't let us down. He knows of the urgency of the situation."

The aide returned with fresh coffee. Meade blew in the cup and took a sip. It was hot, but he could feel it as it entered that empty place in his stomach. *Too much to do to think about eating,* he thought to himself.

There was some commotion outside the tent. Meade turned toward the disturbance. An aide entered with a concerned look on his face.

"Sir, it appears the telegraph lines to Washington are down. We can't get anything through."

Meade was momentarily stunned. Damn it, what else could go wrong? He gathered himself quickly and thought of options. Harrisburg came to mind."Send a wire to Harrisburg and see if they can relay it to Washington."

"Yes, sir." The aide left to carry out his orders.

Meade looked at Williams, rubbed his forehead and exhaled slowly."Is it always this hectic in headquarters?"

Williams smiled and said"Only during combat. You will find yourself getting deluged with information from all over the field. Each corps commander will make it seem as though their sector is the most important one to deal with. They'll want your immediate attention to their particular problem. Other than that, it is usually quite peaceful in headquarters. Good food, a good night's sleep and a good staff to wait on you, hand and foot." He looked at Meade and they both laughed.

"It seems we are on the front stoop to combat, and I'm being tested to see if I've got what it takes to lead an army," Meade replied.

"It's just like corps command, seven times over. The only difference is you're making decisions for the whole army during the ever-changing nature of combat. Nothing to it," added Williams with a gleam in his eye.

"Nothing to it at all, you say. Is this why we have a new commander after every battle?" Meade let the question linger in the air. It was his command now, and all he could do was his duty as he saw fit.

He walked back to the map. What was Lee planning? His army was still scattered across south central Pennsylvania from Chambersburg northeasterly to the Susquehanna River at Harrisburg, a distance of fifty miles.

He spoke mostly to get his thoughts out into the open."Look at Gettysburg. From intelligence, we know Lee has two corps on the road between Chambersburg and Gettysburg. Ewell, however, is on the west bank of the Susquehanna, about fifty miles northerly of Gettysburg. By nightfall, Reynolds will be at Emmitsburg, ten miles southwesterly of Gettysburg, with his three corps. There is a chance he could get into Gettysburg before Lee. He's got 31,000 men under his command. Lee will have 50,000 troops in the two corps. If he finds some good ground to defend, he might be able to hold Lee until we get the rest of the army there. Then it would be a race to Gettysburg between Ewell's corps and our remaining four corps."

Williams absorbed these words, but was considering other avenues."Harrisburg is a bigger prize for Lee. It's the capitol of Pennsylvania and it has a manufacturing base that would supply Lee's army. Gettysburg offers very little for Lee's army. Besides, Ewell already marched through the town and took whatever supplies he could get his hands on. Lee needs supplies to stay in Pennsylvania. Gettysburg has been picked over."

"True, but the Susquehanna still stands between Lee and Harrisburg. She's a formidable river, difficult to cross on foot. Many of the bridges have been burned and others are strongly defended. General Couch is in command of the forces around Harrisburg. He's one tough son of a bitch, and he'll give Lee a fight. Lee may move on Harrisburg, but he's too smart to stay there for any length of time. We'll be coming up behind him and he will not want to put the river at his back. He would be surrounded with no escape route. His move toward Harrisburg could be a feint to throw us off. His intended target could be Baltimore. Many railroads converge there."

"Its capture would put Washington in a state of panic," added Williams.

They paused to take in all that had been said. There was much to consider. Meade knew he had to cover Baltimore. He was glad he had Williams as his adjutant. Williams would offer opinions and keep Meade on his toes. He would not just agree with Meade to placate him. Meade needed men around him who could think independently and not be afraid to offer differing opinions. Except for Butterfield, Meade had a strong and supportive staff. General Warren would find him good ground. Then there was Henry Hunt, his Chief of Artillery. Hell, he wrote the manual for artillery tactics in combat. None better, Meade thought. No matter the strength of his staff, he knew all the decisions in the upcoming fight fell on his shoulders.

An aide entered the tent bringing news that telegraph service to Harrisburg was still in service. They would send to Washington any telegraphs that needed to get through. This relieved Meade. He intended to keep Halleck informed of his movements. Others in his position had not been so prudent.

He turned to Williams."Go get something to eat. I've got matters to think on. I'll see you later tonight to write out tomorrow's marching orders. Thanks for your input. This commander appreciates it."

So·EOCR·S

Late evening

Meade was in headquarters waiting for Williams. What a day it had been. The steady flow of dispatches needing his attention kept him busy. Any free time he had was spent dwelling on Lee, which meant there was no free time. This is what he knew of his army: Reynolds had reached Emmitsburg with his wing command. Hancock, even though delayed by four hours, had marched his corps for fourteen hours to reach his destination at Uniontown by 10 p.m.. Meade knew he could count heavily on these two generals in the upcoming fight. Sykes, the new commander of Meade's old Fifth Corps, had reached Liberty, and Sedgwick, with the Sixth Corps, was encamped at New Market. These two corps were the right wing of his army. They were marching in a northeasterly direction to cover Baltimore. The last he heard from Slocum was around 6 p.m.. His corps, the Twelfth, had only marched twelve miles due to Sickles tardiness and had fifteen miles more to cover to reach Middleburg. In his last dispatch, Slocum wrote he would march his corps through the night until they reached Middleburg. Henry Slocum had a reputation for following through with assigned orders. This was a trait Meade respected.

There was still no word from General Warren. If none came by morning, Meade would send out riders to find him. He needed good ground to gather the army on before Lee attacked. Meade wanted the Army of the Potomac concentrated for the ensuing battle.

"Sir, General Williams is here," announced an aide.

"Send him in."

As Williams entered the tent, Meade nodded at him and said,"We've got work to do. Let's get at it. Get some paper and start writing."

Williams got some paper and sat down at the desk. He looked at Meade to signal he was ready.

79

Meade began."We'll start with the marching orders for tomorrow. Third Corps to Bridgeport; Second Corps can rest; Twelfth Corps to Littlestown; First Corps to Marsh Creek; Eleventh Corps to Emmitsburg; Sixth Corps to Manchester; Fifth Corps to Union Mills."

He waited for Williams to finish writing. He thought of the orders he was sending out. The army would be spread out from Gettysburg to Manchester, a distance of roughly thirty miles. He still had an inside track on Lee and felt he could gather his army quicker than Lee.

"I'm ready for more," broke in Williams.

Meade continued,"Cavalry to the front and flanks, well out in all directions, giving timely notice of positions and movements of the enemy. All empty wagons, surplus baggage, useless animals and impedimenta of every sort to Union Bridge, 3 miles from Middleburg: a proper officer from each corps with them.

"The general relies upon every commander to put his column in the lightest possible order. Staff officers to report daily from each corps with orderlies to leave for orders. Prompt information to be sent into headquarters at all times. All ready to move to attack at any moment.

"The commanding general desires you to be informed that, from present information, Longstreet and Hill are at Chambersburg, partly toward Gettysburg; Ewell at Carlisle and York. Movements indicate a disposition to advance from Chambersburg to Gettysburg.

"Vigilance, energy and prompt response to orders from headquarters are necessary, and the personal attention of corps commanders must be given to the reduction of impedimenta. The orders and movements from this headquarters must be carefully and confidentially preserved, that they do not fall into the enemy's hands."

Meade had Williams read the order to see how it sounded. When Williams was finished, Meade nodded his approval and said,"Good, sign it 'By command of Major General Meade' and have copies delivered to each corps commander immediately. When you're done get some sleep. Morning will come early."

"Try to get some sleep yourself," added Williams as he left.

Meade dismissed his aides for the night. He wanted to be alone and write to his wife. He got out some paper and began to write."We are marching as fast as we can to relieve Harrisburg, but have to keep a sharp lookout that the rebels don't turn around us and get at Washington and

Baltimore in our rear. I am going straight at them, and will settle this thing one way or the other. The men are in good spirits; we have been reinforced so as to have equal numbers with the enemy, and with God's blessing I hope to be successful. Good-by!"

He sat alone. It would be another uneasy night with little sleep. The burden of command weighed on his every thought. He wanted to rest, but knew his mind would not allow it. He turned down the lantern, laid down on his cot and stared at the canvas ceiling of the tent.

CHAPTER 15

June 30th

IT WAS 6 A.M. Reynolds was just finishing breakfast. His marching orders arrived as dawn broke. He was to proceed to Marsh Creek, a short march of six miles. He would let the men sleep. They were weary from the long marches of the last two days. Extra rest and a good meal before the day's march would boost morale considerably.

The air was refreshing. The rain had cleared the humidity. It would get warmer, but he felt it would not be as oppressive.

The men could sleep late, but Reynolds had much to do. He would need to find good ground near Marsh Creek to dig in for the night. Lee was nearby and if his intentions were to advance toward Gettysburg, Reynolds wanted a good defensive position to fight from. This would give Meade time to get the remainder of the army to the fight. General Buford with his cavalry was still to the north and west screening Reynolds' command. If Buford encountered Lee's army moving east through the mountain passes, he would be in a position to engage the enemy and slow their progress. Reynolds knew he had to have his wing dug in on good ground before any fighting took place on his front.

He called for his aides to gather."We have a busy day," he started."We only have to march to Marsh Creek, but we need to find good ground there." He ordered two men to ride ahead and scout the area."I will be along later in the morning to approve of the position you recommend." They saluted and left for their horses.

"General Wadsworth will lead the march with his division. The men can sleep in awhile longer and have a proper breakfast. Nine o'clock will be a good time to commence marching." He assigned an aide to take these orders to Wadsworth.

"Yes, sir," the aide replied. He saluted and was off.

"Get these marching orders to Robinson and Doubleday," said Reynolds to two other aides. He dismissed them and went for another cup of coffee.

ॐ☙❦❧☙

Buford was up early and riding toward Fairfield. He had seen the campfires in the west the night before, but could get no information about the size of the force from the local citizens. They seemed afraid to get involved. One farmer told him the rebels would destroy their houses if they told him anything. Buford was a fighter and could not understand this type of thinking. He was from Kentucky and he knew from an early age life was a struggle, not to be backed down from.

He was leading his two brigades toward Gettysburg, but he would first see what size the enemy force was near Fairfield. Reconnaissance was part of the job of a cavalry commander. Any information he could gather was useful to those in higher command making decisions that would affect the entire army. He was planning to skirmish with the enemy force and see if he could drive them away.

He was informed there were two regiments of infantry and two pieces of artillery. He rode ahead to size up the situation. His men were skirmishing as he had ordered, but the enemy was in too good of a position to be driven away. He did not wish to bring on an engagement so far from the road he was expected to be on. He ordered his men to withdraw. They would ride back to Emmitsburg and then proceed to Gettysburg.

He enjoyed being in the saddle. The steady pace of the horse under him felt natural. Ever since his graduation from West Point in 1848, it seemed he had served in the saddle. He fought against the Sioux in the 1850's. He remembered them as tenacious fighters, a worthy adversary. He thought of his time out west as he rode. The land was so much different than in the east. The plains were vast and treeless. The horizon stretched as far as the eye could see. He remembered the sense of riding all day and not seeming to get anywhere.

Then there was Utah, where he was also stationed. The mountains were magnificent. Their jagged, snow-covered peaks stood in majestic grandeur for all to see. He was even impressed by their beauty.

His eye spotted a hill ahead to the right. While reminiscing of the west he had lost track of time. He quickly returned to the present. The hill was covered with trees. It would not do for artillery. As he rode further, a smaller hill appeared at the base of the first hill. The top of this hill was clearly visible, as the trees had been cleared from the top and from the western slope. He put his hand up to stop his men. He took out his field glasses to get a better look at this hill. He looked for the top. It was clear. Artillery could be placed there with a good field of fire. The western slope was steep and strewn with rocks. At the base he observed a formation of large boulders. The ground dropped away uncovered from these boulders to a stone farmhouse. Here was some good ground. The larger hill to the south would be a natural defense to anchor a line on. Troops posted on this small hill would have a tremendous field of fire to their front. Buford liked what he saw. He needed to see the ground north of this small hill.

He looked up the road and saw in the distance church spires rising up from the town of Gettysburg. He gave the signal to proceed and his men continued their ride up the Emmitsburg Road. He cleared some woods, rode up a small incline and came to a peach orchard on his right. Again, he stopped his men and sent riders to notify his two brigade commanders, Colonel Gamble and Colonel Devin, to report to him. The landscape opened up. There was a ridge that extended from the base of the small hill, northerly to the edge of the town. The land dropped away from the ridge to the road he was on. It was open farmland, covered with wheat and crisscrossed with wood fences. Magnificent, he thought.

"What's up, sir," asked Gamble, with his slight Irish brogue.

"Look at the ground from that small treeless hill up to the town. What do you see?" replied Buford.

Gamble looked at the small hill and followed the land northerly to the town."Looks like excellent ground. An army entrenched there would be hard to dislodge."

"My thoughts exactly. Lee is west and north of here. If we can get Reynolds here before Lee arrives, he can entrench on this ground and perhaps we'll have the high ground this time."

Devin arrived."Sir, you sent for me."

"Look at the ground to our right," said Buford pointing to the small hill and up the ridgeline."Best damn ground I've seen in days."

Devin followed where Buford was pointing and saw the ground."It's fine ground, sir. I'd love to see our army entrenched here and see what old Lee could do against it."

"Knowing Lee, he won't attack head on. He'll go at the flanks. The small hill is protected by the larger one to its south, which will help secure our left flank. We'll have to scout near the town and see what the ground is like for the right flank. Let's ride into town and let the townsfolk know we are here. Perhaps we can get something to eat. I'll see you two in town."

Gamble and Devin returned to their brigades. Buford waved his division ahead towards Gettysburg.

ஃ😜🟩∾

Headquarters was now at Taneytown. Meade picked this spot to be near the center of his army. Dispatches could arrive and depart from headquarters in a timely fashion. He was waiting for his staff to gather after the morning march from Middleburg. It had been a short march of around seven miles. The hard marches of June 29th were replaced by short marches on the 30th. Meade did not want the army too fatigued from marching to fight. The long marches from Virginia to Pennsylvania had been tiresome enough.

General Warren would soon reach headquarters with information about the terrain in the area to deploy an army. Warren was his chief engineer and would have found the best ground to wage a battle. Meade was looking forward to his arrival and report.

An aide entered and said,"Williams, Butterfield and Hunt have arrived."

"Send them in. Let me know when the others arrive. I don't want to start the meeting without a majority of the staff present."

As they entered the tent, Meade nodded and offered them coffee. They poured themselves coffee and exchanged small talk. Butterfield remained silent. He was uncomfortable amidst this group and only wished to speak on military matters. Soon Sharpe, Ingalls, Norton and Letterman arrived. They also poured themselves some coffee and mingled with the other officers. Meade did not wish to start until Warren arrived. The rest of his staff was present.

"Sir, General Warren is here," said an aide.

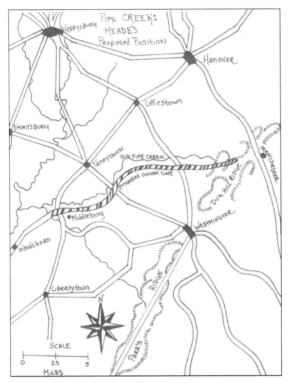

"Send him in. Hold all dispatches, unless Lee is attacking on a broad front. We will be meeting inside and do not wish to be disturbed," barked Meade at his aide. As Warren entered the tent, Meade welcomed him and said he was looking forward to his report, but other matters were to be discussed first.

"Gentlemen," started Meade,"I have received new intelligence that Ewell is pulling away from the Susquehanna River and heading in a southwest direction. I can only surmise he is heading toward Gettysburg to meet with Lee. Ten roads converge at Gettysburg, so it is a perfect gathering place for an army. Hill and Longstreet are west of Gettysburg between Cashtown and Chambersburg. Lee will most likely have his whole army around Gettysburg by tomorrow night. Reynolds has orders to be near Gettysburg today. He started only ten miles away, so he should get there before nightfall. He is in command of the left wing of the army, consisting of the First, Third and Eleventh Corps. He has been instructed to find good ground to fight on and send me instructions to advance the balance of the army if there is any such ground on which to fight. If he is unable to secure good ground, he will fight a delaying action and give us time to gather for a fight. General Warren has been out scouting the terrain and will now give us his report. You have the floor."

Warren walked over to the table, unrolled a map and placed it on the table. He placed weights on the corners so it would stay flat. The map had dirt smudges and some smears of dried blood on it. This map had seen some hard miles.

Warren started,"Sir, we have been out scouring the area for good ground to deploy this army and to protect Baltimore and Washington, per your orders. After lengthy discussions with my staff, we are of the opinion the army should make a stand behind Pipe Creek, between Middleburg and Manchester." He pointed to these areas on the map. He paused to let the others get their bearings. After a moment he continued."This line will defend our supply base at Westminster and cover both Baltimore and Washington. If Lee presses us, we can fall back to Dug Hill Ridge and Parr's Ridge. This secondary line will still protect Westminster. Our cavalry will be deployed at both flanks for protection and to monitor any wide flanking movements by Lee. We still hold an inside track to Lee. This is our best recommendation."

Meade looked at the map and asked for discussion. He did not wish to make the same mistakes as Hooker had by not keeping an open line of communication with his subordinates.

General Hunt, Chief of Artillery, looked at the map and said,"Looks like good ground for artillery. We can place guns to mass fire wherever Lee attacks. I can place reserve artillery on the two ridges, in case we need to fall back. Looks good from my end."

Captain Norton of the Signal Corps expressed his approval."There appears to be a good line of sight up and down the line for keeping communications open. I'm for it, also."

Williams spoke up,"Fine job, Warren. We'll have good interior lines and a fallback position should Lee push us hard. Nothing slows down an attack like a creek crossing. There is no cover. A well-thought-out plan."

Meade listened to these opinions and to the other voices in the room. He would hear them all out before making his final decision. He had not heard anything from Reynolds yet. Meade wondered if Reynolds would find ground as splendid as the area behind Pipe Creek. Warren had found a superb spot for the army to entrench. The question would be Lee's move. He very seldom struck head on against an entrenched army. He preferred flanking movements that exploited weak positions of his enemy. Warren's proposal had both flanks anchored by natural barriers, a ridge to the north end and a creek to the south. Meade liked the plan. If Reynolds was attacked and found he was in an untenable position, he could withdraw his wing command to Pipe Creek. The remaining four corps would have time to entrench behind Pipe Creek before Lee arrived.

"Gentlemen," Meade said. He waited for silence. He wanted their strict attention."I've listened to the discussion and am of the opinion Warren has put forth an acceptable proposal. I'll have Butterfield write up the orders for the army to move to Pipe Creek tomorrow. Dan, I need these orders written up so they can be delivered to all corps commanders before midnight."

Meade shifted gears."Send out orders immediately to all corps commanders to issue each man three days' rations and sixty rounds of ammunition. Everyone will get the message that a battle is imminent. I want all corps commanders to address their men explaining the immense issues involved in the upcoming fight. The enemy is on our soil. The whole country looks anxiously to this army for the defeat of this invading force. Corps and other commanders are authorized to order instant death to any soldier who fails in his duty at this hour." He gazed at each man to ensure they understood the gravity of the situation. He was satisfied they had.

Meade continued."At this time I have no desire to fight on the offensive until I have a better understanding of Lee's intentions. The Pipe Creek line allows us to fight defensively until there is an opportunity to strike at Lee. We should not take the offensive unless we are certain of success. I wish to send a dispatch to Reynolds. If he cannot hold at Marsh Creek, he should fall back to Emmitsburg. We can get reinforcements to him there quicker, providing he has good ground to make a stand. If not we will fall back to Pipe Creek. Let's get to work, gentlemen."

ॐ৪০১৪ॐ

Buford rode toward Gettysburg, still studying the terrain. Emmitsburg Road ran northeasterly, while the ridge off to his right ran in a northerly direction toward the town. The closer he got to the town, the closer the road was to the ridge. He saw a magnificent red barn with three spires on the roof to the right of the road. It was the largest, most magnificent barn he had seen this day. Upon passing it, he saw wood fences run back from the barn to a stone wall just before the crest of the ridge. The stone wall would afford cover for infantry. He looked to his left to see the ground slope away for roughly half a mile before disappearing into woods. Here was clear field of fire for artillery. The more he saw, the more he thought this would be good ground to fight from. He checked the time. It was close to eleven in the morning.

The ridge ended at a cemetery on the south side of town. The cemetery was on high ground. He halted his men, sending word to have them rest while he rode over to the cemetery. He sent for Devin and Gamble to meet him at the cemetery. When he got to the cemetery, he dismounted so he could study the view. The ridge ran south to the base of the small treeless hill about five miles away. There were open fields to the west dotted with wood fences running in every direction. These fences served to delineate different pastures. The cemetery sloped away in all directions surrounded by open fields. The town stood roughly half a mile to the north. Looking off to the east, he observed an open saddle of land that rose up to a wooded hill. He was impressed with this ground. This was a place to entrench an army.

Devin and Gamble rode up together. They dismounted and walked over to Buford.

"Lovely ground," said Buford."Both ends of the line can be anchored by tree covered hills, affording a natural fortress. The cavalry can be posted at both ends protecting the flanks."

"It is lovely ground," agreed Gamble.

Buford continued as if he didn't hear Gamble speak."Artillery can be placed along the ridgeline with clear fields of fire in all directions. The infantry can be posted in front of the artillery behind the stone walls and wood fences that run down to the treeless hill. We'll have good interior lines to move quickly to positions that are being threatened. I intend to send a dispatch to General Reynolds to hasten to this place before Lee gets here." *Lovely ground,* he repeated to himself."Now let's get the men into town."

They rode back to Emmitsburg Road and led their men the last mile into Gettysburg. As they entered, the people came out into the streets cheering and waving. Some children sang patriotic songs. Food and water were offered to the riders. Buford listened to the townsfolk. The enemy had been through town on two different occasions in the past few weeks, demanding supplies. If they did pay, it was with worthless Confederate money. Some reported Confederate infantry had been spotted this morning marching towards Gettysburg from the west. There were no enemy troops in the town at present, he was told.

Buford looked at his watch. Eleven fifteen. He would send scouts on the roads to the north and west of town. He let the rest of his men enjoy the food and drink they were being offered. A small break was in order. *Let them savor the moment*, he thought. His next move would depend on what the scouts discovered.

He got down off his horse and was offered a warm piece of bread from a young lady, who smiled and nodded her head. He thanked her and took the bread. It was smothered in butter. He took a bite and a faint smile came across his face as he chewed on the warm, butter-soaked bread. It reminded him of bread his mother had made when he was young. He would be allowed a piece as it came out of the oven. Bread would never be better than at that moment. He took another bite, smiled at the young lady and tipped his hat. War had its gentle moments, and this was one of them.

⚜

Reynolds established his headquarters at Moritz Tavern, a large brick building about a mile south of Marsh Creek. He had spent the day posting his corps in a strong defensive position behind the creek. Pickets were posted in forward positions. He knew from Buford's dispatch that Lee was nearby. Reynolds would not let his command fall victim to any surprise attacks by the enemy. The Eleventh Corps and the Third Corps were four miles away at Emmitsburg.

Reynolds had sent an invitation to General Howard to dine with him that evening. No such invitation had been sent to Sickles, as Reynolds had no intentions of entertaining that rascal. He shook his head as he thought of the two corps under his command. The Eleventh Corps, under General Howard, was filled with German and Dutch men. It had been overrun at Chancellorsville by Jackson's flank attack. Their reputation had taken a severe hit after they crumbled before Jackson, putting the rest of the army in jeopardy. Perhaps they would fight with a viciousness to restore their reputation. Reynolds could only hope so.

General Sickles, commanding the Third Corps, was another matter entirely. He was a political general, with no formal military training. His rank was due to his political connections in Washington. Sickles had been a solid backer of Hooker. He would need to be watched carefully in the upcoming fight. His two division commanders were from different ends of the spectrum. General Birney was a political general like Sickles. Unlike Sickles, Birney had distinguished himself in combat and his promotions were based on merit. Birney had been with the Third Corps since its inception in 1862, so the men knew him and his abilities.

General Humphries, the other division commander, was a West Point graduate. He had a reputation as a tough, demanding leader. He had been a division commander under General Meade at Fredericksburg and Chancellorsville. Reynolds recalled that Meade was livid after the battle of Fredericksburg, when Sickles was promoted to corps command over Humphries. Now Humphries, the more qualified of the two, would serve under Sickles as a division commander. This event happened due to bad timing. After Chancellorsville, most of Humphries division went home as their service time had expired. His remaining men were transferred into other divisions within the Fifth Corps. Humphries had no command, so on May 23rd he was ordered to the Third Corps to lead the Second Division. This concerned Reynolds, for no matter how solid one's reputation for leadership, there was a feeling-out process when a new commander was assigned to troops from outside of their ranks. Reynolds would have to keep his eye on the Third Corps.

An aide entered the room,"Sir, General Howard has arrived."

"Excellent. Send him in. Have my staff join us, then get word to the cook everyone is here and dinner can be served."

Howard entered the room and they greeted each other. Before they were done exchanging pleasantries, Reynolds staff entered the room. Howard was introduced to each staff member. They sat down and were served dinner, a meal consisting of chicken, potatoes and freshly baked bread. The conversation was of far away homes, family and tales of hunting exploits before the war. The hunting tales brought laughter to the room. For a few moments the war was not the topic and they were just men telling exaggerated stories, each one a little more outlandish than the previous.

When dinner was over, Reynolds excused the aides. He and Howard went into another room with maps spread out on a table. They walked over to the table and gazed at the maps.

"It seems a fight is imminent very shortly," started Reynolds."This afternoon's orders from HQ to issue sixty rounds of ammunition and three days rations to each man has everyone's attention."

"Yes, it does. My division commanders are asking me what is up. I haven't the faintest idea and tell them to carry out orders as they come in. What do you know?"

"I know what everyone else does before a battle: rumors and hearsay. The enemy is massing in force over there. The enemy will show up early in the morning with a force twice the size of ours. We are in that uncertain time before a fight, with no knowledge of Lee's intentions or any decision of where we will meet him. Earlier today I received a dispatch from Meade informing me to fall back to Emmitsburg if Lee should make a move towards Gettysburg. General Humphries, an engineer with the Third Corps, was assigned the task of finding suitable ground where I could deploy the three corps under my command. He found a position we could occupy behind Middle Creek, just north of Emmitsburg. This is why I countermanded your orders from HQ to march to Marsh Creek. By the time First Corps was on the road and you were to begin your march, I had received the orders from Meade to fall back to Emmitsburg."

"I was wondering that, but realized you had most likely received new orders and didn't have time to expound on them. My corps is near Middle Creek. The men are rested and ready."

"I sent word to Meade of our intentions. It seems he wants to fight a defensive battle, but is not sure where to gather the army. I hope he has time to gather the army before any fight against Lee. We are so spread out, Lee has an opportunity to attack individual units and put a serious ass whipping on us."

Howard cleared his throat. Reynolds remembered that Howard was quite religious and profanity was not to his liking. Reynolds had told himself this before the evening began, but damn it, they were in a war where men were dying. Profane language paled by comparison.

Reynolds spoke."I understand your dislike for profanity. However, it spills over into my conversation and I won't apologize for it. If you think my talk is vulgar, you should hear Humphries, Hancock or even the commanding general. I'm an altar boy by their standards. So, I would appreciate you not attempting to scold me when I let fly with some hellish phrase!"

Howard looked down at the floor."Yes, sir. Continue please."

Reynolds would much rather be in conference with those whom profanity was a natural occurrence, spewing forth as thick as a driving rainstorm. Reynolds used profanity sparingly, but was not offended by those who thought every noun needed to be salted with a descriptive profane adjective. He would make an attempt to keep profanity absent while speaking with Howard. Strategy was a more important topic and he wanted Howard's input.

"Buford sent word he entered Gettysburg. He mentioned seeing excellent ground to the south of the town. He was told of enemy forces just to the west of town and was sending out riders to recon the area. That was the last I've heard from him. So I'm sitting here with Buford telling me to come forward to occupy some good ground and with Meade ordering me to fall back if Lee makes an advance toward Gettysburg. If I advance to Gettysburg and run into Lee, I've got 31,000 troops to put in the field against roughly 80,000 of the enemy. These are not good odds. Is Meade close enough to reinforce me? It does not appear so from today's marching orders. I need more information."

Howard looked at the map."Sir, our last reports have Ewell's corps at York and Carlisle. This puts them thirty to forty miles from Gettysburg. If they make it to Gettysburg, it won't be until late tomorrow night and they would not be ready to fight until July 2nd. That brings down the number we'll have to hold against to 55,000. The Twelfth and Second Corps are close enough to get to Gettysburg tomorrow. Adding their 24,000 troops to ours and we can have 55,000 troops in the fight by tomorrow night. This seems to even the odds quite a bit."

"If in fact Ewell is still at York and Carlisle," added Reynolds."There is some talk that Lee will hunker down in Cashtown, throw up a strong defense at Cashtown Pass and wait for us to attack his fortified position. He would control the high ground, and it would be Fredericksburg all over again. I hope Meade learned from that debacle and would not order a frontal attack as Burnside did."

"I'm not sure Lee has the time to hunker down in a defensive position and await our attack. We could get behind him, cut off his supply line and his escape route. He would have to fight his way out. That might be to our advantage."

"You may well be right, but I'm not sure Washington will allow us to take a siege mentality. They'll be screaming at Meade to evict the invader from northern soil. The noise from Washington was one reason I would not accept the position of commander."

An aide entered with a dispatch from Buford. Reynolds took the dispatch and looked at his watch. 11:45. Almost midnight. Reynolds read the dispatch. Buford had spent the day ascertaining the whereabouts of the enemy. When he had entered Gettysburg that day, Confederate infantry were discovered about a half-mile west of Gettysburg. Upon seeing the Union cavalry troops, the Confederates retreated to the west on the Chambersburg Pike. Buford had sent riders out in all directions seeking information on Lee's army. He could find no other sign of infantry, but ran into some small detachments of enemy cavalry. Buford set up camp four miles west of Gettysburg on both sides of the Chambersburg Pike. The enemy campfires could be seen to the west. He was certain the enemy would attack him in the morning. He was requesting Reynolds to advance to Gettysburg as early as possible in the morning.

Reynolds shared the information with Howard. Reynolds spoke first,"I have no marching orders from Meade. My last order from Meade was to fall back to Emmitsburg if Lee should advance on Gettysburg. I sent him a dispatch confirming my adherence to these orders, even telling him of the position behind Middle Creek I would deploy on. Now Buford wants me to advance to Gettysburg, which would run counter to standing orders. I've no idea of Meade's overall strategy and could jeopardize it by moving to Gettysburg."

Neither general spoke. The silence filled the room with a deafening roar. Reynolds went to a chair and sat down. He crossed his arms just below his chest. Then he rubbed his forehead with his right hand. It would be a long agonizing night.

He looked up at Howard and said,"Tomorrow will be an interesting day. I'm tired and I have decisions to weigh if I don't hear from Meade. Head back to your troops and be ready for just about anything in the morning. I'll see you tomorrow."

"Goodnight, John. We're fighting Lee on our soil. I think the men will give a good account of themselves. Get some sleep."

ᔓᕉᘓᘎᘐ

During the night of June 30th, the busiest people in the Army of the Potomac were the couriers. Dispatches were being sent from headquarters to corps commanders throughout the night, into the wee small hours of the morning. The couriers were glad to get away from headquarters, for Meade was in a foul mood and snapping at everyone. He was especially upset with Butterfield, who did not have the Pipe Creek orders ready by midnight.

Meade was heard damning Butterfield for his inability to have the orders written up in a timely fashion. The Pipe Creek orders might or might not reach corps commanders by morning.

Meade had received a dispatch from General Buford around midnight. Buford had deployed his cavalry forces between three and four miles north and west of Gettysburg. The enemy was four and a half miles west of his position, encamped on both sides of the Chambersburg Pike. Buford wrote of good ground south and east of Gettysburg. He requested that Reynolds and his command be advanced to Gettysburg the next morning, to secure the ground before Lee took possession of it. Buford would fight a delaying action west of town until Reynolds arrived.

This information concerned Meade. From intelligence Meade knew Ewell was marching toward Gettysburg with his corps. It was possible for Ewell to reach Gettysburg sometime on July 1st, in which case, Lee would have his whole army concentrated at Gettysburg. This could spell trouble for Reynolds if he moved forward, as he would be seriously outmanned. Meade knew the Fifth and Sixth corps were two days away from Gettysburg. Events were rendering the Pipe Creek plan obsolete before it was even written.

Williams arrived."I came as fast as I could after receiving your summons. Has Butterfield completed the Pipe Creek orders?"

"No!" barked Meade."Damn that son of a bitch. He's taking his sweet ass time. I'll replace him when this fight is over. He's being most uncooperative."

Meade continued."I've received a dispatch from Buford. He's found good ground south of Gettysburg and requests Reynolds be ordered forward to secure it with his wing command. Reynolds has informed me he has good ground north of Emmitsburg, behind Middle Creek. He will fall back there if Lee approaches Gettysburg. This message complies with my orders to him earlier today. Now Buford requests I move a third of my army to Gettysburg. If I do this and Lee decides to attack, Reynolds could find his command seriously outnumbered."

"Twelfth Corps is nearby," added Williams."And Second Corps could reach Gettysburg tomorrow night. If the ground is as Buford describes, Reynolds could dig in and maybe hold off Lee until we get the rest of the army to him. If he can't hold, we can order him to withdraw to Pipe Creek, where the balance of the army will be entrenched and waiting."

"I need to get marching orders out for tomorrow, seeing that the orders for Pipe Creek will not be ready until later."

"Reynolds is the best you've got. He was given wing command for this reason. Send him to Gettysburg in the morning. He can scout the terrain and give you an informed opinion of its value to this army. I'd trust his judgment." Williams spoke with conviction.

"Perhaps you're right." Meade walked over to the map and studied it for a moment. He turned to Williams and said,"Get a pen and paper." When Williams was ready, Meade began issuing marching orders for July 1st."First Corps to Gettysburg; Eleventh Corps to Gettysburg; Third Corps to Emmitsburg; Second Corps to Taneytown; Twelfth Corps to Two Taverns; Fifth Corps to Hanover; Sixth Corps to Manchester. Get these orders written and to couriers to be delivered immediately."

"Yes, sir. It's past midnight. Try to get some shut eye. You're looking tired."

"We have our duty to attend to. Now get out of here," said Meade with a hint of a smile.

"Yes, sir."

Meade was alone. He needed to write to the Misses, if for no other reason than for some relaxation. He started writing:

I continue well, but am much oppressed with a sense of responsibility and the magnitude of the great interests entrusted to me. Pray that I may be permitted to be an instrument to save my country and advance a just cause.

He finished the letter. Then he sat, awaiting the Pipe Creek orders.

ഔ·ഴഄഓ·ഔ

Reynolds was asleep on the floor of the tavern. He heard a voice."Sir, new orders have arrived." He was not sure where he was. He sat up and looked around. His head was starting to clear. He was at Moritz Tavern. He must've fallen asleep on the floor.

"What's up?" he asked.

"Orders from headquarters just arrived."

"Let me see them."

The aide handed the orders to Reynolds, who looked at them. He was to proceed to Gettysburg in the morning. Eleventh Corps would be right behind him. So much for falling back, he thought. He hoped the ground would be as good as Buford proclaimed.

Reynolds thanked the aide."You're excused. If I'm not up at first light, please wake me."

He put his head back down on the floor and fell asleep.

❧⬩ℰ❁Ꮐ⬩❦

Buford was checking the lines. Gamble was deployed south of Chambersburg Pike. Devin was north of the Pike. He had pickets out and told them to be alert. He could see the campfires of the enemy, and they were numerous.

He was in Devin's camp discussing the situation.

"There'll be a fight here in the morning," started Buford."I hope we can hold until the infantry arrives."

"Sir, the boys are ready for a scrap. We'll keep those Secesh away all day, if need be," replied Devin.

Buford looked at him with steely eyes."No, you won't. They will attack you in the morning and will come booming, skirmishers three deep. You'll have to fight like the devil to hold your own until support arrives. The enemy must know the importance of this position, and will strain every nerve to secure it. If we are able to hold it, we shall do well. Be vigilant and keep alert."

Buford rode back to the Eagle Hotel, his headquarters for the night. He would grab some sleep, but as he rode, he knew he would be up early the next morning.

PART III
AN UNINTENDED CLASH

CHAPTER 16

July 1ˢᵗ

GENERAL ABNER DOUBLEDAY, commander of the Third Division in the First Corps, was enjoying his second cup of coffee. He had finished his breakfast over an hour ago. It was past 7 a.m. ,and he still had no marching orders for the day. Strange, he thought. Yesterday the men were issued ammunition and three days of rations. This meant a battle was imminent. It did not make sense that orders had not come down from the top. But where would the battle be? The enemy was to the west of the mountains, last he knew. It did not seem a battle would be brewing anywhere this day.

Riders were approaching. As they got closer, he recognized they were from Corps headquarters. They rode up to Doubleday and saluted.

"Sir, General Reynolds sends his compliments," said one of the riders."He wishes to speak with you at headquarters. We are to escort you to him."

"Fine. I'll get my horse and we'll head over."

He looked at his watch. It was 7:20. Something was up. Orders would normally arrive by courier, but Reynolds was requesting a conference. Would the other division commanders be present? He wasn't sure, but he would soon find out.

He mounted his horse and followed the others to headquarters. The sky was blue, sprinkled with fair weather clouds. The rainstorms of June 29ᵗʰ had cleared the humidity, leaving dry, pleasant air. If they were to fight, today would offer optimum conditions. The air would be temperate and dry. The heat would not be a burden on the men.

They reached Moritz Tavern. Reynolds was outside amongst his aides. He was issuing orders, and riders were heading off to deliver them.

Doubleday rode up and saluted."Morning, sir."

Reynolds returned the salute."Morning. Come inside, we've urgent business."

They walked into the tavern. Reynolds led him to a table covered with maps.

"I received marching orders from Meade very early this morning," began Reynolds."We are to proceed to Gettysburg. The latest information from Buford is the enemy is at Cashtown and Mummasberg and is advancing on Gettysburg. He is skirmishing with them on the roads west of Gettysburg." He pointed to the towns on the map and Buford's position. He gave Doubleday a moment to study the map. Then he continued."I've already ordered Wadsworth forward with his division accompanied by a battery of artillery under Captain Hall. I will ride forward with them. I'm placing you in charge of bringing the rest of the corps forward. Howard will come up behind you with the Eleventh Corps." He paused to gather his thoughts, and then went on."I have no idea of the ground or what we'll find when we get there. If you hear gunfire, just march to the sound of it."

"Any idea of the number of troops we may encounter?" asked Doubleday.

"Not really. Buford writes that A.P. Hill's corps is half a mile to his west and Longstreet is behind Hill. He's not sure where Ewell's corps is."

"What do you know of the position of our army?" Doubleday inquired.

"We're spread out. Slocum will be marching to Two Taverns, so he'll be close by. The other three corps are deployed from Taneytown, easterly to Manchester. They'll be of no help today, if we're drawn into a fight. They're too far away."

Reynolds paused. After a moment he continued."I'm riding forward with one division, to ground I've never seen, to take on any number of rebels. It's going to be a hell of a day!"

"I'll get to you as quick as I can. Perhaps we'll surprise Lee. I'll see you at the front."

Doubleday put out his hand. Reynolds found it and they exchanged a firm handshake. Doubleday looked at Reynolds and said,"Give 'em hell, John." Reynolds nodded.

⊱❧❦⊰

Doubleday rode back to his camp. He had much work to do. He had to call in the pickets and get the remaining two divisions on the road quickly. He needed to study the maps a little more thoroughly to be familiar with the roads to Gettysburg.

When he arrived in camp, he sent a rider to the west to General Rowley. Rowley was the First Brigade commander, and his troops were camped closer to the mountain passes to the west. Rowley would become division commander and General Biddle would take over the brigade. Rowley would march to Gettysburg via the westerly roads, keeping an eye on the passes. He also sent a rider to order General Stone to report to headquarters.

He then sent a message to General Robinson, the Second Division commander, to ready his men for marching. Then he was to report to Doubleday for orders.

Doubleday waited for them to arrive before going over the situation. He only wanted to say things once. After they arrived, he went over what he knew from his meeting with Reynolds. He then issued the order of the day's march. Stone would lead. General Robinson would have his division fall in behind Stone. The wagons would come up behind the infantry, so as not to clog the roads. Doubleday dismissed his commanders to their tasks.

It was 9 a.m. before the march got underway. Doubleday watched as the march commenced. When he was certain all the units were under way, he rode to the head of the column. The march proceeded at a normal pace. It was a pleasant morning for marching.

They marched northerly on the Emmitsburg Road. He marveled at the beauty of the landscape. Well-maintained orchards gave way to fields of hay and sprouting rows of corn. There were worm fences separating fields. The road was lined by post and rail fences. Farmhouses and barns were interspersed among the fields. They were well maintained structures. He sensed these people took pride in their farms.

Soon he heard the sounds of a fight. There was rapid cannon firing going off in the distance. Doubleday gave orders for the men to move forward at double time. Buford's cavalry was in a scrap and he intended to get his corps to the front as quick as he could.

Up ahead, he saw the end of Wadsworth's division crossing the open fields, heading toward the sounds of the cannon. There were holes in the fences and they were passing through at a rapid pace. He fell in line behind the First Division, moving with alacrity as the cannon fire grew louder.

"Lieutenant Marten to the front," he yelled to his aides.

Marten rode up alongside him."Yes, sir."

"Ride ahead and find Reynolds. With my compliments, tell him we are on the heels of Wadsworth's division and will be on the field right behind him. What are his orders for this command? Be quick about it."

"Yes, sir." Marten kicked his horse and galloped off to the front.

There were woods ahead. They were not too thick and Doubleday followed Wadsworth's men through. Coming out the other side, he noticed the land falling away. They were on a ridge that extended northerly. He saw the seminary building with the white cupola on top. He could see the smoke from the cannons rising in the fields west of the seminary. The smell of gunpowder overtook him. The sound of musketry was now evident. This was more than a skirmish. He rode ahead of the corps, passing Wadsworth's division, to observe for himself the battle. He got to the seminary building and rode to the west side.

Lieutenant Marten came riding up to Doubleday."Sir, General Reynolds sends his compliments and wishes you to attend to the area of Hagerstown Road. He is deploying Cutler's brigade north of Chambersburg Pike. You are to move forward to the next ridgeline and put up a stout defense. He says you are to fight for every inch of ground and hold off the enemy as long as possible, so Meade can bring up the army and secure the heights on the south side of town. He has sent riders to Meade, Howard and Sickles to get to this place with all possible speed."

"Well done. You may carry on." So, this would be where the battle would be fought. Buford had found good ground, and now Reynolds would fight a delaying action on the ridges west of Gettysburg, so the Army of the Potomac could advance and hopefully secure the high ground.

Doubleday looked to the west. There he saw enemy troops pressing the cavalry. He studied the terrain. The ground sloped away from the seminary, came to a low point and sloped up to the next ridgeline. There was a barn and farmhouse on the next ridge near the Chambersburg Pike. These buildings could be used for cover. He would need to get troops there. To the south was a small piece of woods, which appeared to be halfway between the Chambersburg Pike to the north and the Hagerstown Road to the south. He thought these woods would make an excellent defensive position. Troops deployed there would have excellent cover and be able to fire across open fields at any approaching enemy.

He saw Reynolds on the north side of the Chambersburg Pike deploying the brigade of General Cutler. Corps commanders needn't be so close to the front, but Reynolds was not one to lead from the rear. Doubleday rode off to the left to scout the ground near the Hagerstown Road. He heard a yell coming from the woods and knew the enemy had entered from the west. Wadsworth's division was at the seminary. Doubleday rode back to order Wadsworth to get his division to advance on those woods and clear them of the enemy.

The Second Wisconsin was the first regiment to arrive. They shifted from marching formation into line of battle with two ranks. They charged into the woods. The rest of the brigade came up on their left, one after the other. The Seventh Wisconsin fell into the left of the Second Wisconsin. Next came the Nineteenth Indiana, followed by the Twenty-Fourth Michigan. These regiments were known as the Iron Brigade. It was made up of men from the northwest frontier and they had a reputation of being fierce fighters. Doubleday watched as they charged into the woods taking on superior numbers."Rider!" he yelled.

An aide rode up next to him on horseback."Yes, sir."

"Go find General Rowley. Have him deploy Biddle's brigade on the left, protecting that flank. I want the line extended to cover the Hagerstown Road. General Stone is to deploy his brigade up by that barn. He needs to fill the gap between the Iron Brigade and Cutler's brigade. Understood?" Doubleday yelled over the noise of the battle.

"Yes, sir." The aide replied and rode off to find General Rowley.

Doubleday saw the Iron Brigade disappear into the woods. They were pushing the rebels back. Odd, he thought. There appeared to be only two Confederate brigades in the fight. Where was the rest of Lee's army? Lee had a reputation of showing a small force and then attacking an exposed flank with a larger force. He was renowned for using this tactic known as front and flank. Buford had riders to the north, to protect that flank. When the First Corps was deployed and the cavalry could be pulled back, Doubleday was certain Reynolds would send Buford to the left.

Doubleday saw Reynolds ride over behind the Iron Brigade, so he rode off to the left to scout the ground Biddle's brigade would be deployed on. They would reach the field after the Sixth Wisconsin, the last of the Iron

Brigade regiments to reach the seminary. He paused as he saw Rebel prisoners being marched out of the woods toward the seminary. There were numerous captives.

A rider approached,"Sir, we have driven the enemy out of the woods. There is a hill that drops down into a creek. We chased them across the creek, and the Twenty-Fourth Michigan got around their right flank into their rear. We've captured quite a few. They are with General Archer's brigade of Hill's corps. You're the first senior officer I've run into, so I'm reporting this to you."

"Marten, take this information to Reynolds. He'll want to know."

"Yes, sir," said the Lieutenant who rode off to find Reynolds.

Doubleday turned to the rider."Have your men bring the prisoners to the rear."

A young private from the Second Wisconsin was leading a prisoner towards Doubleday. The prisoner appeared to be a high-ranking officer. As they got closer, Doubleday recognized the prisoner. It was General Archer. They had served together before the war and knew each other.

Doubleday spoke,"Good morning, Archer. How are you? I am glad to see you."

"Well, I'm not glad to see you by a damned sight!" replied Archer.

"Take him to the rear with the others."

Marten came riding back and his face was ashen."Sir," he said with a trembling voice,"General Reynolds has been killed. You're in command of the field."

Doubleday was stunned.

ঔ৵৪৩৹ও

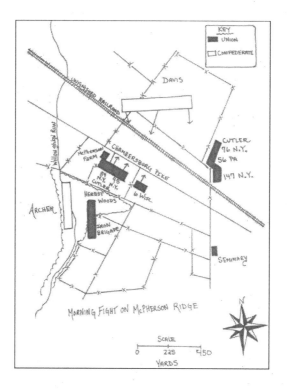

KEY
Union
Confederate

DAVIS

CUTLER
96 N.Y.
56 PA
147 N.Y.

CHAMBERSBURG PIKE

McPHERSON FARM

UNFINISHED RAILROAD

Willoughby Run

84 N.Y.
95 CUTLER N.Y.

6 WISC.

HERBST WOODS

ARCHER

IRON BRIGADE

SEMINARY

MORNING FIGHT ON McPHERSON RIDGE

N

SCALE
0   225   450
YARDS

Meade was in his headquarters at Taneytown. The Pipe Creek orders had been sent out early in the morning. It was his intention to fight Lee at Pipe Creek. General Hancock, whose corps was now at Taneytown, had spent some time with Meade. Meade discussed the Pipe Creek plan with him. He explained that Reynolds was moving to Gettysburg to encounter Lee, then to withdraw to Pipe Creek by way of the Taneytown Road. Meade hoped Lee would chase Reynolds all the way to Pipe Creek, where the Army of the Potomac would be entrenched on high ground. This was the plan Meade would follow.

Meade would send a telegram to Halleck, informing him of his intentions. He called for an aide, and one entered the tent quickly.

"I wish to send a telegram to General Halleck," said Meade to the aide."Get some paper at the table and get ready to write."

The aide moved to the table and took a seat. He got out some paper and reached for a pen."I'm ready, sir."

Meade started:

Headquarters Army of the Potomac

July 1, 1863—11 a.m.

Major Gen. H. W. Halleck
General-in-Chief:

General Buford has informed me that General Ewell is coming over the mountains from Carlisle, moving towards Gettysburg. The news proves my advance has answered its purpose. I shall not advance any, but am prepared to receive an attack in case Lee makes one. A battlefield has been selected at Pipe Creek and orders sent to all commanders with marching routes to reach Pipe Creek.

Geo. G. Meade, Major-General.

"Get this to the telegraph office and have it sent out immediately."

"Yes, sir," the aide replied. He stood up and left the tent.

Meade felt a growl in his stomach. He was hungry. He had consumed a large breakfast early this morning, but the stress seemed to be consuming his food at a rapid pace. His stomach was now empty and was barking at him. It would soon be time for lunch.

An aide reported,"Sir, Captain Weld of Reynold's staff has arrived."

Meade looked at the time. It was 11:20. He stepped out of the tent to meet with Weld.

Weld saluted,"Sir, I've a message from General Reynolds, sent with his compliments."

"Thank you, Captain. I can tell by looking at your horse that you've ridden hard. What's the message."

"Reynolds gave me explicit instructions to get here as quick as I could, even if it meant killing the horse. Fortunately, that didn't happen. He's a fine animal. The enemy is approaching Gettysburg in force. There's excellent high ground to the south of the town, which Reynolds intends to keep out of their hands. He is committed to fight for every inch of ground, even through the town. Reynolds is requesting that you bring the army to Gettysburg with all possible speed and secure the high ground."

"What of the Pipe Creek orders?"

"We never received any orders for Pipe Creek. Our last orders from you were to proceed to Gettysburg."

"Damn that Butterfield," Meade bellowed with some force. There was fire in his words. Butterfield's tardiness in having the orders ready was now proving to be a problem. If Reynolds were to get overwhelmed by Lee, his last orders were to fall back to Emmitsburg. This would leave a gaping hole on the Taneytown Road for Lee to exploit. Meade wondered who else did not receive the orders.

He turned to Weld."Cool your horse down and get something to eat. I may need you to ride back with new orders for Reynolds. You're dismissed for the time being. Stay where I can get in touch with you."

Weld saluted and left.

Meade walked into the tent and looked at the map. The Twelfth Corps was at Two Taverns. They were covering the Baltimore Pike. The Second Corps was at Taneytown. He would send them forward to cover Taneytown Road. He would get word to Hancock to amend his marching orders.

What else could go wrong, he lamented.

ﻬ

Reynolds was dead. Doubleday had trouble catching his breath. He took a moment to grasp the news. It was unfathomable. Corps commanders just didn't get killed. They were too far from the front lines. They remained in the rear to observe the action and direct their forces on the ever-changing battlefield. Their job was to manage their corps during combat.

Doubleday was now the senior commander on the field. He did not know the big picture, he only knew Reynolds wanted to contest every inch of ground, so Lee could not gain possession of the high ground south of Gettysburg. Perhaps General Howard had received new orders from headquarters. When Howard reached the field, he would have seniority to Doubleday and be in charge. Until then, Doubleday would do all he could to follow Reynolds last order.

The Iron Brigade had repulsed the advance of Archer's brigade and were falling back to the top of the ridge in the woods. Brigade Commander General Meredith was deploying them. Doubleday approved of his deployment. The position was strong. It was quiet in front of the Iron Brigade. Doubleday heard increasing musketry to the north. He rode over to see what was happening.

The right flank was collapsing. The two regiments on the extreme right were moving to the rear. Had Cutler ordered a retreat? Doubleday was unaware of any order to fall back. There appeared to be only one Confederate brigade attacking. Why would Cutler withdraw? Doubleday observed one Union regiment remaining on the north side of the road. They would soon be pressed on the front and flank by a Confederate brigade. Their flank had been exposed when the two right regiments retreated. Doubleday saw their commanding officer bend the right of the regiment back to refuse the line. This would buy some time.

Doubleday sprung into action. He turned to an aide,"Ride over to those two regiments up by the barn and order them forward to the road. Have them pour enfilading fire on the enemy advancing across those fields."

"Yes, sir." The aide rode off at a gallop to convey the orders.

Doubleday rode over to the Sixth Wisconsin, near the seminary building. They had been deployed there in a reserve position. He rode over to their commander, Lt. Colonel Dawes.

"Get your unit over to the Chambersburg Pike," Doubleday ordered."I want you to place your left onto the right of the two regiments that will be advancing to that position from the barn."

As they looked to the north, they saw the last regiment retreating. Its position was getting overrun and many of the men were down. There were now six pieces of artillery exposed on the north side of the Pike with no infantry support. Doubleday looked at Dawes and said,"Damn, the whole line is collapsing and those guns are on the verge of being captured. Get over there on the double and see if you can salvage the guns and restore some order. Reynolds orders are to hold this ground as long as possible."

"We'll get to the road and then charge the bastards," Dawes answered with steely determination.

It was a critical moment. If those six guns were captured, they could be turned on the Union forces, and create havoc. Doubleday watched as canister was unleashed from the cannons tearing holes in the oncoming

Rebels. Their advance slowed in the face of this canister. Doubleday saw the artillery commander, Captain Hall, riding hurriedly behind the guns, pointing in all directions and exhorting his men to fight. The gun furthest to the right was being withdrawn. Enemy skirmishers fired on the gun and its crew. Four horses went down. Then he watched in amazement as the remaining canoneers withdrew the piece by hand. Other canoneers were fighting in a fierce hand-to-hand struggle, using whatever piece of equipment was available as a weapon, to save as many guns as possible. Doubleday gave a silent shout to those brave men.

Dawes was now at the road behind a wood fence. He had hooked up with the other two regiments. All at once, they unleashed a galling fire into the unsuspecting Confederates. Doubleday watched their lines dissolve. They changed their front to meet this onslaught. The Confederates faced the road and were advancing when they dropped from sight. At this moment Dawes ordered all three regiments forward. Doubleday saw them at the far side of the field aiming down and firing. He sent an aide to see what was happening. The noise of musketry was lessening and that fierce Rebel yell was silent. The smoke was clearing.

Soon the aide returned."Sir, we've captured two Rebel regiments along with their battle flags. They were trapped in a railroad cut. The third regiment escaped to the west. The two units are the Second and Forty Second Mississippi. They are with the brigade of General Davis, which is attached to General Heth's division. We have recaptured all the guns and secured the right flank."

"Excellent," said Doubleday. He looked over the field. It was now quiet. Two Rebel brigades had been stymied and many prisoners were taken. He looked at his watch. It was 11:15. All this had taken place in thirty minutes. He had no idea what the rest of the day would bring, but he had held the ground.

ঔৎ৪৩৫৬৯

Meade sat on a camp stool outside his tent alongside General Williams. They had just finished eating and were discussing the unfolding predicament facing the army. Meade was furious with Butterfield and laid the blame for the mess squarely at his feet. Williams let him vent. A commander needed an ear once in a while, if for no other reason than to get an issue off his chest. The burden of command was heavy enough without having to carry it around, bottled up inside.

When he was done with his diatribe against Butterfield, Meade took a deep breath. He looked off into the distance, staring blankly at nothing. Then he turned to Williams and started talking in a more composed manner.

"Well, it seems we're in a hell of a mess. I'm not sure how many commanders received the Pipe Creek orders. By the end of the day we could have troops marching all around Maryland and Pennsylvania in a disjointed fashion. If Lee gathers his forces he could fall on a portion of this army and put a serious whipping on it. I wonder whom Halleck will replace me with. One battle and done. It seems to be a pattern with this army."

"Don't worry about Washington. Lee is your major concern, and getting control of the army. You'll just have to adapt to the situation as it unfolds. This has been the problem for generals throughout the ages. The ones that adapt quicker to the battlefield as it is, and not how they want it to be, have been proven to be the more successful tacticians. We've learned all about them at West Point."

"Yes, we studied military tactics, but do they talk about the human factor? Do they teach us about generals unable to get along and petty differences between officers sabotaging plans? I think not!"

"You're an engineer, and I understand you want to fix problems. This is how engineers are wired. Even General Washington had difficult subordinates to deal with, but he had his eye on the success of the revolution and utilized men for their strengths. You have to deal with the issues, not the personalities. If the job is not being done, you can reassign anyone. But for now, we must deal with all possible contingencies and make the best choice based on what we know. I'll say this; unlike Hooker, you're keeping an open line of communication with your staff and asking for input. It's a more professional command style."

"Good to know I'm being viewed as the opposite of Hooker. He didn't win many allies while in command," said Meade with a slight chuckle.

"No, he didn't," agreed Williams."What if Reynolds has found good ground at Gettysburg? Should we make plans to advance the army in that direction?"

"Sedgwick with the Sixth Corps is two days away and the Fifth Corps will not reach the field until late tomorrow afternoon. They'll both be fatigued after long marches. Is it fair to throw them into some ongoing battle after hard marches? I still think we have time to regroup and get the army marching to Pipe Creek in good order."

An aide came forward saluting."Sir, General Pleasonton requests to speak with you most urgently."

"I'll see him now," said Meade.

Pleasonton was in command of the cavalry. Meade looked at Williams and said,"Perhaps he has some news from Buford. Any news from the front will be welcome."

Pleasonton rode up and dismounted. He walked toward Meade with a paper in his hand. The look in his eyes screamed something's terribly wrong.

"Sir, I just received this dispatch from Buford. Reynolds is dead." His voice was trembling and he tried to continue, but found it hard. He handed the dispatch to Meade.

Meade looked at Pleasonton in disbelief. He took the dispatch and started reading:

I am satisfied that Longstreet and Hill have made a junction. A tremendous battle has been raging since nine and one-half a.m. with varying success. At the present moment the battle is raging on the road to Cashtown, and in short cannon range of Gettysburg; the enemy's line is a semi-circle on the height from north to west. General Reynolds was killed early this morning. In my opinion, there appears to be no directing person—we need help now.

When he finished reading, he handed the note to Williams,"Read this. We've lost the best one of us, and all hell's breaking loose."

Williams took the dispatch and read it. He couldn't speak for a moment. There was a deafening silence surrounding the generals, each lost in his own thoughts.

Meade broke the silence."This changes everything. Who's senior officer in the First Corps?"

Williams thought for a moment and then answered,"It would be Doubleday. He should take charge until Howard arrives."

Meade shook his head. He didn't have much confidence in Doubleday. Hell, he had never even led a division into combat and now he was in charge of a corps. The dispatch was two hours old. Meade wondered what changes had taken place since the dispatch was written. He needed to act.

He turned to Williams and spoke,"I'm riding over to see Hancock. I'm sending him to Gettysburg to assess the situation. If the left wing is getting hammered by Lee, we may have to fall back to Pipe Creek with seriously diminished numbers. Stay close to headquarters in case more dispatches arrive from the front. After I talk with Win, I'll be back."

ം•ജ)(ഔ•ം

Buford rode over to check with Devin. Gamble's brigade had done a marvelous job slowing down the advance of two Confederate brigades until Reynolds arrived with the infantry. Gamble had 1500 men fighting against 3500. Gamble had fought a brilliant tactical fight, losing very few men in the process. His two-hour fight from Herr Ridge to McPherson's Ridge ensured Reynolds could deploy on McPherson's Ridge and fight on good ground. Reynolds death was a great blow to Buford. He didn't know a finer general in the Union army. Buford had no use for Doubleday, whom he considered nothing more than an average general. Others Buford had talked to during the war held this view as well. However, he had watched as Doubleday took control quickly after Reynolds death and turned impending danger into a victory, capturing many prisoners and restoring order on the field. Maybe there were some leadership qualities in Doubleday. They were apparent this morning. Buford would still deploy his own men as he saw fit. He was still intent on holding his ground north and west of Gettysburg until the rest of the army came forward. He had sent the dispatch to Pleasonton in hopes it got to Meade. He wanted them to know of the urgency of getting the army forward with all possible speed. The heights south of Gettysburg were still waiting for one army to deploy on. Buford hoped it would be the Army of the Potomac.

He reached Devin's position."How goes it, Devin?"

"It's all quiet at the moment, sir. I've got riders out to the north. They report Ewell's corps is headed this way, but they're still an hour or more away. What are your orders?"

Buford responded."I want you to hold these roads that approach Gettysburg from the north. The First Corps has repulsed the morning attack and is entrenching on McPherson's Ridge. General Howard will be arriving soon with the Eleventh Corps. I'll try to impress on him the importance of moving his corps north of town to relieve you. When he relieves you, I want you to cover his right flank. I'm going over with Gamble to cover Hagerstown Road and the left flank of the First Corps. You need to hold your ground until the infantry relieves you. Understood?"

"Yes, sir. We put up a hell of a fight this morning and I'm hearing we took light casualties."

"You heard correctly. Keep me posted."

Buford rode off to find Gamble and post his brigade. His two brigadiers were fighters and they had not let him down this day. They had performed admirably.

ɷ๛ʊʊɷ๛

There was a lull in the fighting. Doubleday was busy reforming the lines. The Iron Brigade was deployed at the top of a ridge in the woods. Their formation was in the shape of a"C" following the contour of the ridge. Below them was a slope that bottomed out in a creek named Willoughby's Run. They had clear fields of fire to the west and the southwest.

General Cutler's brigade was posted to the north near the Mummasburg Road. They were deployed in front of some woods, facing north and west. Doubleday could see there were gaps to fill. Cutler's brigade could not fill the land between the Chambersburg Pike and the Mummasberg Road. Fortunately, the remaining divisions of the First Corps were arriving on the field.

Colonel Roy Stone and his staff rode up to Doubleday. Stone had three brigades of men from Pennsylvania. They were itching to get a shot at extricating the invaders from their state. Stone addressed Doubleday,"Sir, the One hundred forty-third, One hundred forty-ninth, and the One hundred fiftieth regiments are reporting for duty. My men are anxious for a fight."

"They'll get that and more. See that farmhouse and barn on the next ridge?" asked Doubleday, pointing to the northwest."I want you to deploy your brigade there. Connect your left with the Second Wisconsin's right, which you'll find in the woods. Extend your line to the road, which is the Chambersburg Pike. Hill and Longstreet will be coming down that road later today. You'll have artillery on your right extending your line to an unfinished railroad cut. You're to hold the line as long as possible. I'll have troops in reserve ready to move forward if you get hard pressed."

Stone smiled and replied,"Hell, we won't need any reserve, we'll whip old Bobby Lee ourselves. You can count on us, sir. You take care of the rest of the field."

Doubleday liked this confidence."Is General Robinson behind you?"

"Yes, he is, sir. I'll go deploy my brigade."

Doubleday watched Stone and his staff ride forward to check out the ground. He rode back to the seminary to meet General Robinson when he arrived. He noticed a wood fence running north and south near the top of the ridge just to the west of the seminary building. He may have seen this fence before, but he was too busy deploying troops to actually notice it. This fence afforded cover for infantry. Here would be his first fallback position if he were pressed. He would post some brigades from Robinson's division here to build breastworks and fortify the position.

He spotted Robinson and his staff approaching the seminary. They exchanged greetings.

"How goes the fight?" asked Robinson.

"We turned back two brigades from Hill's corps. We took many prisoners, who inform us the whole Rebel army is coming down this road and will send us to hell today. I've no doubt we'll be in a heavy scrap before this day's out. Reynolds is dead. My orders are to hold this ground, so the rest of our army will have time to deploy on the heights south of Gettysburg."

"I noticed the ground riding here. Thought it could be of some use for an army."

"Reynolds told me this morning it is the place to fight. He sent riders to Meade to bring the army up quickly. I want you to place one brigade at yonder fence. Fortify the position. Tear the fence down and use the rails for breastworks. This will be our first fallback position. Send your other brigade north to extend Cutler's line. I'm waiting here for Rowley to arrive. After I put him in position, I'll ride up and check out your position. I haven't had a chance to get up to that end of the field yet."

Robinson looked to the west."This is a fine position, sir. Excellent field of fire. We'll pour some lead into Johnny from here. I'll send General Baxter north and deploy General Paul here."

"Get to it. I don't know how long this lull will last."

Rowley would be arriving from the west. Doubleday rode down the Hagerstown Road and waited for Rowley. His brigade would be deployed to the left of the Iron Brigade. When this was accomplished, the First Corps would be in a position from the Mummasberg Road, south to the Hagerstown Road. The three major roads entering Gettysburg from the west would be covered. This should slow Lee down. For how long, he was not sure, but he hoped long enough to enable the Army of the Potomac to grab the high ground. Would they get here in time? This was beyond his control. Doubleday would do his utmost to carry out Reynolds' orders.

He saw Buford with his cavalry going into position south of the Hagerstown Road. Buford had sent a rider to inform Doubleday of his intentions. Devin's Brigade was still deployed north of Gettysburg and would hold until Howard arrived with the Eleventh Corps.

Rowley arrived with his brigade. Since Doubleday was now corps commander, he told Rowley he was in charge of the Third Division and he should appoint a brigade commander to replace him. Rowley said General Biddle would be the new brigade commander. Doubleday rode with Rowley and pointed out the area to the left of the Iron Brigade where he was to deploy. When this was done, he rode north to check on Cutler and Robinson.

ౚ•౪)(౧•౼

General Howard reached Gettysburg well ahead of his corps. He had received the message from Reynolds to make haste and get forward as quickly as possible, for he had made contact with the rebels. The march had started in a torrential rainstorm, muddying the roads and making the men miserable. When the corps crossed into Pennsylvania, the roads were dry and the sky was sprinkled with fair-weather clouds. When Howard caught up to the tail end of the First Corps on their march up the Emmitsburg Road, he left the road and passed the marching men. He got to a peach orchard and heard the sound of the battle raging in the north. He rode ahead with Colonel Meysenburg of his staff to scout the ground. They arrived at Cemetery Hill and stopped to survey the landscape. They came to the same decision that Buford had yesterday.

Howard looked across the open fields sloping away in three directions, and said,"This seems to be a good position, Colonel. This must be the position Reynolds alluded to in his message. He spoke of heights to the south of the town that he hoped he could keep the enemy from attaining."

Meysenburg nodded his head and replied,"It's a fine position, General."

"Let's go into town and have a look around," said Howard.

They rode into town looking for a tall building to observe the fighting from. They rode up to two young men who appeared to be in their teens.

"Son," said Howard"can you direct me to a building where I can see the battle."

"Why, we've been watching the fight from the observatory on the roof of my dad's dry goods store. I'll take you there," said one of the young men.

"Thank you, son. What's your name?"

"Daniel Skelly, and this is my friend, Gus Bentley."

"Nice to meet you, I'm General Oliver Howard of the Eleventh Corps. Now let's go have a look at the battle."

They led him to the building on Middle Street and took him into the observatory on the roof. Howard pulled out his large field glasses and looked out over the fields where two brigades of the First Corps were fighting. He then looked to the north and saw the cavalry in position blocking the incoming roads. There was no sign of Confederates coming down any of the north roads.

Captain Hall, one of his aides, came riding down the street. He spotted Howard and yelled up,"Sir, General Reynolds is dead. You're the senior officer on the field."

Howard looked at his watch. It was 11:00.

"God help us," was all he could say. Being a religious man, he said a quick prayer for Reynolds' soul. We must hold this place until the army arrives.

"Captain," he yelled to Hall,"ride to General Schurz and inform him General Reynolds has been killed. Tell him he is in charge of the Eleventh Corps, as I am acting commander of the field. Tell him to get forward as quickly as he can. You'll find him marching up the Taneytown Road."

"Yes, sir." Hall kicked his horse and galloped south out of town.

Howard turned to Meysenburg and said,"Let's head back to the cemetery. I will use this as my headquarters position." He thanked the young men for bringing him to this observatory, and then he went down to the street. As he was riding south to the cemetery, more of his staff arrived. He called for Captain Pearson. The captain came over and saluted.

"Captain," said Howard,"Ride down to General Barlow and tell him we are engaged with the enemy and to come forward with his division quickly. Then ride to General Sickles at Emmitsburg. Inform him of the situation here and tell him to have his corps ready to advance if the need arises."

"Yes, sir," the Captain replied. He turned his horse around and headed south.

Howard and his staff rode up to Cemetery Hill. If Reynolds wanted this spot held, Howard would do his best .

ɷ☙ɷ☙☙ʚ☙

General Hancock was at his headquarters tent with his chief of staff, Lt. Colonel Charles Morgan. They were discussing the Pipe Creek orders and going over the marching order for the corps. Hancock had studied the map and liked the position for the army. He wondered if Lee would take the bait and attack a well-entrenched Union army. It did not seem to fit what he knew of Lee's style.

An aide appeared in the tent,"Sir, General Meade is riding up."

"Meade?" said Hancock in a puzzled tone. Commanding generals usually sent their aides to convey any messages."Let's go meet him outside," he said to Morgan.

They stepped out of the tent and watched Meade ride up. Hancock saluted and said,"I'm guessing this isn't a social call."

Meade returned a brisk salute and got off his horse."Correct." Meade was not one to waste words."Reynolds has been killed at Gettysburg this morning. Buford tells me he is heavily engaged with Hill's corps and there seems to be no one worth a damn in charge. Doubleday would be the senior commander in the First Corps. I've worked with him and am not impressed with his abilities. I may need to assign some other general to take over the First Corps. All hell seems to be breaking loose at Gettysburg, and I have no idea what the ground looks like. Both Reynolds and Buford informed me there were heights south of the town this army should occupy. I need you to ride to Gettysburg and check out the ground. I need your opinion that it is indeed good ground and I'll have time to order the army there."

"Damn, Reynolds was the perfect general. We've lost a good man. What of the Pipe Creek order?"

"It seems he never received it. That bastard Butterfield was so slow putting the orders together that they never went out until this morning. Reynolds' aide told me they never received any orders concerning Pipe Creek. So if the First Corps is pushed hard, they will retreat towards Emmitsburg, for these were the last orders they received from me. This will leave a huge hole in the army on the Taneytown Road, the road Reynolds would have marched to Pipe Creek by. I'm assigning Gibbon to take over your corps and placing you in charge of the left wing in place of Reynolds. I want Gibbon to move the corps forward about five miles on the Taneytown Road. He will deploy on good ground and protect the road from falling into Lee's hands."

"General Howard is senior to me. Won't this cause a problem?" asked Hancock.

"I've got these handwritten orders signed by me putting you in charge. He'd damn sure not make it a problem. You show him these orders if he balks at relinquishing command! I'm having an ambulance sent over with maps to take you to Gettysburg. You can study maps in the back on your way there. I'm counting on you, Win. Hell, this army is counting on you. The Twelfth Corps is four miles from Gettysburg at Two Taverns and your corps could reach the town by nightfall. The Fifth and Sixth Corps won't be able to reach the town until tomorrow night at the earliest. The ground may be good, but I'm still intent on gathering the army at Pipe Creek to fight Lee there. If you feel the ground at Gettysburg is good, and we can hold it until the whole army arrives, well, you let me know, and I'll mobilize everyone to your position. With Reynolds gone, you're the best I've got. Take care of yourself."

"Thank you, sir. You can count on me. Nothing will give me more pleasure than choosing the battleground on which to repel those damn invaders."

Meade smiled inside. Hancock was confident and brash, but thoroughly competent for this task. He'd like to be at the front when Hancock met Howard with orders to take command. Hancock was known for his sharp, salty tongue that could spew forth profanities at a rapid clip. Howard was an overtly religious man, who abstained from vulgar language. Meade thought it would make for an interesting meeting. No time for hurt feelings, there's a battle to prepare for.

CHAPTER 17

Afternoon

DOUBLEDAY WAS ON MCPHERSON'S RIDGE looking west. Confederate soldiers were going into battle formation on Herr's Ridge. Their ranks were growing by the minute. This would be Hill's Corps preparing to advance. Doubleday had roughly seven thousand troops ready to fight. Hill could put nineteen thousand in the field. It would be a rough go for the First Corps. If Longstreet was behind Hill with his twenty-five thousand men, the First Corps would be vastly outnumbered.

The corps had fought valiantly in the morning, but would now face superior numbers. He knew Slocum and Sickles were within striking distance. If they arrived on the field soon, they would greatly even the odds.

An aide came galloping up and saluted,"Sir, General Robinson sends his compliments and wishes to inform you that Confederate forces are massing on his front."

Doubleday took out his field glasses and looked to the north. Rebel banners were swirling in the wind and troops were forming in battle formation behind the flags. This must be Ewell's Corps.

He lowered the glasses and said to the aide,"Ride over to General Howard, who is on Cemetery Hill and inform him of this development. At the moment only one brigade of cavalry is on my right. We'll need reinforcements or we will get flanked."

"Yes, sir." The aide saluted and took off for Howard.

Doubleday turned to an aide and said,"Ride up to Robinson. Have him refuse the right of his line, so he'll have troops facing north and west. He'll have to hold with what he's got, until help arrives and bolsters his line."

The aide rode off to deliver the order.

Doubleday looked back to the west. The enemy line was growing in both depth and length. If their line extended north and they hooked up with Ewell's corps their front would be formidable, potentially overlapping each end of his line. He looked south and saw no dust arising from marching troops. Would Sickles and Slocum arrive in time?

He called for another aide."Ride over to Colonel Stone. Have him deploy the One Hundred Forty-third Pennsylvania from a reserve position to the Chambersburg Pike, facing north. The One Hundred Forty-ninth Pennsylvania needs to extend their line down the pike so their right rests on the One Forty-third's left. The One Forty-ninth will now face west and north."

The aide rode off toward McPherson's farm where Colonel Stone was located.

A rider hurriedly approached from the left."Sir, General Meredith sends his compliments and wishes to inform you of a situation. Colonel Biddle's brigade has pulled back from his position, exposing the left flank of Meredith's brigade. Meredith's left flank has no support and is hanging in the air. Colonel Morrow of the Twenty-forth Michigan is madder than hell and wishes to file a complaint against Biddle."

"Go back and inform Meredith I'm looking into the situation." Doubleday turned to one of his aides and said,"Ride over to Biddle and find out why he retreated. I need him forward to the left of the Iron Brigade."

Doubleday looked across to the Confederate troops forming. More were amassing to the west and north. They'd be coming soon.

৸৵৵৩

Things were not going well for Howard on Cemetery Hill. He had sent General Schurz forward to deploy on the right of the First Corps. When Schurz went forward, the high ground he was ordered to station his troops on was filled with enemy troops. He deployed on ground to the right of the First Corps facing north. The ground was low and not suitable for defense.

General Barlow had been deployed north of Gettysburg between the Carlisle Road and Harrisburg Road. According to Buford, General Ewell would be marching down these roads with two divisions. Howard viewed the position of his two divisions, and saw the land was too vast for him to cover it properly. By hooking his right with Barlow's left, Schurz's left flank could not reach the right of the First Corps. There was a hole in the line.

Howard had sent a dispatch to Sickles and Slocum at 1 p.m. informing them of the morning's fight. He did not seek their help at that time. Seeing his lines unable to cover all the ground north of Gettysburg, he knew he needed help. He looked at his watch. It read 1:55.

He wrote out a dispatch to both Slocum and Sickles requesting they come forward immediately as a battle was brewing. He then wrote another dispatch to Meade informing him of the overall situation and that he, Howard, had requested Sickles and Slocum to advance to his position. He sent three different riders to deliver these dispatches to their destinations.

"Sir," said an aide,"Look to the north. General Barlow is moving his division forward."

Howard looked in the direction of Barlow's Division. They were advancing.

"Ride up to Schurz and ask if he ordered this movement," barked Howard to his aide.

The sound of cannon fire from the west caught his attention. The Confederates were unleashing artillery from the west and northwest. This generally preceded an advance by infantry. The First Corps were dug in on good ground, but they barely had enough men to hold back what the Confederates were about to unleash. His Eleventh Corps was deployed on poor ground with too few troops. Now, Barlow was moving forward increasing the amount of ground he would have to cover. The Eleventh Corps took a beating at Chancellorsville and were known as the corps that ran in the face of the enemy, causing the Union flank to collapse. The men needed to atone for their poor showing, but events were quickly spiraling out of control. Howard knew reinforcements would not reach the field in time.

છ∞જી

The enemy was advancing. Doubleday looked to the north and saw the troops moving forward, wheeling to the right, like a door shutting. They were heading for General Robinson's troops north of the Chambersburg Pike. He looked to the west and saw the lines on Herr's Ridge moving forward. Many a good man would be shaking hands with the devil before this day was over.

There were issues to contend with, but it was now too late. The first issue was the retreat of General Biddle's men. In their forward position, they were under a tremendous barrage of artillery fire and General Rowley ordered them to withdraw. Biddle withdrew acting on orders from his superior commander. Doubleday could find no fault with Biddle. Rowley had made the decision that threatened the overall deployment of his troops in this sector. The Iron Brigade was forward with their left flank hanging in the air. There was now no time to redeploy Biddle's brigade, with the advance of the enemy. Doubleday was aware that battles, once started, took on a life of their own and a commander had to respond quickly to the ever-changing ebb and flow of lines being swallowed up by smoke and confusion.

The second issue was the poor deployment of the Eleventh Corps. General Robinson had sent a rider to inform Doubleday that the Eleventh Corps was not anchored on his right. They were about four hundred yards to the east. Robinson's right flank was in the air. Enemy troops were now headed for that hole in the line. Their commanders would take advantage of this gap and attempt to breach it so as to get behind the exposed Union flank. Doubleday sent an aide to General Paul, who was being held in reserve at the seminary. His orders for Paul were to move north to help plug that gap. Doubleday sent a rider to Robinson informing him of Paul's advance to his sector.

Doubleday watched as the Confederates to the north continued their wheel movements until their lines were perpendicular to the Mummasburg Road. They advanced across an open field, but he noticed there were no skirmishers leading the attack. *Odd,* he thought, *infantry advancing in battle always sent skirmishers ahead, to probe for the enemy.* He moved his glasses to view Baxter's line. They were lying behind a stone wall with their regimental flags down. They could not be seen from the other side of the wall. The Confederates were advancing toward a perceived hole in the line that was devoid of Union troops. Three cheers for Baxter, the crafty bastard.

Doubleday looked to the west. The troops advancing from this direction would not reach the Iron Brigade for another twenty minutes. He told his staff he was moving north to get a better view of the impending fight. He left a few aides behind with orders to forward all messages to his new position. He rode north with his remaining staff. They found a spot to watch the events in this sector unfold.

The Confederates were marching forward in battle formation, howling that fierce Rebel yell. It sent shivers up his spine. He counted four regimental flags leading the formation. It was a whole brigade advancing. Within fifty yards of the wall, he watched Baxter's men rise from behind the stones and unleash a galling fire. The Rebel line was torn to pieces. They fell like wheat before the scythe. Huge gaps appeared as men fell in their tracks. The advance halted as if running into an imaginary barrier. They tried to close their lines, but this proved fruitless. They were in the open and were getting cut down at a torrid pace. Baxter's men poured unrelenting fire into their ranks. Any attempt to reform their ranks was unsuccessful. Some ran to the rear and others started waving white flags. Baxter's men moved forward and brought the captives back. This was another small victory for the boys in blue.

Doubleday saw more brigades filling in behind this shattered one. Their lines were lengthening and soon would merge with the troops advancing from the west. He thought of bees. *We just killed one, but a swarm is coming our way.* He heard the sound of musketry to the east. He looked that way and saw a Union line well in advance of other troops in that sector. Their flanks were hanging in the air and a much larger Confederate force was advancing. These were Eleventh Corps troops. What the hell were they doing so far forward? He shook his head. Another poor deployment for that corps. No wonder their reputation was deplorable. They were Howard's problem. Howard had ridden over to see Doubleday earlier. Howard approved the deployment of the First Corps, and ordered Doubleday to hold as long as possible. How ironic that he should approve the fine position picked by Buford and Reynolds, while his corps looked to be in such a poor position to the east.

The Rebel yell drifting over the farm fields brought him back to matters on his front. The enemy lines approaching all had skirmishers leading them. He looked to the north and west. The Confederate advance would soon be an uninterrupted line two miles long. He had very few reserve troops to call upon.

The fight was intensifying. The sounds of the battle filled the air. Musketry, cannon, orders barked by commanders at their lines and the piercing Rebel yell. The lines were holding. Initial thrusts to dislodge the Union troops failed. If a position was breached, hand to hand combat ensued. Second and third ranks of Union troops charged into the melee with bayonets, repelling the Confederates and restoring the lines.

Doubleday saw the enemy being reinforced in large numbers. Their lines were now advancing two and three deep. Colonel Stone's brigade was pressed on front and flank. Smoke spewed forth from muskets discharging lead into opposing lines. Men fell on both sides. Gaps were filled and lines reformed. The firing was steady from both sides. More men fell. Doubleday saw that the enemy would have more men to replenish their ranks than he would. The terrible toll in blood could surpass Shiloh or Antietam before this day was over.

Stone's brigade was finally overwhelmed by superior numbers and forced to fall back. To their left was the Iron Brigade, standing tall in the woods exchanging fire with Confederates in ever-increasing numbers. Their left flank was unsupported due to Rowley withdrawing Biddle's brigade. Now with Stone's retreat, their right flank was vulnerable to a front and flank attack.

Doubleday saw new Confederate brigades forming in battle formation on Herr's Ridge. He had one regiment, the One Hundred Fifty-first Pennsylvania, in reserve. His First Corps would pay dearly to hold this ridge.

A rider galloped up."Sir, General Robinson sends his compliments. He wishes to thank you for sending Paul's brigade to his sector. He's being hard pressed and requests more troops."

"Go back and tell him I have no reserves to spare. He must hold with what he has."

"Yes, sir."

The Rebel yell grew in intensity on the left. He looked over and saw the left end of the Iron Brigade falling back. This would be the Nineteenth Indiana, he thought. They were paying the price for Biddle's retreat. The men fell back forty yards, reformed their lines, turned and fired at pursuing Confederates. They weren't conceding ground without a struggle.

Doubleday watched through his glasses as the Twenty-Fourth Michigan, now at the left end, refused their line. They now faced west and south and were pouring fire into the enemy on two fronts. Men were falling everywhere, but neither side backed away. He looked at his watch. It was almost four o'clock. The Iron Brigade had reached the field at ten this morning and they were still standing strong in the fury. Their name, earned in previous battles, was being tested and resoundingly upheld today. They had repulsed one Confederate brigade in the morning, captured a general, and were now holding their position against superior numbers.

Doubleday turned to Lt. Marten and said,"Damn fine showing by the boys. We're giving Johnny hell on all fronts. Reynolds would be proud."

"Yes, he would, sir. We're fighting on our soil now, defending our homes from a foreign invader. The boys have a different mindset."

"You make a good point. We may be fighting with a new mindset, but before long, we'll be outnumbered three to one. Numbers win in combat, not some intangible concept. Without reinforcements, we'll be pushed from this position before day's end."

"Look, sir, the Twenty-Fourth Michigan is withdrawing," said Marten pointing to the left.

Doubleday turned in his saddle and saw the Twenty-Fourth pulling back. They fell back to where the remnants of the Nineteenth Indiana were now fighting. They planted their flag and formed a new line to the right of the Nineteenth. There was no quit in these boys.

"Damn, the enemy's numbers are too great to hold those woods any longer. We need to pull back to the seminary and entrench in our reserve position," Doubleday said as he watched the fight rage on. The last two regiments of the Iron Brigade were now withdrawing before they got surrounded. The enemy was in close pursuit.

Doubleday turned to Marten,"Ride over to the One Hundred Fifty-first Pennsylvania and send them forward. They are to slow Johnny down and give us time to withdraw all our forces south of the pike back to the seminary. Remind them they're fighting on their home soil."

Marten rode away to deliver the orders.

A rider approached from the north."Sir, General Robinson sends his compliments and wishes to inform you the Eleventh Corps has collapsed. His right is in danger. What are your orders?"

"Tell him to hold as long as he can. I'm withdrawing the rest of the corps to the seminary. He needs to hold until we are able to establish our lines there."

"Yes, sir. I'll deliver the message on the double."

Doubleday shook his head and said to no one in particular,"That damned Eleventh!" They were running again. He had deployed his corps on the ground Reynolds wished to hold. The First Division had been in the field for six hours, fighting on and off. He had sent his one reserve brigade to stabilize the lines in the north and he was sending forward his last reserve regiment. He had done his duty. He could only hope the rest of the army would reach the field and secure the heights south of town. At least all the blood his men had shed would not have been in vain.

The Iron Brigade was fighting as they withdrew. Damn, he was proud of them. This enabled the One Hundred Fifty-first Pennsylvania Regiment to get forward and deploy in battle formation. He watched as they fired by ranks into the oncoming Confederates, slowing their advance. He had ordered all other regiments back to the breastworks at the seminary.

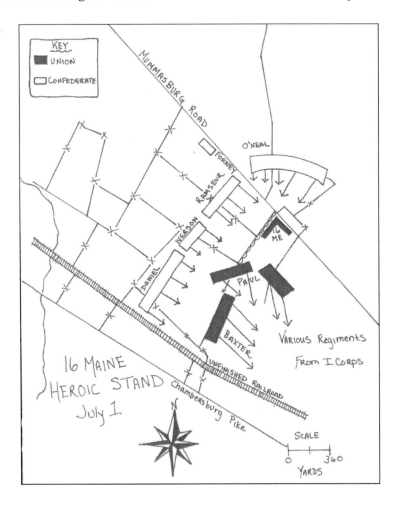

The One Hundred Fifty-first was taking heavy casualties, but the Confederate advance seemed to be losing its steam. The troops were firing, but not advancing. Doubleday soon saw the reason. Three fresh brigades were marching forward out of the woods. Was there to be no end to this fight, he wondered. His men were spent and many out of ammunition. He could stretch his remaining men to form one long line at the seminary, without any reserves. It was only four forty-five, by his watch. Too much daylight left. He sent an aide to the One Hundred Fifty-first to order them back. They had fought valiantly and bought him time to deploy the balance of the corps. The seminary was the last line he could hold before the outskirts of town.

His men waited for the Pennsylvanians to get behind the breastworks, before they unleashed a steady volley of death at the oncoming ranks. He couldn't remember when he had seen the boys in blue fight with such tenacity. They were still outnumbered, but they were giving a damn fine account of themselves.

The fight at the seminary raged for twenty minutes. If the men were exhausted, Doubleday saw no outward sign of it. They methodically shot at the enemy, reloaded their weapon and shot again. They seemed composed under fire. All of the training was paying off. Sure, the men grumbled about too much training, but this fight showed them why they trained.

A rider came up to him and saluted,"Sir, General Robinson wishes to inform you he has ordered his men to withdraw. The enemy is beginning to swing around his right and with no support there he will lose his whole division. He has ordered the Sixteenth Maine to hold at all costs while he withdraws the rest of the men."

Another regiment sacrificed. Doubleday would lay their sacrifice at the feet of the Eleventh Corps in his report. He looked at the rider and said,"Tell Robinson we will hold the line at the seminary as long as we can. His men can withdraw behind us through the town to Cemetery Hill."

"Yes, sir." He turned his horse and galloped north.

Cemetery Hill. General Howard was there with a division. It was to be the fall back position for the First and Eleventh Corps. The whole of the Eleventh Corps was probably there already, having put up a feeble effort on their front. Earlier in the day, Reynolds had told Doubleday of the strong position that Cemetery Hill commanded. This fight on the westerly side of town was to keep Lee away from it. Now, Howard would probably take credit for establishing a line on it. He wondered if the Twelfth Corps had arrived. They were only four miles away at Two Taverns. Doubleday knew Howard sent for help at two p.m. They should be in the area by now.

The Confederate lines were beginning to overlap the end of his left flank. He was receiving reports that ammunition was exhausted for many of the men. He couldn't ask any more of these gallant boys. They have given their all this day. He turned to his aides and gave them orders to be sent to all commanders. It's time to retire to Cemetery Hill.

General Winfield Scott Hancock was galloping toward Gettysburg over the Taneytown Road with several members of his staff. When he first left

Taneytown, he rode in the back of an ambulance with his chief of staff, Lt. Col. Charles Morgan. They studied maps of the area around Gettysburg so they would have an idea of the ground. When Hancock had a firm grasp of the terrain in his head, he ordered the ambulance to stop. He would proceed the remaining distance on horseback, as it would get him to Gettysburg quicker.

At 3 p.m. he reached Cemetery Hill. He heard the sounds of the battle raging to the north and northwest. He halted his staff and took out his glasses. He looked to the north and observed the Union forces rapidly retreating, with the Confederate forces in hot pursuit.

"Damn it!" he barked,"It's a carbon copy of Chancellorsville. Let's go find General Howard."

After a brief ride, Hancock spotted Howard with his staff. To Hancock, Howard appeared quite passive as the army was withdrawing. He was probably praying for divine intervention, thought Hancock, who felt God didn't care to take sides when people were killing each other. Battles were fought by men and it was men who would decide the outcome. He rode up to Howard and inquired in a forceful tone."What in the hell happened here today?"

"General Hancock, I'm pleased to see you. Is your corps nearby? We could use some reinforcements.

"General Meade sent me forward to take command of the left wing when he heard of Reynolds death. I know you have seniority, but I have written orders from Meade putting me in charge of this wing. So damn it, fill me in on what's happening."

"Reynolds ordered me forward this morning after he became engaged with the enemy on the roads west of town. Upon my arrival, I was notified that First Corps was heavily engaged with forces from A. P. Hill's corps and I was to deploy my corps to their right and cover the roads on the north side of town. Buford had reports that Ewell's corps was headed toward Gettysburg from that direction. Shortly after my arrival, I was told of Reynolds death and that I was senior commander on the field. I offered up a short prayer for his soul and got to work. This hill seems to be the ground Reynolds hoped to hold for our army, so I deployed one division here and sent the rest of my division forward, north of town. General Schurz informed me Confederate forces were massing on the high ground northwest of town, so he could not deploy there as ordered. He was forced to place his troops on low ground, which in his estimation was a poor position. I discovered I didn't have enough men to cover all the roads north of town adequately. Ewell's corps attacked around 2 o'clock. Our position became compromised when the First Corps withdrew, exposing my left. If Reynolds were still alive, he never would have withdrawn so quickly, but Doubleday is no Reynolds."

"Son of a bitch, are you telling me that Doubleday ordered his men to withdraw?"

"That I am. My only option was to order the Eleventh Corps to withdraw to this hill. The men had to fight while retreating, as they were pressed hard by Ewell's corps. I had to send one brigade from my reserves forward, to slow the Confederate advance."

Hancock digested this news. He would have to mention this incident to Meade. Doubleday was already not in good standing with Meade.

"Have you heard from the Twelfth or Third Corps?" inquired Hancock.

"Not a thing and I sent out requests for help at 2 p.m.. I understand Slocum is only four miles away at Two Taverns. I cannot begin to imagine why leading forces of his corps are not within sight. Sickles is at Emmitsburg, and even if he began marching when he received my order, he would not arrive until after dark."

Hancock looked over the ground. This certainly was a position to entrench an army. Lovely fields of fire for both artillery and infantry. Meade had sent him forward to ascertain whether the army should move forward to Gettysburg or retreat to Pipe Creek. Hancock looked over the field and said,"I think this the strongest position by nature upon which to fight a battle that I've ever seen."

Howard agreed.

"Damn it, then. I select this as the battlefield." Hancock shifted gears,"Did you ever receive orders for Pipe Creek?"

"I've never seen or heard of any orders for Pipe Creek," replied Howard.

Hancock shook his head. Two corps did not receive Meade's orders for Pipe Creek. Meade would be madder than a hornet and his anger would be directed at Butterfield. Hancock was glad he was not in Butterfield's shoes, but the chief of staff's tardiness caused this mess.

Hancock turned to Howard and said,"Let's form some battle lines on this hill. It's imperative we keep it out of Lee's hands. I want you to post the Eleventh Corps; I'll bring some order to the First Corps."

"Captain Parker," yelled Hancock."I want you to take a dispatch to General Meade, with my compliments. Inform him the position at Gettysburg is a very strong one. We can fight here as the ground appears not unfavorable with good troops." And we've got some damn fine troops fighting on home soil, he thought."Now get to it!"

"Yes, sir. I'll write this up quickly and be on my way."

Hancock saw a battery of artillery arriving on the field. He rode over to the commander and pointed to a knoll between Cemetery Hill and Culp's Hill."Post your battery there and prevent the enemy from coming up that ravine!" ordered Hancock.

The commander of this battery was Captain Stevens with the First Corps Division of artillery. He did not recognize the general barking orders at him. He replied"By whose order?"

"General Hancock's! Get your damn guns there on the double."

Stevens placed his guns as ordered.

Hancock was all over the field posting troops, barking orders and spewing forth profanities. His actions were well-received by the men who responded quickly to his orders. His bearing seemed to instill a new confidence in the men, and the panicked retreat became an army with spirit digging in to protect vital ground. Hancock was restoring order.

Hancock spotted Doubleday and rode over to him."General, I need you to send some men over to that hill, known as Culp's Hill. We need to protect it from a flank attack. Our supply trains will be arriving up the two roads to the west of the hill, so it must not fall into enemy hands."

"Sir, my men are fought out and short of ammunition. My corps has been fighting . . ." began Doubleday.

Hancock stopped him short and thundered,"I don't give a damn how long you've been fighting. I'm in command here and I order you to send every available man to that hill. This is not a request!"

Doubleday glared at him in disbelief. Then he rode off to comply with the orders.

Hancock looked over the entrenched army. Skirmishers had been deployed forward at a stone wall near the town and were holding off any advance by the enemy. The remaining regiments were formed in battle formation on good ground, backed by numerous pieces of artillery. Hancock had stabilized the army. He felt energized and alive. Today he had arrived on a battlefield to an army on the verge of being swept from the field. He rode amongst the panicked men posting regiments and demanding order be restored by junior officers. They responded to his authority. Winfield Scott Hancock, named after the hero of the Mexican War, was born for this.

The Twelfth Corps was arriving on the Baltimore Pike. A general with his staff rode up to Hancock."Sir, General Geary arriving on the field with the Second Division of the Twelfth Corps. General Williams with the First Division is somewhere behind me on this road. Who's in charge here?"

"I am," answered Hancock."Do you have any orders?"

"My orders from Slocum were to get to Gettysburg. I've received no other orders from him. Is he here?"

"If he is I haven't seen him. How many brigades do you have?" asked Hancock.

"Three brigades."

"I want you to send one brigade to General Howard on Cemetery Hill. Tell him to deploy the brigade in a reserve position. I will take you over to the left and show you where to deploy your other two brigades."

Geary barked these orders to his staff. Riders went off in three different directions to carry out the orders. Geary turned to Hancock and stated he was ready to ride to the left. They rode past a small white house on Taneytown Road, then up a slope to its crest. The view from the top was magnificent. The land sloped gently away to the west. There were open fields for at least a mile before they were swallowed up by forests. Emmitsburg Road, bordered by a post and rail fence, ran down the middle of the field from the cemetery southwest, until it dropped out of sight beyond an orchard down by a farm building. There were post and rail, and worm fences crisscrossing the open fields in all directions.

Hancock spoke to no one and everyone,"Look at those fields. An army attacking across them would be butchered. I don't think Lee will attempt to attack on this front. He'll probe our flanks. We need to secure these heights anchoring our left on that treeless hill to the south."

Hancock saw a stone wall heading west, then take a ninety degree turn and travel south, until it ended. A wood fence arose at its end and continued as far as he could see toward the barren hill. This was an excellent barrier to entrench an army.

Hancock turned to Geary."Post your brigade to Howard's left and extend it down this ridge line to that hill." He pointed toward Little Round

Top."Dig in behind that stone wall and wood fence. You stay in this position until the Third Corps arrives and relieves you."

"This is one fine position, sir."

"Yes, General, it's damn fine ground. Post your brigades so we can secure it."

ভ–৪০৫৪–৻

It was dusk. The Confederate army seemed done for the day. There was still sporadic firing, but it was spread out, not concentrated in a single area. Doubleday had been out riding amongst his men. He was proud of them. They had fought all day and still had the determination to create breastworks to bolster their new position on Culp's Hill. They had worked diligently cutting down trees and piling the wood on top of a low stone wall. They now had a strong fortification.

His six brigades had fought for seven hours against a foe with superior numbers. From reports of his division commanders, he counted ten Confederate brigades that had taken part in the attack on his front. They could have held longer if the Eleventh Corps hadn't collapsed. He would address this issue with his superiors after the battle.

Hancock's arrival on the field was welcome, after Howard's poor showing. There had been harsh words, but Doubleday attributed it to his tiredness and Hancock's energy. This energy helped to bolster morale and refocus exhausted troops to the task of fortifying their new positions. Doubleday saw the men responding with renewed fervor to Hancock's orders. He certainly knew how to inspire men. Doubleday would give Hancock credit for restoring order out of chaos in his reports.

Doubleday had checked on the condition of his corps. The casualty figures staggered him. The First Brigade had 691 men present for duty. This morning at Marsh Creek the roles had been answered by 1883 men. The Twenty-fourth Michigan reported a casualty rate of eighty percent. He personally checked on two regiments that played a special role in the day's fight. They had been asked to hold their lines and slow down advancing enemy troops. This allowed other regiments to retreat and reform lines. These two heroic regiments were the One Hundred Fifty-first Pennsylvania and the Sixteenth Maine.

The One Hundred Fifty-first was sent forward from a reserve position to buy time for regiments to regroup at the seminary. Their casualty rate was at seventy-eight percent. The Sixteenth was ordered to hold a stone wall at the Mummasburg Road to the bitter end. This was the regiment General Robinson chose to be sacrificed so his men would not get surrounded and cut off. The Sixteenth went in with 298 men. There were over 230 missing this night. How many were captured and how many still lay wounded he could not be certain. Final figures after the battle would show more accurate casualty numbers.

Four of the six brigades that fought had casualty rates over sixty percent. Doubleday had trouble comprehending the numbers. His mind went numb. All he knew was he had done his duty and the heights Reynolds coveted were still in the hands of the Army of the Potomac.

ॐ⊷༄❀❁༄⊶ॐ

Hancock and Meade were at headquarters in Taneytown discussing the events of the day.

"It was a shameful display of impotence when I arrived on Cemetery Hill" started Hancock."The army was falling back in complete disorder with the enemy in close pursuit. Fortunately, Howard had posted one division on Cemetery Hill or we might have lost it. After a brief consultation with Howard, I began posting retreating units on the hill. They responded to my profane urgings and soon the army was settling in on the hill in a fine defensive position. The enemy seemed spent and did not attack us with any concerted effort after 6 p.m.."

"So, amidst this turmoil, you felt this was the place to fight instead of Pipe Creek?" asked Meade.

"Meaning no disrespect to you or your staff, Gettysburg is the place to fight. The ground is superb."

"I've ordered all corps commanders forward with the utmost speed. The Fifth Corps is one hard days march away. They could be on the field tomorrow morning. The Sixth Corps is further east and will be hard pressed to reach Gettysburg tomorrow. If Lee attacks in the morning, will we be able to hold with only five corps?"

"I'm confident we'll be able to hold. The Third and Twelfth Corps arrived on the field before I left. Our lines extend from the cemetery in both directions. To the east is Culp's Hill, which has been fortified by the First Corps. One division from the Twelfth Corps is behind them in reserve. Cemetery Hill is covered with artillery and men of the Eleventh Corps. As an engineer, you'll like the salient created at Cemetery Hill. Damn fine fields of fire. There is a ridge that heads south from the cemetery to a barren hill, known as Little Round Top. Elements of the Third and Twelfth Corps are entrenched on this ridge behind stone walls and wood fences. We get some artillery up there and we'll have one hell of a formidable fortress! Lee would be a fool to attack across such open ground. I think he'll probe our flanks and try to attack there. The beauty of this position is the natural barriers anchoring both flanks, and the open fields which will provide Lee no cover to move around us."

"I heard from Howard that we were up against Hill and Ewell. What are your thoughts on this?"

"From what I could gather, we fought against elements of those two corps. There was no sign of Longstreet today. We don't know how far behind Hill's corps he is. Lee may not be ready to attack in the morning. He does not know the ground here as he does in Virginia. This will be to his disadvantage."

There was a pause in the conversation. They were digesting events, knowing they had cast their lot on Gettysburg as the place to fight, but not knowing how the fight would unfold.

Hancock broke the silence."By the way, Howard informed me that Doubleday withdrew the First Corps without orders. Their withdrawal jeopardized the position of the Eleventh Corps. Howard had to order his corps to retreat to Cemetery Hill before they were surrounded from the left, the ground which Doubleday deserted."

Meade shook his head,"Howard already informed me of this development. I thought Doubleday was an average commander, but not a shirker. I've already sent for General Newton, a division commander with the Sixth Corps, to proceed to Gettysburg and take command of the First Corps. I'm heading to Gettysburg shortly. I'm anxious to ride the lines and get a feel for the ground. Hell of a job today, Win."

"Thank you, sir. Lee does not have time to sit on the defensive. His army is vulnerable to being cut off from its supply line if he stays in Pennsylvania too long. I think he will attack and it will be on one or both flanks."

"Flank attacks are his preference. Let's be ready, we'll see how it plays out. I'm hoping to attack tomorrow after the Fifth and Sixth Corps arrive on the field. If Longstreet is not up, we'll have numbers on our side. I'll see you on the field."

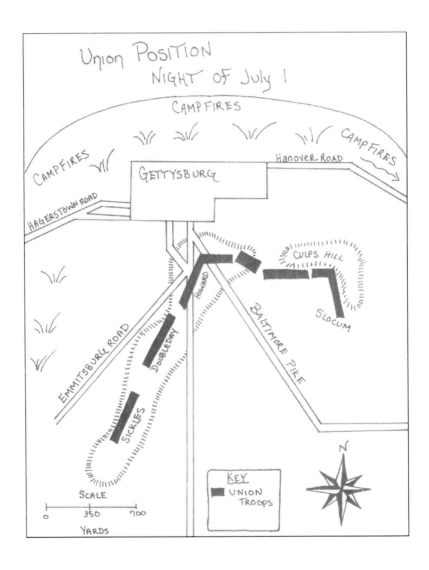

PART IV
THE RIVERS RUN RED

CHAPTER 18

July 2nd

IT WAS ONE IN THE MORNING when Meade arrived at Gettysburg. He was accompanied by General Hunt, his chief of artillery, and seven aides. They arrived at the cemetery gatehouse and dismounted. Slocum, Howard, Sickles and Warren were present to meet them. Meade looked across the fields and saw numerous campfires in the distance. Lee's army was there in force. There would be a battle today, Meade was sure of this.

"Gentlemen, is this the place to fight?" asked Meade.

They all assured him it was, and that it was splendid ground.

"I am glad to hear you say so," answered Meade,"for it is too late to leave it. The numerous campfires lead me to believe Lee is also planning to stay and fight. I wish to inspect the ground. Howard and Hunt, you'll accompany me. Captain Paine, you'll sketch the ground as we ride, so I can have a map for posting the troops. The rest of you are dismissed. Look in on your men and then get some rest. I'll need some generals who are awake and alert tomorrow."

He mounted his horse and walked slowly thru the night. The full moon cast her light across the fields of Gettysburg. The campfires were plentiful in the west, northwest and north. He looked into the cemetery and saw many troops asleep amongst the tombstones. How ironic, he thought.

Clearing the cemetery, they continued riding south along the ridge. They stopped at a stone wall and glanced over the open fields to the west. Each man was lost in his own thoughts. Captain Paine was sketching from his saddle, a skill he had perfected. This skill was the reason Meade had chosen him to accompany them on the ride.

Meade spoke to General Hunt,"Henry, this position is an artillerymen's dream."

"I was just thinking that. We can bring fire down on any portion of these fields Lee attempts to cross. If he decides to mass an attack at one point, I'll have the ability to reposition guns and pour fire from all sides. I doubt Lee will attack across these fields. It's not his style."

"I'd have to agree with you. Still, I want you to position guns on this ridge and make it a fortress."

"A dream come true! I'll come back at first light and get a better look," replied Hunt.

Captain Paine said,"I'm done here, sir. We can continue south."

"Win tells me there is a hill devoid of trees that we can anchor the end of our line on. To the south of that is a larger hill covered with trees, which will protect the end of the line. Let's continue in that direction." Meade said these words and urged his horse forward.

They rode until they came to a farm lane. Meade halted everyone, so they could observe the terrain. Meade looked up and down the line. Men were sleeping behind the wood fence all along the ridge. They had been marching hard to reach this spot. They deserved their rest. For many it would be their last night of sleep on this earth. He wasn't sure where, but he knew tomorrow death would once again visit these fields.

"I'm ready to move on, sir," said Paine.

They continued their ride in silence toward Little Round Top. As they neared the base of the hill, Meade called for a halt. He looked at the boulder-strewn hill and decided against riding up in the dark. He looked off to the west and saw no campfires. They were well off to the north. Lee must be planning to attack the area around Culp's Hill. Meade would have to check on the defenses there later on.

Meade looked to the west and spoke from his saddle."I don't think Lee will attack on this flank. The ground is too strong. Plus, all their campfires are up north. I believe he'll attempt an attack around Culp's Hill. I'll station Buford with his cavalry on this flank, up at the Emmitsburg Road. He'll keep us apprised of any movement in this direction. Let's ride back and find an area for headquarters. We'll certainly have good interior lines."

They rode back to the north. The faint color of gray was beginning to pierce the eastern sky. Dawn was approaching. They rode to a small white farmhouse on Taneytown Road. Meade decided this would be the best spot for headquarters as it would be in the center of his lines. They dismounted and entered the house.

"Captain Paine, bring your sketches over so we can have a look at them," said Meade standing by a table. He looked at the sketch."The First Corps is on Culp's Hill facing north. The Twelfth Corps is behind them in reserve. We'll ride over when it gets lighter and see if we need to shore up the lines. The Eleventh Corps is to their left on Cemetery Hill, facing north and west. Henry, I saw artillery covering this area. Check it out when you make your rounds and make damn sure there is enough artillery to support the infantry. I think Lee will hit us on this flank first."

Hunt looked at the sketch and nodded his head in acknowledgement.

Meade continued,"The Second Corps is three miles away and will be here shortly. I want them posted to the left of the Eleventh, running south down the ridge. They can use the stone walls and wood fences as breastworks. The Third Corps will deploy on their left and extend the line to Little Round Top. For the moment that hill will be the anchor at the end of our line. I'll send Warren down later to see if we need to occupy it. Lee has no troops in that area yet and Buford is out guarding the extreme left. The Fifth Corps will be held in reserve behind Culp's Hill. My initial plan is to attack on the right when the Sixth Corps arrives on the field. We'll have the Twelfth, Fifth and Sixth take part in the attack. I'd like to hit them before Longstreet gets up. They might be tired from yesterday's fight. Any discussion on these plans?"

Meade listened as they spoke approval of his plans. He wanted to allow his subordinates time for input and disagreement. Hooker took no advice from any of his commanders, which lost him a battle and their respect. Meade would not duplicate this command style.

"It seems we're all in agreement. Captain Paine, you're to make copies of your sketch with troop positions and get them to every corps commander. I want each commander to know their positions as well as the positions of the other corps," ordered Meade."Let's try to find some food. Who knows when we'll be able to eat again?"

৯৵৪৹৻৶

Meade was at headquarters as messengers arrived constantly with news from different sectors of the field. It was 10 a.m. and Lee had shown no signs of a concerted attack. There were exchanges of musketry across picket lines, but this seemed to be the extent of the morning's excitement. The Second

Corps arrived at 5 a.m. and were posted on cemetery ridge. The Fifth Corps was on the field at 7, which surprised Meade. They had marched hard throughout the night and made better time than he anticipated. General Sykes was doing a splendid job with Meade's old corps. Meade posted them in a reserve position near Culp's Hill. He still felt this would be the front Lee would attack.

Meade had ridden over to Culp's Hill at daybreak. The First Corps was deployed on the hill facing the north. Their right was hanging in the air. He ordered General Slocum to post his Twelfth Corps to the right of the First and extend the line down Culp's Hill to Rock Creek, facing east. The Baltimore Pike was the key to the Union position, for it was the road leading to the supply base at Westminster. Meade had it in the back of his mind that if he was forced to retreat, it would be down this road. He had Butterfield write up orders for withdrawal, but not issue them unless ordered to. Holding Culp's Hill would keep Baltimore Pike safely in the hands of the Army of the Potomac.

With the Fifth Corps present, Meade was contemplating an offensive movement. He sent Warren over to Culp's Hill with orders to scout the ground on the right with Slocum for the possibility of an attack when the Sixth Corps arrived. The attack would consist of the Fifth, Sixth and Twelfth Corps. Meade was awaiting their findings.

Meade knew he was running on pure adrenaline. He was in his fifth day of command of the army. Sleep and food had been erratic. There was no one above him to make the call anymore. All the decisions concerning the upcoming fight rested squarely on his shoulders. Reynolds was dead. This left him with Hancock, Slocum and Sedgwick as capable corps commanders. He could count on them to take charge on their front. Slocum was at Culp's Hill, so he could keep an eye on the First, Eleventh and Twelfth Corps. Hancock was on cemetery ridge with his corps, so he could watch the Second and Third Corps, which comprised the left of the Union line. Meade would talk to both commanders and convey his thoughts to them concerning this idea.

An aide came into the house."Sir, General Warren is here."

"Send him in," said Meade.

Warren entered. They exchanged greetings.

Meade got right to the point."What's your opinion of the ground on the right?"

"Henry and I both agree this is not the place to mount an attack. The ground bottoms out in Rock Creek. Upon crossing, we would be attacking uphill through murky ground. The enemy has the high ground and is entrenched in a good defensive position," reported Warren.

Meade pondered this for a moment. Then he spoke."So the right's no good for an attack. Hell, we're in a damn fine defensive position ourselves. Perhaps we'll await Lee's attack. He's still across the field. I don't think he intends to leave. I think he'll want to slug it out here."

∽ঞ৹ OCৣ ঔ

General Winfield Scott Hancock spent the morning riding the length of his corps line. He stopped and discussed the preparedness with each of his Division commanders. He had seen this ground yesterday and envisioned how strong it would look with an army entrenched on its forward ridge behind stone walls and wood fences. His corps had been assigned this ground to deploy on and seeing it now heavily secured by his corps gave him a deep sense of satisfaction. He had regiments two and three deep behind the aforementioned walls. Behind them were reserve troops ready to be moved anywhere along his front that was being threatened. If Lee attacked on his front he would be exposing his men to a mile of open field. Hancock thought of how his artillery would be able to pour shells down upon advancing enemy troops with a devastating effect. If Lee's men somehow managed to reach the Emmitsburg Road, they would then come under heavy musket fire with no cover on their front. Hancock did not see this as a strategy Lee would employ.

There had been firing going on throughout the morning, but it was the fire on the skirmish lines that were a part of every battle. Hancock continued riding the lines with no concern for his safety, as the sound of musket fire was heavy in the air on his front. He could see movement across the fields, as the enemy extended their lines southerly to his left. He would send a message to Meade concerning this development. Hancock knew that cavalry was posted at the end of the line and would keep Meade informed of any movement by the enemy in that direction.

General Sickles was posted to his left. This worried Hancock. Sickles was not a man with any formal military training. His money and political connections were the only rational reasons Hancock could see that got him his position as a corps commander. He was viewed as a controversial figure with a shady reputation. Hancock was not sure how he would hold up in the upcoming fight. He was a loose cannon, and at the moment was guarding the left end of the Union line. With Lee's propensity for flank attacks, Hancock was not sure how Sickles would fare having to hold the end of the line. Hancock would keep a careful eye on developments to his left.

It was past 11 a.m., and there was still no sign of Lee's intentions. Hancock thought this strange. Perhaps he could enjoy some lunch before any action began. He rode back towards his headquarters. It was time to put the cooks to work.

ॐ☙�***☜ॐ

General Doubleday's pride was still stinging from being replaced. General John Newton had arrived early in the morning with the news he was the new commander of First Corps. Doubleday was returned to his old position as commander of the Third Division of the First Corps. The only explanation he could get from Newton was that Meade had ordered him to Gettysburg at all possible speed to assume command of the First Corps when he arrived. Newton was in command of the First Division with the Sixth Corps, when he received Meade's order. Many of the men with the First Corps who had witnessed Doubleday's exemplary handling of the corps on July 1, were more than a little displeased with Newton's arrival as commander. He wasn't even one of them. He was an outsider who was transferred in to take charge in the middle of an important battle. This did not sit well with Doubleday or the men who had fought under him.

Doubleday had other matters to contend with. General Rowley, who was in charge of the Third Division on July 1, had been arrested for drunkenness during the fight. He was observed giving orders to troops not under his command. When he called men from the Iron Brigade cowards, he stepped over a line they could not forgive. Men of the Sixth Wisconsin arrested him at bayonet point. Doubleday could not afford the loss of another brigade commander. Colonel Stone had been wounded and then captured. Rowley would retain his position for the duration of the battle. Doubleday had Rowley sent to his tent under guard until he sobered up.

His Third Brigade arrived at twilight on July 1st. They missed the day's fight as they were left behind to guard the supply trains. The Third Division, under the command of General George Stannard, was comprised of men from Vermont who had never seen combat. They were nine-month volunteers, whose enlistments would be expiring this month. Doubleday was not sure how they would fare in combat, never experiencing it, and being so close to their date to muster out. However, having missed the day's fight, they were at full capacity. The army needed men at the moment.

Doubleday rode up to General Stannard and dismounted. Greetings were exchanged.

"Are your men ready for combat?" asked Doubleday.

"These Vermont boys will surprise a few people. They are chomping at the bit to show their mettle in combat. They signed up to fight, but have been stuck around Washington doing garrison duty. I've drilled them every day for five hours. They are trained, disciplined and ready," answered Stannard.

"Let's hope so. You cannot duplicate combat conditions while drilling, and no one ever knows how they will respond to being shot at until it happens." Doubleday stared across the fields, his mind still numbed by the casualties."We took numerous casualties yesterday. First Division lost over sixty percent of its strength." His voice cracked.

"I've heard," said Stannard."I spoke to other commanders last night. They say the corps gave Johnny hell. You were cited by many for your extraordinary handling of the corps after Reynolds' untimely death."

"I've heard that too, but it seems Meade didn't. He's replaced me with General Newton, who wasn't even on the damn field yesterday!"

"It's a damn shame, after the way you fought yesterday. Most of the officers I spoke to thought you got a raw deal. They all support you."

Doubleday changed the subject."How was the march from Washington?"

"It was seven hard days of marching through the heat. The boys slept well last night. I had one incident I'll inform you of. One hot afternoon a young lieutenant, named Stephen Brown with the Thirteenth Vermont, fell out of rank with some canteens. He was heading to a well to get water for his troops. I had strict orders that men were not to fall out for water. A cavalry officer was guarding the well and ordered Brown back to formation. Brown told the man his name, rank and the unit he was with and said he was getting water for his men. That young man had some spunk. He filled the canteens and returned to disperse them to his marching troops. The cavalry officer followed him and placed him under arrest after he handed out the canteens. Brown was forced to surrender his sword. I had to ease the water restrictions after this. I don't think I will bring the young man up on charges. He has been in no trouble that I can see and he will be heading home this month. It's hard for men who have been in the army for such a short duration to be expected to adhere to discipline that they perceive as foolish. I know an army needs discipline, but at times common sense has to take precedence."

"That and we'll need every available man for this fight," said Doubleday."I think you made the right decision. We'll keep this between you and me. It need not go any further. Tend to your men. I'm sure they'll be needed for today's action."

"Any word from above?" asked Stannard.

"Nothing yet. Lee's out there somewhere and it seems we will sit here and await his next move. I'm impressed with the ground and the position of this army."

♥☜ℰℐℭℬ⚬ᛃ

Meade was irritated. Sickles had appeared at headquarters complaining of the position his corps was assigned. The ground was too low and not good for artillery. He also felt the position was vulnerable to a flank attack, similar to Chancellorsville. Sickles spoke of some good ground up near the Emmitsburg Road he wished to occupy. Meade told him he would send General Hunt to his sector to check out the situation. Damn political generals, he thought. Sickles was not content with following orders; instead he wanted to alter the position of the left flank of the army.

Meade turned to Hunt,"Henry, ride down to Sickles position. He's bitching about his assigned spot and desires to move forward. We haven't seen this area in daylight. Check out the terrain, hear Sickles out and then report back to me."

"If he asks, do I have the authority to approve of any forward movement?" asked Hunt.

"No. I have plans and his standing pat is a considerable part of them."

"I'm off to see the lawyer-general. I'll be back as quick as I can with my report on the situation."

Lawyers, thought Meade.

As if reading Meade's mind, Williams spoke,"They're good in court, but their training can cause them to create havoc in the military."

Meade turned his head towards Williams and said,"That's the damn truth. I just need him to follow orders, not plan strategy that benefits only him. I've got plans to move the Fifth Corps to the left behind Sickles, in a reserve position. I'm just waiting for John to arrive with the Sixth Corps. They will be posted in reserve on the right, in the area where the Fifth Corps is currently occupying. If Lee hasn't attacked by then, we'll have all seven corps on the field in a strong position. The longer he waits to attack, the more favorable our position becomes."

An aide entered."Sir, a report from the signal corps on Little Round Top. The enemy is extending their line southerly. They are massing troops in front of Sickles' position on the ridges to the west."

"Thank you," said Meade."What do you make of this news?" he asked Williams.

"Lee prefers attacking on the flanks, usually the weakest one. We have fortified Culp's Hill and Cemetery Hill, so his main thrust may not be there. He could be holding Ewell's Corps in position there, while moving around to the left. We still don't know where Longstreet is."

Meade thought for a moment. *We are weakest on the left. Sickles is deployed there, with no troops in a reserve position. Could this be Lee's plan, moving around to our left and attacking on that flank?* It was conceivable. Meade was so concerned with the area around Culp's Hill he had not spent much time thinking of this possibility. When he was near Little Round Top early this morning, he detected no signs of enemy activity in this area. There were no campfires directly to the west. He wondered why there were no reports from Buford of enemy movement. He would send a courier to General Pleasanton and inquire if he had any news from Buford.

"You make a good point," Meade said to Williams."We've got work to do on that front. I want a courier sent to Pleasanton, seeking any reports from Buford. I want you to find Warren and tell him to get down to Little Round Top. We need good information about any enemy movements in that area."

An aide entered the house."Sir, a rider has just arrived from Sixth Corps with a message to be delivered to you in person."

He turned to Williams."Let's go out and hear the news from John."

They walked out of the house into the sunshine. A young captain walked forward to Meade, saluted, handed him a note and said,"Sir, General

Sedgwick sends his compliments and asks me to hand this dispatch to you personally."

"Thank you, Captain," replied Meade. He read the note and turned to his gathered staff."Sedgwick has marched his men straight through the night. His lead elements are five miles away. He expects to have his whole corps here within the next two hours. We'll have all seven corps on the field by 2 p.m.. Captain, ride back to Sedgwick and give him this message from me—'Damn fine job.'"

"Yes, sir," replied the captain. He mounted his horse and gave a hard kick.

Williams excused himself to attend to his orders. Meade sat in a chair on the porch. Perhaps there was a chance for him to take the offensive. The area around Culp's Hill was not good for an attack, but with Sedgwick approaching the field, Meade could explore the possibilities of an attack on the left. He would wait for word from Hunt and Warren about the ground down there.

CHAPTER 19

Afternoon

GENERAL HANCOCK WAS TALKING with John Gibbon, his Second Division commander. They were standing behind their entrenched troops, looking across the fields to the west. They had noticed the enemy moving to the south in the tree line across the fields. Hancock had been to headquarters to discuss this with Meade.

"What's the news from headquarters?" asked Gibbon.

"The signal corps on Little Round Top informed Meade that enemy troops were extending their line well to the south. This confirms what I reported to him about movement in the trees across the way. It seems Lee is attempting to get around our left flank. Meade has sent Warren down to look at the ground and see if it needs bolstering up. Evidently, that bastard Sickles was bitching about his position and wants to move his corps forward. Hunt was sent down by Meade to look into the situation. Meade assured me Hunt has no authority to allow any move by Sickles. His Third Corps guards our left, and if he moves, he puts our position in peril. Damn that man. On a different note, Sedgwick should be on the field within the hour. He drove his men through the night, and they still love him. He's like a father to his men. They call him Uncle John, but it seems to work for him. Crafty old son of a bitch."

"How about we start calling you Uncle Win?" asked Gibbon.

"Don't start with me John," shot back Hancock. They both laughed.

They both heard drumming off to the south. They looked in the direction and were astounded. Third Corps was moving forward as if on parade. The drums were beating; the flags were unfurled, dancing in the wind and leading the corps forward across the valley.

"What in the hell can that man Sickles be doing!" blurted out Hancock.

Gibbon just stared in amazement. He was dumbfounded.

Hancock glared at Gibbon and said,"Did you get any orders to move, because I certainly haven't."

"I've received no orders to move."

They watched as skirmishers marched ahead of the main line and cleared enemy skirmishers from their front. On and on marched the whole corps until they reached the Emmitsburg Road. There they halted and planted their flags. This would be their new position.

Hancock looked at his pocket watch. It read 1:45. Then he spoke."It seems Mr. Sickles has stuck his neck out and will soon find out how it can be lopped off. His right flank is unsupported and hanging in the air. I've no idea where his left will end up. In the meantime, our left is now uncovered and we'll have to make some adjustments in the line. I'm heading over to see General Caldwell. It may be necessary to send his division over to cover the area Sickles just vacated. After that, I'm riding over to headquarters to see what I can find out about this move. What a damn mess."

ೋ❦ಌ

General Hunt was at headquarters conferring with Meade and Williams, after returning from Sickles' front.

"Sickles' present position has some drawbacks," Hunt explained."It's not ground I would pick for artillery placement, as there are areas the enemy could advance over that the guns couldn't cover. There are woods to the west and southwest that Lee could exploit to gather his troops. Those woods would shield their strength, and they could hit Sickles from two directions with perhaps a corps, if not more."

Meade broke in."I'm sending the Fifth Corps to that flank to act as a reserve. We can plug any holes in the position with them. What of Sickles desired position?"

"It's higher ground and is better suited for artillery deployment. The ground before it is more open, so any advance by Lee would come under heavy fire. The issue is this; Sickles does not have enough men to cover the ground between Hancock and Little Round Top. His lines would be too thin to provide adequate defense. I told him that. I also told him you had to approve any movement he makes from his current position."

"Well done, Henry," said Meade. He posed a question to Williams."Have you heard anything from Warren?"

"Worse than that, we haven't been able to locate him, yet. We're still looking for him."

Meade replied,"He's out somewhere checking our lines. He'll show up."

General Hancock burst through the door."What in the hell is going on with Sickles?" he asked in an agitated tone.

Meade looked at him and said,"Nothing should be going on. Why?"

"The son of a bitch has marched his whole corps forward to Emmitsburg Road. Our left is completely uncovered!" roared Hancock.

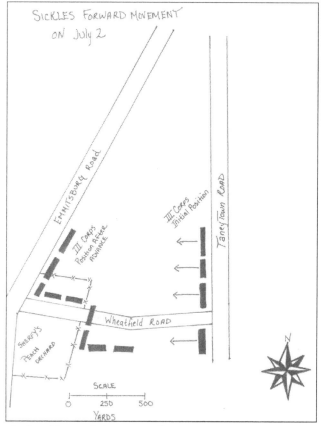

Heads looked at Hancock in stunned amazement.

Hancock continued,"Did you order him forward?"

Meade put his hand up."No, dammit. He has no orders to move." Meade turned to Williams and said sharply,"I want all corps commanders to report here immediately. We'll have to amend some lines. Send riders out now to deliver that message. I'm going over to Hancock's position to have a look at what Mr. Sickles has done."

∾⳾⳾ೞ⳾⳿

The corps commanders were gathering at headquarters. They were told to wait for Meade. He had ridden over to Hancock's position and would be back shortly. Williams would not give them any hint as to the meeting's purpose. He would leave that in Meade's hands. It was still fortunate that Lee had not pressed an attack anywhere. Time was marching on, leaving about six hours of daylight left.

Meade arrived with Hancock. Meade looked around the room taking a mental inventory of who was present. Everyone was there with the exception of Sickles. Meade turned to Williams and asked,"What have you told them?"

"Nothing, sir," replied Williams,"except that you would fill everyone in when you returned."

"Where's Sickles?" asked Meade.

"He sent a message informing us he was too busy deploying his corps to attend a meeting at headquarters," answered Williams.

Meade snapped."Send a stern message that he needs to get his ass here immediately!"

Meade took a deep breath. He needed to calm his temper and be in control. He looked around the room."Gentlemen, we have a situation. Sickles has moved his corps forward, without orders, might I add, to a new position. The move is completely unauthorized by this command. He's created a large gap between his Third Corps and the Second Corps. I have no idea where the left end of his line is. I'll be riding down there after this meeting to get more specific information on his whole front. I've ordered Hancock to send his First Division south to occupy as much of Sickles' old line as he can. One lone division will be unable to cover all the ground, but it's a start. The Fifth Corps is also heading to that sector. They were going to be held in reserve, but will now have to help secure Sickles' old position. I may need to order other units there. As you all know, Lee has been moving to his right throughout the day. There's a good chance he may attack on that flank. I've recently discovered that General Buford is no longer guarding our left with his cavalry. He requested to be pulled off the line, as his men were tired from yesterday's fight and needed to be refitted with supplies.

Pleasanton granted this request, but never informed me. So, Sickles is forward, in an unsupported position and the cavalry screen he assumed was protecting his left is no longer in the area."

Meade stopped to let the information sink in. The room was overtaken by a deafening silence. Meade had nothing else to add. He was lost in his thoughts. First Dan Butterfield had undermined him and now it was Sickles' turn to be rebellious. These two were loyal to Hooker. Perhaps they thought Meade had worked to get Hooker replaced. This might explain their lack of cooperation with him. But he hadn't sought the position, and when approached, would not take part in any revolt against Hooker.

Hancock broke the silence."I've moved three regiments forward to Emmitsburg Road to connect with Sickles' right. But they're sticking out with no damn support on their right. I just don't have enough troops to move forward. I hope there'll be a serious reprimand for Sickles."

"After the battle," replied Meade.

The sound of artillery reached their ears. They went outside to get a better idea where it was coming from. The noise came from the southwest. They all knew an artillery barrage usually preceded an infantry assault.

"It appears Lee may be attacking on our left," said Williams.

There was agreement amongst the other generals.

So it begins, thought Meade. *Lee has found our weakest flank to begin his attack. He has an uncanny ability to do this time and again.* One could not help but be in awe of Lee's genius. Now Meade would be put to the test.

Meade saw Sickles riding in to headquarters. He was hoping to keep his temper in check. Sickles pulled his horse up. Before dismounting, he began barking at Meade,"I'm deploying my corps and you demand . . ."

"Against my orders," broke in Meade very loudly. His anger was evident in his voice."Your forward movement has threatened the left flank of the entire army, and by the sound of the artillery, I am guessing Lee is planning to attack on your front!"

"Let him attack; my corps is ready," shot back Sickles.

"Your corps is unsupported and in a vulnerable position . . ."

"My old position was vulnerable; my new one is far better . . ."

Meade's eyes were shooting out fire at Sickles."This is not Sickles private enterprises. This is an army, and you're to obey orders . . ."

Sickles cut him off quickly and roared,"I've obeyed orders in the past and watched all you damn West Pointers lose one battle after another!"

They were glaring at each other, Meade on the ground, Sickles on his horse. This was not the time for a confrontation, even though one had erupted. Meade took a deep breath.

"Ride back to your men," ordered Meade."I'll be along shortly to see what we can do about your lines."

Sickles turned his horse, kicked hard and galloped off.

"That's one insubordinate son of a bitch," Meade blurted out to no one in particular, but for everyone to hear. He turned and looked at his commanders.

"Gentleman, you all have work to do. Warren, you're to ride with me. I want you to scout the position on Little Round Top, while I go to Sickles' lines. Maybe there will be time to withdraw his corps before any attack."

"We can only hope," said Williams.

෨ᚹᚻᚳᚷ

General Warren was on Little Round Top with his aides. Looking off to the west, he saw two Confederate divisions in battle formation advancing across the open fields. They were about two miles away, so he had some time before they reached this position. At the moment a signal station manned by a small contingent of troops was all that occupied the hill. He needed to get reinforcements up here. He looked to the north. If the enemy took this position, they could post artillery and fire upon the Union line on Cemetery Ridge. Their infantry would be able to mass and attack an exposed flank. Little Round Top had to be held.

He looked down at the Third Corps position. They were spread far too thin for the ground they occupied. At the base of Little Round Top were huge boulders. There were Third Corps troops deployed on these boulders, but to their left was nothing. This was the extreme left of the Third Corps line and it was hanging in the air with no support. The advancing Confederates would hit this position from front and flank. It was too late to withdraw Third Corps now. What a mess Sickles had created. Warren was certain Meade would deal sternly with Sickles after the battle.

He turned to Lieutenant Meese and said,"Take down this message and deliver it to General Meade. Little Round Top is unoccupied, except for the signal station. It is the key to the left end of our line and must be held at all costs. We need a division rushed here to defend this place."

Meese finished writing the note and put it in his pocket. He mounted his horse and rode off to deliver the dispatch to General Meade.

Warren turned to Lieutenant Mackenzie and said,"Ride to General Sickles and order him to send a brigade to this place."

"Yes, sir," responded Mackenzie.

Warren looked to the west. More troops appeared from the tree line, advancing on Sickles' forward position. He thought this might be Longstreet's Corps, as it had been unaccounted for all day. If this was the case, Sickles' Third Corps with 10,700 men would soon be confronted by 25,000 Confederates. The odds were not good for the Third Corps.

৩৪৮০৫৪৩৯৩

Lieutenant Mackenzie rode his horse hard after his meeting with Sickles. Sickles had told him he had no men to spare. They were all needed to defend his position. Mackenzie had stood on Little Round Top and knew how important it was for the Union army to secure and hold the position. If Sickles could not spare any men, Mackenzie had to search elsewhere to get troops. He would not return to Warren without fulfilling his mission.

He headed for the area of Fifth Corps, to see if they would send some troops. He rode up the small rise in the road and saw troops being deployed. He saw the command flag of the Fifth Corps around a group of men on horseback, and rode over and saluted.

"General Warren sends his compliments. He needs a brigade to help secure yonder hill," said Mackenzie, pointing to Little Round Top."The enemy is approaching, and the hill is devoid of troops."

"I'll send a brigade immediately. Go and tell General Warren that the Fifth Corps will respond to his request," replied General Sykes, commander of the corps. He turned to an aide."Captain, ride over to General Barnes and order him to dispatch one brigade to that hilltop."

"Yes, sir," the captain responded. He rode off in the direction of General Barnes.

"Lieutenant," said Sykes"you are dismissed to deliver your message, with my compliments."

"Thank you, sir. I'm sure your cooperation with be duly noted in General Warren's report."

Mackenzie rode off with the knowledge he had carried out his orders. He had secured a brigade as ordered, even though it was not from Sickles' Corps. He did not think Warren would rebuke him too harshly.

ഏ≈ೞഇ≈ഋ

The captain was looking for General Barnes, but could not find him. He came upon Colonel Vincent, one of the brigade commanders.

"Sir, I'm looking for General Barnes. I have a message to deliver from General Sykes."

Vincent did not know where Barnes was. He said to the courier,"Captain, what are your orders?"

"I need to deliver an order to General Barnes," repeated the captain.

Vincent could hear the sound of fighting to the south and west. He knew a battle was commenced, and there was no time to be wasted in delivering orders. He outranked the captain and would use this card if necessary.

He again said to the captain,"What are your orders? Give me your orders."

"General Sykes told me to direct General Barnes to send one of his brigades to occupy that hill yonder," the captain responded, pointing to Little Round Top.

"I will take the responsibility of taking my brigade there," said Vincent."You may report back to General Sykes that Colonel Strong Vincent is leading his brigade to that hill. You're dismissed"

Vincent rode over to the Forty-fourth New York, which was the southernmost regiment in his brigade. He found Colonel Rice and ordered him to lead the brigade to the hill as quickly as possible. Colonel Vincent galloped off toward Little Round Top with his flag bearer Oliver Norton. They followed a farm lane and rode around the east side of the hill. When they got to the south side of the hill, they were confronted by a larger hill further to the south. The ground before them dropped off to a saddle between the two hills. Trees were abundant, so it was not open ground. Nevertheless, Vincent felt an attack would come from this direction and this side of the hill needed to be secured. He eyed the ground to find the best place to deploy his brigade. He found a spur of land partly covered by boulders and smaller rocks part way down the southern slope. This would be the ground on which his brigade would make their stand.

Artillery shells began bursting in the trees behind them. Tree limbs were blown off their trunks and came crashing to the ground. The enemy had found the range and was shelling the top of this hill. The regiment would be marching through this fire to get to the southerly slopes.

Colonel Rice soon appeared leading his regiment. They had taken the same route as Vincent, around the east side of the hill. Vincent placed Rice's regiment on the right end of the line, facing southwest. To their left, he placed in succession, the Eighty-third Pennsylvania, the Twentieth Maine and the Sixteenth Michigan. These three regiments were facing more southerly, then the Forty-fourth. As Vincent inspected his lines, he shifted the Sixteenth Michigan from the extreme left to the extreme right end. They were now posted to the right of the Forty-fourth New York, facing southwesterly. Vincent was now content with his brigade's position. From behind the position of the Sixteenth Michigan, he could look down at the large boulders at the base of Little Round Top. He witnessed the enemy overrunning the blue troops and taking possession of the rocks. They would soon be heading for his brigade.

Vincent rode over to the position held by the Twentieth Maine. He found Colonel Chamberlain walking among his troops. Vincent called him over to a spot further away from his men.

"Your position is the extreme left end of the Union line," Vincent began."You are to hold this ground at all costs. Do you understand?"

Chamberlain looked into Vincent's eyes. He saw steely determination. This was a no nonsense order.

"I understand, Colonel," replied Chamberlain.

Vincent put out his hand. Chamberlain took it, and they exchanged a firm handshake. They nodded at each other, and then Vincent walked back uphill to the right.

ഏ•ഉ⦂ഌ•ல

General Warren was on Little Round Top looking intently to the west. The Confederates had captured the boulders at the base of the hill and heavy fighting was taking place in a large field of wheat, northerly of those boulders. Warren was getting worried. Lieutenant Mackenzie had returned thirty minutes ago with the news a brigade would be sent from Fifth Corps to this position. No troops had arrived yet. If Union troops did not arrive soon, the enemy could end up taking the hill without a fight. This would threaten the whole Union line on Cemetery Ridge. Where were the Fifth Corps troops?

Shots rang out from the back side of the hill."That's odd," Warren said to Mackenzie."Go and see what's happening."

As far as Warren knew, there were no troops there. If it was Confederate musketry advancing on the signal station, the hill would soon be lost. Union reinforcements would reach the top too late to prevent it from falling into enemy hands. Warren observed more Confederate brigades in battle formation advancing toward Sickles' front. His corps would pay a terrible toll in blood for his blunder.

Mackenzie returned."Sir, Colonel Vincent has posted his brigade on the south side of this hill. It seems they marched up the east side. This is why we didn't see them."

"And the gunfire?" Warren asked.

"The rebels are mounting an attack from the south. We are fortunate Colonel Vincent deployed his brigade where he did. He's in a strong position to hold off an attack."

"Damn good fortune," replied Warren."We still need a brigade up here. Let's ride down to Fifth Corps and get another brigade."

A young lieutenant approached Warren and his aides."Lieutenant Hazlett reporting, sir. I'm bringing artillery up this hill."

"By whose orders?" asked Warren.

"I'm with Fifth Corps. We were down in the valley waiting to be deployed. Captain Martin saw these heights and ordered me to place my guns up here. He felt we could pour some lead on Johnnie from here."

"I'm General Warren with headquarters staff. I'm up here to recon the area. Let's have a look and see where your artillery will be the most beneficial."

They walked along the ridge top. It was poor ground for artillery. The ridge was too narrow from front to rear. Both artillery and caissons would be unable to fit on the ridge. The caissons would have to be left below the summit and ammunition constantly hauled up.

Warren looked around with Hazlett. Warren shook his head and said,"It doesn't look good for artillery placement. The slope is too steep in front of the guns. They will not be able to depress their muzzles enough to provide fire power on any advancing troops."

"Never mind that," said Hazlett,"the sound of my guns will be encouraging to our troops and disheartening to the others. Besides, my battery's no damn good if this hill is lost."

"You make a good argument, Lieutenant. Let's get them up here," said Warren.

They watched the teams struggle to get the cannon to the crest. The horses were of no use near the top, so the men were hauling the guns up by hand. Warren and his aides lent a hand hauling the guns to the top. The men were surprised to see a general pitch in and do some of the grunt work. There were nods of admiration sent his way, after the six guns were settled on the ridge.

As the guns and their crew became evident on the ridge, Confederate sharpshooters, perched in the boulders at the base of the hill, began finding the range and picking off members of the gun crews. General Warren felt a sting in his neck. He reached up with his hand and felt a warm liquid. He withdrew his hand and saw blood."Son of a bitch got me," he exclaimed.

"Let me have a look," said his aide Lieutenant Roebling. Roebling looked at the wound."You've been grazed. No vital parts got hit. You'll be fine, sir."

"That's certainly good news. We still need to get troops up here to protect the west face. Let's ride down to Fifth Corps and grab another brigade," said Warren.

Warren and Roebling walked over to their horses, mounted and rode down the north side of the hill. They expected to find Fifth Corps in this area. Warren was intent on commandeering the first troops he encountered for Little Round Top.

Warren came upon the One Hundred Fortieth New York, led by Colonel Patrick O'Rorke. Fortune smiled on Warren, as these were troops from his old brigade, now under the command of General Stephen Weed.

Warren galloped over to O'Rorke and yelled,"Paddy, give me a regiment!"

"Good to see you alive, sir," said O'Rorke. "General Weed has ridden ahead and we're to follow him. These are my orders."

"Never mind that, Paddy! Bring them up on the double-quick. Don't stop for aligning! I'll take the responsibility. Lieutenant Roebling will lead you to the top and show you where to place your regiment. But you've got to get up there damned fast. Johnnie's advancing up the hill and the west face has no troops defending it now. We can't let them get a foothold on the ridge. Vincent's brigade will be cut off and the left end of our line will be in danger. Now, go!"

"On the double, sir," replied O'Rorke.

Warren turned to Roebling."Get them posted quickly. I'm riding up to have General Sykes send the rest of the brigade to you on the crest. Then I'm riding to headquarters. General Meade will be expecting my report of conditions on Little Round Top. Keep your head down."

"Heed your own words, sir. I'm not the one that got shot today," said Roebling. He turned on his horse and led Colonel O'Rorke's regiment up the hill.

Warren watched until they were at the top of the hill. He felt he had done his job and Little Round Top was secure from falling into enemy hands. Colonel Vincent had played his part, by posting his brigade in the exact spot it needed to inhabit. He would commend Vincent when this was over. He turned on his horse and headed back to headquarters.

৯৲৪৵৶৶

General John Caldwell, commander of the First Division, Second Corps, was watching intently the battle raging to the southwest of his position. His position was the extreme left of the Second Corps, a position that became unsupported when General Sickles advanced his corps. Fifth Corps troops were hurrying behind his position to fill the area vacated by Sickles. From where Caldwell stood, the attack appeared to be the first main thrust of the day by the Confederates. He could still see enemy troops to the west in the distant tree line. They did not seem to be making any attempt to get into battle formation. He wondered if they were waiting for the attack to reach their front before they advanced.

An aide from Hancock's staff rode up."Sir, General Hancock sends his compliments. You are to move your entire division to the south and report to General Sykes of the Fifth Corps for further instructions."

Caldwell thanked the young officer and dismissed him. He turned to his staff and began issuing orders."All brigade commanders are to move quickly to the south. Colonel Cross is the left end of our line. He'll lead the corps with his brigade. The other three brigades will follow keeping the same alignment they're now in. I'm riding ahead to find General Sykes and get orders for our new position."

Some aides rode off to deliver his orders. The other aides stayed with him. They rode south seeking General Sykes. As they rode closer to the fray, the smell of gunpowder became more prevalent. The sounds of battle increased in volume. Officers were barking orders, musketry spewed forth its death and destruction and that strange howl, felt in the spine of every Union soldier, bellowed from the Confederate mass as it advanced.

An officer galloped toward them. He came to a halt."I've been sent by General Sykes to lead you to your new position. It's hot there. The Third Corps is hard pressed. You'll be thrown right into the fight."

"Lead on," said Caldwell.

He was led to a spot overlooking a field of wheat bordered on three sides by woods. There was a road on the north end of this field running east and west. Caldwell saw a hill off to the left, barren of trees, its west face strewn with boulders and Confederate soldiers attempting to advance up its steep slope, while Union troops fired down on them from the crest. It did not appear to him the Confederates would be successful in their attempt. He looked across the wheat field and saw numerous Confederate brigades firing on Union troops.

"Fifth Corps troops are on top of the hill," began Sykes aide."Down in the wheat field are members of the Third Corps. They are being pressed from the south and west. The enemy is breaking through on the right. Strike him quick."

With this order given, the aide rode hard away.

Caldwell, who had never before led a division, was now ordered into a situation that was deteriorating quickly before his eyes. Colonel Cross appeared with his brigade. Caldwell barked orders at him."I want you to advance obliquely across that field in a southwesterly direction. The enemy has pushed back our forces on the right and I want you to hit them in the flank. No time for skirmishers. Head through that field of wheat to the woods on the westerly side. I'll put Kelly's brigade on your right. Get your brigade down there at the double quick."

"We're on it, sir," replied Cross to his orders.

Caldwell rode over to issue orders to Kelly's brigade. They were to connect their left with the right of Cross' brigade and advance in the same oblique manner. Caldwell then sought out Colonel Zook. He would be advancing on Kelly's right. Most of his brigade would be advancing through woods. These were the woods on the westerly side of the wheat field. He told

Zook to try to hook up with the Third Corps forces on his right. He should expect to encounter enemy forces in those woods. Caldwell rode over to his Fourth Brigade, led by Colonel Brooke. He was being held in reserve and would be sent in where the situation dictated.

That damn Sickles, he thought. He had advanced his corps without orders, and now many other troops were being called in to clean up his mess. Caldwell, like Sickles, was not a professional soldier. He was a teacher and then a principal at Washington Academy in East Machias, Maine, before the war. Even though he had no military experience, he was elected colonel of the Eleventh Maine regiment early in the war. His advancement was based on merit and not political connections. Sickles' action on this day irked Caldwell to no end. Caldwell knew that those that attended that school on the Hudson River scrutinized the generals not from West Point more thoroughly. What Sickles did by moving his corps forward without orders was a black mark against all non-professional officers.

Caldwell watched Cross lead his brigade across the wheat. Suddenly, a galling fire was poured on them from the south. This fire came from behind a stone wall at the edge of the woods. The ranks were thinned considerably as men fell with wounds, many of them mortal. Cross stopped his men so they could return fire. The air was thick with lead, and the boys in blue were out in the open. They stood and exchanged fire with the enemy in the woods, but they were falling quickly to Confederate bullets. Caldwell felt they had to advance or stand and be eviscerated. He saw Cross move to the left of his line. Then he went down in a barrage of lead. Caldwell did not know how bad Cross was. As if reading his mind, the brigade charged forward into the woods. They climbed up and over the stonewall firing at their foe. The boys in gray withdrew from the position. Those that didn't were taken prisoner.

A staff officer from the regiment rode up to Caldwell."Sir, Colonel Cross has been killed. A bullet tore into him, and he was killed instantly. He ordered the charge before he died. The boys went forward like wild animals seeking revenge for their colonel. It appears they have exacted their revenge. They are spent and almost out of ammunition. We request you send in the reserve brigade."

"Ride back to your men and tell them to hold their current position until Colonel Brooke arrives with his brigade. Then they can retire to get refitted," said Caldwell.

The staff officer turned his horse to deliver the orders.

Caldwell sent a staff officer to General Brooke with orders for him to advance his brigade on the left to the position now held by Cross's Brigade. If he could, he was to clear the woods of enemy troops.

Caldwell looked in the direction of his other two brigades to check on their progress. Kelly's brigade, no longer taking flank fire from the front, wheeled to the right and advanced into the west woods. Their attack was now in a westerly direction, running perpendicular to General Zook's brigade, which was advancing in a southerly direction. The smoke was thick as muskets erupted from both sides at close quarters. Caldwell watched as men from each brigade fell in this murderous hail of lead. Within ten minutes, he watched his two brigades advance into the woods. *Clear those woods my brave boys,* he cried to himself. *Give 'em hell!*

The battle carried on before him. His boys were driving the rebels from the woods. General Brooke's brigade charged gallantly through the woods and gained a position at the crest of a small hill on the far side of the woods. Caldwell rode up to inspect the position. He thought it an excellent position to defend. He looked off to the right and saw both Kelly's and Zook's brigades in a similar position to the north. They were behind fences and rocks at the crest of a small hill, facing west. He thought his troops were in an impregnable position from a frontal assault if their flanks were properly supported.

He rode over to the left and asked General Ayres of the Fifth Corps to advance his two brigades forward to connect with the left of Brooke's brigade. Before they could begin their advance, a tremendous volley of fire opened upon Brooke's left. More Confederates were advancing upon his exposed flank. He refused the line of his left regiment, the Second Delaware, and bought himself some time.

Caldwell saw the right of his line begin to crumble. A fresh Confederate brigade had fallen on their flank and would soon get in their rear if they did not retreat. The Third Corps had not held on his right and now his men were in peril. He sent orders for all regiments to fall back to the north side of the wheat field. His men were forced to retreat through a heavy crossfire of enemy musketry. He was taking numerous casualties, and he again cursed Sickles under his breath. His division had fought gallantly, coming to the aid of the Third Corps, securing the wheat field and the woods on its far side. They had pushed Johnny completely from the woods and were in a good defensive position. They were then abandoned by the same Third Corps, allowing the enemy to attack their exposed flank and force them from the field. Caldwell would not hide his displeasure of the Third Corps when telling General Hancock of his fight in the wheat field.

The Confederate army pressed the left flank of the Union army hard. Caldwell had done his best, but had to retire with numerous casualties. He had lost two brigade commanders in the fight. Colonel Cross and Colonel Zook were both killed. *Damn that Sickles.*

♫♥ꝏ♥♫

General Hancock and General Gibbon were riding slowly behind their Second Corps lines. There was no fighting on their front, so the men began yelling out their names as they rode by. Exuberant yells of"Hancock,""Gibbon" and"Our Generals" were heard filling the air. Hancock knew these boys were ready to fight. They were defending their nation from a foreign invader, as he saw it. They were ready to give Johnny hell. Both generals raised their hats to their men in acknowledgement of their cheers. They stopped their mounts and looked to the southwest, where the battle was raging in full fury.

"It's going to be a long damned day for the Third Corps," said Gibbon.

"And for the rest of the army," added Hancock."Sickles' forward move has unhinged the left flank of this army. Meade is doing all he can to minimize the damage caused by that bastard Sickles. But in doing so, he is weakening our lines elsewhere. The whole Fifth Corps has been moved to that flank and word is the Sixth Corps is being sent to that vicinity. Hell, we've sent a whole division down there. Lee is famous for flank attacks and he's hit us where we're vulnerable."

Hancock looked through his field glasses from the southwest in a northerly direction to the west. He lowered the glasses and continued speaking."It appears Lee is sending brigades forward one at a time, with a certain interval between each brigade stepping off. There are still numerous troops and artillery across these fields to our west. They'll be heading for our front soon, you can damn sure bet on that. Our ranks are extremely thin and our reserves are negligible. It will be hot on our front soon enough."

A rider came galloping up to them. Hancock recognized the young man as a staff officer from headquarters.

The officer halted his horse and spoke with great excitement in his voice."Sir, General Meade sends his compliments. He needs more help on the left immediately. Third Corps is hard pressed to hold the line. He requests you to send one brigade to the assistance of General Birney whose division is the extreme left of Sickles' corps. He also needs two regiments sent to General Humphries, who occupies the right of the Third Corps."

"Tell Meade the help he requests will be there shortly," replied Hancock. The young officer rode off.

Hancock turned to Gibbon and said,"Damn, I've already sent one division to the left. Sending another brigade and two regiments will seriously thin our ranks."

"Must be more trouble down there than we can see," responded Gibbon."Who should we send?"

"Send a message to General Hays that Colonel Willard's brigade from his division is to be sent to the left and report to General Birney, immediately. I want you to send two regiments from your division to General Humphries. Then we'll have to spread our men even thinner to cover all the ground on our assigned front."

They looked to the west once again through their field glasses."They're stepping off," exclaimed Gibbon, pointing in the direction for Hancock to look. Hancock looked through his glasses and saw what Gibbon was alluding to. Three Confederate brigades were advancing simultaneously. They would be heading for his front. *Damn*, he thought, *our lines are being thinned, and the enemy is now approaching on this front. Time to see how much fight these cheering boys have in them.*

An aide spoke up,"General Meade is approaching, sir."

Hancock looked south and saw Meade and his staff riding up. He rode up beside Hancock and spoke tersely,"It's a hell of a mess on the left. Sickles has lost a leg and is being sent to the hospital. Win, I'm putting you in charge of the left wing, to include the Second, Third and Fifth Corps. Sykes has two brigades on Little Round Top and seems to be in good condition there. I need you to get over to the left to stabilize an uncertain situation. Third Corps was being hard pressed when I left."

"Sickles loses a damn leg," said Hancock"but he cost this army an arm and a leg. I hope you'll deal harshly with him when this is over."

"Right now I've got my hands full with Lee," replied Meade."I'll deal with Sickles later. I'm riding over to Twelfth Corps for reinforcements. I'll order them to report to you. You have complete authority as to where they'll be deployed. I trust your judgment. With Reynolds dead, you're the best I've got left. Keep me informed of developments on your front. Don't be afraid to ask for more men. Our line will be in trouble if Lee collapses our left."

"The men are ready to fight, sir. Hell, we'll throw rocks at Johnny, but we'll keep him off this ridge," answered Hancock with some grit in his voice. He turned to Gibbon,"You're in charge of the Second Corps. Let's get to work."

Meade kicked his horse and rode off towards Culp's Hill followed by his staff. Gibbon went in the direction of the two regiments he would send to the left. Hancock saw General Willard leading his brigade to the left.

"We'll ride together," said Hancock,"and see where the hell you'll be needed."

"What do you know of the situation?" asked Willard.

"Probably as much as you do. Sickles has lost a leg, so Meade has put me in charge of the left end of our line. Sykes has stationed troops on Little Round Top and is holding his own. The fighting has been raging for over an hour, and by the noise and smoke, it been a heavily contested front for both armies."

"Sir, my men are ready to bloody some noses and kick these damned invaders out of our country!"

Hancock smiled."That's the spirit."

They rode in silence for a few moments. The roar of the battle grew louder as they led their horses into the sector. Hancock observed Confederate troops on a wide front steadily advancing while Union forces were heading to the rear. It was worse than he anticipated. The Third Corps troops were paying a heavy price for the folly of their commander. Where was Caldwell's Division, he wondered.

General Birney rode up alongside Hancock."Where are you headed, sir?"

"Meade has put me in charge of the Third Corps," replied Hancock."I'm leading this brigade to the left to give you support. What's the situation?"

"The left has collapsed. We were overrun by a Confederate corps. My division has been driven to the rear. I'm heading back to reform what is left of my division."

"What of Caldwell's division?" asked Hancock.

"His men came up and relieved our line. They pushed the enemy back and were in an advanced position. The rebs kept pressing, clearing the troops on his right. He had to withdraw his corps or get surrounded. His men fought their way to the rear suffering numerous casualties," said Birney.

"Go reform your command. We still may need them to fight today," ordered Hancock.

He looked off to the west. He saw two Confederate brigades advancing toward the ridge. There were Union forces attempting to slow the attack. They were too few to succeed, but they would buy him time.

"Willard, put your brigade in battle formation along this ridge, two regiments in the front and two in the rear for support. Those two Confederate brigades will soon overrun our troops down below us. Then Johnny will head up into this gap. After you form into battle formation, I want you to attack. Don't hold anything back. They've been fighting for over an hour. They'll be tired and low on ammunition."

"You can count on us, sir," answered Willard with a confident air. He rode off to post his brigade.

Hancock looked to the south. Fifth Corps held the hill known as Little Round Top. It did not appear it would fall into enemy hands. Its west slope was too steep and strewn with boulders for a concerted attack to be waged on the defenders. He then looked off to the west. The enemy was approaching a narrow patch of trees that was on the west side of a small creek. They would pass through these trees, cross the creek and then advance uphill, through dense underbrush, toward the ridge he was on. He had arrived in time with Willard's brigade. They were deploying into battle formation and would attack an unsuspecting enemy. Meade was responsible for ordering a brigade to this sector to stem a Confederate surge. And now Meade was off to find more reinforcements to be sent to this front. Hancock was gaining a new admiration for George Meade.

General Humphries rode up with his staff. He was agitated and let it be known."Sickles and Birney have about ruined my division. First Sickles advances to an unsupported position, without orders I've heard. I posted my division as best I could under the circumstances. I had adequate troops in reserve, and felt I could have held off the enemy. Birney requested a brigade be sent to his front, as he was attacked first and needed help. I was ordered to send one brigade to him, which stripped me of my reserves and made my line weaker. Well, Birney got overrun, Sickles got his damn leg blown off and put Birney in charge of the corps. One political general, with no military training, appoints another to lead the men. I'm fighting like a bastard to hold my position, when I get an order from the new corps commander, that son of a bitch Birney, to retreat. I'm being hard pressed by rebels and then I have to retreat. My men put up stiff resistance, during this withdrawal, contesting every inch of ground taken by the enemy. We made them pay in blood, but we also paid a heavy price."

Humphries paused for a moment to collect himself. He put his hand to his forehead and rubbed it a few times."It's good to see you, Win. Did Meade send you over?"

"Yes, he did. He also put me in charge of the Third Corps, although it seems a little too late. He wants me to stabilize the left end of our line. He is off looking for more reinforcements to send my way. I've been watching your men fight, and they did you proud. Post your men up on the ridge behind that wood fence. You'll be my reserve. The Sixth Corps is also headed here. I'll post them near you. See to your men."

"Yes, sir. I feel more confident with you in the area. Give 'em hell, Win," said Humphries. He rode off to tend to his troops.

Hancock turned and looked to the west. Willard's brigade was advancing down the slope and through the underbrush. They did not stop to fire, but fired as they advanced. Many of their numbers fell as the enemy was holding their line and pouring lead into them. The boys in blue were not deterred. They kept advancing in the face of this terrible volley, intent on driving the enemy back. Willard's right was unsupported. Hancock turned and rode to the north to get some troops to fill the gap. As he passed Willard's advancing men, he saw another Confederate brigade advancing toward the gap in his line. He galloped forward and came upon a lone regiment.

Hancock rode over yelling,"What regiment is this?"

"First Minnesota, sir," replied its commander Colonel Colvill.

"Charge and take those colors," ordered Hancock, pointing to the advancing brigade.

"Yes, sir," replied Colvill. He turned to his men."Attention, First Minnesota; right shoulder shift; arms. Forward, double quick march!"

Hancock watched the small regiment of eight companies charge into an enemy brigade of 1300 soldiers. He estimated the regiment to have roughly 250 men. He knew it was a suicide mission, but it was necessary to buy time to plug the hole in the line. He sent an aide to Colonel Willard to order his reserve regiment, the One Hundred Eleventh New York, to leave its reserve position and attack to the right, giving support to the boys from Minnesota. He watched the charge, and to his amazement, the enemy brigade stopped its advance. The Confederates pulled back and the boys from Minnesota reached the creek bed. There they took up a defensive position and exchanged fire with the enemy. They were still vastly outnumbered, but they were fighting as ferocious as cornered lions. Hancock watched as the enemy advanced their lines on both flanks, continuing to exchange fire with the boys from Minnesota. He looked to the left and saw the One Hundred Eleventh New York Regiment advance to the left of the First Minnesota.

Willard's other two brigades were exchanging fire with the Confederate brigade to the left. The smoke was thick, and the noise of musketry constant. Willard had also advanced to the creek. The steady stream of fire poured on the enemy wore them down, until they withdrew from their position, retiring back to the Emmitsburg Road. Hancock was recovering ground lost when Sickles advanced.

Hancock turned his attention to the One Hundred Eleventh, bearing down on the left of the First Minnesota. They unleashed their fury on the Confederate brigade on the west side of the creek, dropping many men in their tracks. The field was littered with dead and wounded men from both armies. Hancock watched as this brigade also withdrew to the Emmitsburg Road. Damn fine job by his boys, he thought.

However, his work was not finished. Two new Confederate brigades were advancing on his front, to the north of the previous attack. Lee still had numerous brigades that could enter the fight and tip the scales in his favor. Hancock saw two of his regiments at the Emmitsburg Road to the right of the red barn. Seventy-five yards behind them were six pieces of artillery. To the left of the barn was another battery of artillery, consisting of six cannons. These troops were now under assault by the two Confederate brigades.

Doubleday arrived with his division from the First Corps. He found Hancock and reported to him."Meade ordered us to come to your aid. Where would you like my men deployed?" asked Doubleday.

Hancock led him to the spot recently vacated by the First Minnesota."I need your men here filling in to the left. As you can see, we are still being hard pressed from the west. If Lee keeps sending brigades one after the other, he just might break through. How are your men after yesterday's fight?"

"Pretty used up, but I've got a fresh brigade of boys from Vermont, who missed yesterday's action. They're ready for a scrap. They're nine-month boys who've never been in combat and are due to muster out this month. Their commander says they are ready and willing to fight."

"We've got no other options. Throw them on the line and we'll see what they're made of. Hopefully they've got some Ethan Allen in them," said Hancock, alluding to revolutionary war heroes from Vermont who fought under Ethan Allen.

Gibbon rode up to Hancock."Son of a bitch, they keep coming!" Gibbon exclaimed.

"Well then, we'll keep showing those bastards what we're made of," replied Hancock."We've pushed them back on the left, and that portion of the line seems stabilized. Give 'em hell, John, and don't let them break through your lines."

"We'll feed them all the lead they can stand!" responded Gibbon. He rode off to his lines, which were now under attack.

The regiments at Emmitsburg Road were forced to fall back or be captured. Johnny crossed the fences on both sides of the road and began advancing toward the ridge. They were met by artillery spewing forth canister, and even though this canister tore deadly holes in their lines, they were too numerous, and soon the artillery was in their possession. They let out their Rebel yell and continued their advance toward the Union lines waiting behind a stone wall on the front slope of cemetery ridge. They reached the wall and the fighting became primal. Men fought each other at close range, using their rifles as clubs and thrusting bayonet points at human flesh. Every man was consumed by seven devils in his desire to survive and lash out at anyone attempting to end his life.

Hancock noticed this Confederate brigade was alone. Units to their left did not advance further than the house on the west side of the road. The units on their right had retreated. He didn't know why this brigade was alone and at the moment didn't give a damn. He was going to smash this brigade. He ordered troops to get around both flanks and in their rear. Union regiments held in reserve appeared at both ends of the line and attempted to surround this lone brigade. The boys in gray, not wanting to be surrounded, gave a good account of themselves and fought like hell in order to get as many back to the road before they got captured.

Hancock rode over to the left side of his line where the boys from Vermont were flush with their first taste of combat. They had helped repel the brigade and were firing into the retreating rebels. Hancock wanted these boys to recapture a battery taken by the rebels in the assault. He pointed out the guns to their commander and asked if he could retake them.

"I'll give it a try," replied Colonel Randall, commander of the Thirteenth Vermont.

"It's a hazardous job, and I won't order it, but if you think you'd like to try, have at it," said Hancock.

"For the Union, sir, we'll give you our all," said Randall.

Randall gave the orders to his men and rode on his horse to lead the charge. Early in the charge, his horse was hit and he was pinned under it. His men held up to free him, but he barked at them, "Go forward boys, I'll be at your head as soon as I get out of this damn saddle!"

The Vermont boys charged down the slope over dead and wounded men, shouting and firing at their foe. They captured many men and had to hold up their charge to gather the prisoners.

Hancock rode up and yelled at Randall, "Press on for the guns. I'll take care of the prisoners."

Randall turned to his men and said, "You heard the General, at the double quick. Charge!"

They charged forward and retook the four guns the enemy had captured. They also took more prisoners. Randall was proud of his boys. They might be nine-month volunteers, but they showed they had steel in their spine today.

The Rebel assault had come to a halt. No more brigades were advancing. Hancock offered a silent prayer for the day's victory. Colonel Randall returned to cemetery hill and was met by Hancock.

Hancock looked him in the eye and said, "Damn fine job, Colonel. Give me Vermonters for a charge."

"Thank you, sir," said a delighted Randall.

CHAPTER 20

Evening

HANCOCK AND GIBBON PUFFED on their cigars on Cemetery Ridge. They were behind the lines of the Second Corps. The guns of war had ceased, and their silence was felt deep in the soul of every living being. The sun was setting in the west, painting the sky orange and red. The ambulances and their crews were collecting the wounded men from the fields between the armies. Their work would continue through the night.

Hancock inhaled on his cigar and slowly let the smoke escape from his mouth."Hell of a day, John. The corps fought magnificently."

"That they did. We took casualties, but from the look of the carnage, it appears they lost more than we did."

"I can't understand why the attack just stopped. The last brigade that came forward consisted of boys from Georgia in General Wright's brigade. I talked to some prisoners, and they don't know why the attack faltered. They feel betrayed there was no support on their left. I'm certain the breakdown was not part of Lee's plan. He's too good to have a brigade advance unsupported."

"Whatever the reason, it played to our favor," said Gibbon."We lost many of our commanders today. General Caldwell lost two brigade commanders, Colonel Cross and General Zook. General Willard was cut down leading his brigade. Colonel Ward of the Fifteenth Mass and Colonel Horton of the Eighty-second New York were killed fighting with their troops at Emmitsburg Road. I pin all these deaths on Sickles and his forward movement which was a dereliction of duty."

"You'll get no argument from me. I'm certain Meade will deal with him harshly when this is over. I don't think his political connections will help him this time. His corps was badly mauled, and if it weren't for the excellent work of Meade plugging forces into the void, the army could have suffered a major defeat today. It was close."

"You did some outstanding work today too, sir," commented Gibbon.

"I did my duty and reacted quickly to each crisis on the field. Meade kept sending men to the points in the line where they were needed. Don't forget the men. They responded to our orders without question and fought like the war would be won or lost today. I sent the First Minnesota on a suicide mission against a brigade with over five times the number of troops. They went forward without hesitation. I checked on them earlier. They went bravely forward with two hundred and sixty two men. When they returned, their ranks numbered forty-seven. Incredible courage." He puffed on his cigar and let the smoke escape."Their brave charge bought me time to plug a gap in our line with fresh troops from other parts of the field, troops, I might add, sent by Meade. I also witnessed courage from a regiment of nine-month volunteers, who have never before been in combat. The men of the Thirteenth Vermont charged into Wright's Georgians, capturing many and then recovered some artillery that had fallen into enemy hands. These are only some of the incidents of courage I witnessed today."

A staff officer from headquarters rode up."Evening, sirs. General Meade is holding a council of war at headquarters and requests your presence."

"Thank you. We'll be there," replied Hancock.

He turned to Gibbon."A good cigar ruined. Let's enjoy these babies a little while longer before we get back to business."

"You're the boss, sir," said Gibbon with a chuckle.

⇜✵⌘✵⇝

Headquarters was a farmhouse on Taneytown Road belonging to the widow Lydia Liester. The generals gathered in a small front room consisting of a table with a candle, five straight-backed rush-bottomed chairs and a bed in the corner. The generals had all gathered for Meade's council. In attendance were General Newton of the First Corps, General Hancock in command of the left wing, General Gibbon of the Second Corps, General Birney head of the Third Corps, General Sykes of the Fifth Corps, General Sedgwick with the Sixth Corps, and General Howard of the Eleventh Corps. Also present was General Slocum, who appointed himself as right wing commander and General Williams as Twelfth Corps commander. When Williams saw

Slocum, he asked Meade if he should leave. Meade told him to stay and give his opinion on matters.

General Meade was present, as was Dan Butterfield, his chief of staff. General Warren was asleep in the corner of the room, exhausted from his day's work. Meade let him sleep. Cigar smoke filled the room.

After everyone had gathered, Meade spoke to his generals,"Men, you've all performed admirably today. I sent a dispatch to Halleck informing him of the enemy's fierce attack and how it was repulsed at all points. I then told him we would remain in our present position tomorrow, but was uncertain if operations would be of an offensive or defensive nature. I have called you all here to get a sense of the condition of the army. I want each of you to give me the hard facts of your corps' strength."

Each general spoke in turn laying out the hard numbers this fight had cost them, and what they could put in the field the next day. Butterfield took notes while each general spoke. When they all had their say, Butterfield sat at the table tallying the numbers.

"Sir, it appears we will have 58,000 infantry troops available for tomorrow," said Butterfield.

Meade nodded. He again spoke to everyone,"I've heard from Colonel Sharpe with intelligence that prisoners have been interviewed and they represent nearly 100 Confederate regiments that have been involved in the two days of fighting. He tells me that General Pickett's division with three brigades is the only unit Lee has not thrown into the fray. They are now in bivouac nearby and will be ready to attack tomorrow. I consider this excellent news for us. Lee has thrown his whole army at us, with the exception of one division, and he has failed to move us off this ground."

The room was filled with congratulatory cheers and men back-slapping each other. This was a moment they could be proud of. Meade allowed them their time. When the room quieted down, he again spoke to everyone.

"I am proposing three questions to you. Each one will answer from junior to senior in rank. I have written these questions down for Butterfield to read. You have the floor, Dan," said Meade.

Butterfield spoke,"Question one. Under existing circumstances, is it advisable for this army to remain in its present position, or to retire to another nearer its base of supplies?"

Gibbon voted first."This is the correct position for the army. I would not retreat."

Williams spoke next."Definitely stay!"

Birney and Sykes agreed with Williams.

Newton then spoke."This is the correct position. I would not retreat."

"Remain," said Howard.

Hancock offered his vote."We rectify our position without moving. We don't want to give up the field."

Sedgwick voted like Howard,"Remain."

Slocum had the last vote."We stay and fight it out."

"Here is the second question," started Butterfield."Shall the army attack or wait the attack of the enemy?"

Gibbon again voted first."We are in no condition to attack. We wait."

Williams, Birney and Sykes all voted to wait for Lee's attack.

"By all means, we don't attack," voted Newton.

Howard voted to wait until 4 p.m. tomorrow.

"We don't attack," said Hancock"unless our communications are cut."

Sedgwick and Slocum both voted to await an attack.

Butterfield posed the third question."How long shall we wait?

"Until Lee moves," said Gibbon.

One day was the vote of Williams, Birney and Sykes.

Newton said,"If we wait, it will give them a chance to cut our line."

"If they don't attack, we should attack them after 4 p.m.," said Howard.

"We can't wait long; we can't be idle," offered Hancock.

Sedgwick voted to stay at least one day.

Slocum again offered these words,"We stay and fight it out."

Meade looked around the room and said,"Such then is the decision. We remain for one day and see what transpires." Meade thanked everyone in the room and dismissed the gathering.

Meade walked over to Gibbon and said,"If Lee attacks tomorrow, it will be on your front."

"What makes you say this," responded Gibbon.

"Because he has made attacks on both our flanks and failed, and if he concludes to try again it will be on our center."

"Let him try, for we will certainly defeat him," said Gibbon confidently.

After the commanders had left, Meade sat thinking. Would Lee still be around in the morning? If Lee was gone, it would not be the first time he retreated after night fell. If he was still across these fields, what would his plan be? Meade still believed he would attack the Union center. Tomorrow would bring the answers.

Part V

A Thunderous Fury

CHAPTER 21

THE SOUND OF ARTILLERY woke Meade up. He was not sure where he was. He was exhausted, and it seemed he had just closed his eyes to catch some needed sleep. He sat up in his bunk. More guns boomed in the distance. It wasn't a dream, he said to himself. He stretched and took a deep breath. His head started clearing. The attack on the right. Yes, it must be starting. Before he fell asleep, a courier appeared at headquarters from General Slocum. The enemy had occupied some of the Union breastworks at the base of Culp's Hill during the fighting on July 2. These were breastworks that had been abandoned by the Twelfth Corps forces sent to the left to help counter the Confederate attack there. When these forces returned to Culp's Hill, they found the lower breastworks on the extreme right occupied by rebel forces. General Slocum wished to attack these forces early in the morning and drive them out. Meade had sent the courier back to Slocum with his approval of the plan.

He pulled out his pocket watch and read the time. It was 4:30. He needed to get up and inspect the lines. He was certain there would be more fighting today and even more certain it would be precipitated by Lee.

When he stepped outside, he saw some of his staff awaiting him on the lawn. They were prepared to execute his orders. The commander got all the glory, but it was these young, willing officers that rode to and fro delivering dispatches to every part of the field that got the work done. He knew how fortunate he was to have such loyal lieutenants.

He turned to an aide."Ride down to General Sedgwick and tell him to send a brigade to Culp's Hill. They are to report to General Slocum for further orders when they arrive."

"Yes, sir." The aide walked quickly to his horse, mounted and headed south to deliver the order.

Meade spoke to another aide."Wake General Warren. I want him to ride the lines with me."

The early morning gray was beginning to be pierced in the east by an orange hue. It was a spectacular sunrise. He knew for many men on both sides, it would be their last sunrise. A generation of young men was being decimated by this war. The scourge of slavery was destroying this nation. He thought of some lines from the book of Isaiah;"'Woe to the obstinate children,'" declares the Lord,"'to those who carry out plans that are not mine, forming an alliance, but not by my spirit, heaping sin upon sin. This sin will become for you like a high wall. It will break in pieces like pottery, shattered so mercilessly that among its pieces not a fragment will be found.'" Slavery was this sin.

"Morning, sir," came Warren's voice, bringing him back to the present."I hear we're inspecting the lines."

"Indeed," replied Meade."Our mounts are being saddled and we'll be on the move soon. How's the wound?"

"Just a graze. The grim reaper had too many other victims to grab. I'll be fine."

"He'll be just as busy today," said Meade.

"Sir, your horses are ready," said an aide.

"Thank you, Captain," said Meade. He mounted his horse, turned to Warren and said,"We'll head to Culp's Hill and see how the fighting is going. Williams is minding headquarters and will inform us if any important dispatches arrive."

They rode off to the north followed by some staff members. They headed toward the sound of battle. It could be a long day, thought Meade. The fighting yesterday didn't start until four in the afternoon. It was now five in the morning, and hostilities were commencing. There were fifteen hours of daylight to contend with. His day would be busy.

They arrived at Culp's Hill and were greeted by General Slocum."The attack is going well, sir. The artillery placed by General Hunt during the night is finding the range and reigning hell down on the enemy in our breastworks. This should dampen their spirits to stay within our lines. Our infantry will advance soon."

"Excellent. I've sent for a brigade from Sixth Corps to report to your front. Post them where you'll need them," said Meade.

"Thank you, sir. The extra brigade will certainly be of help."

Meade looked at Slocum intently and said,"We need this hill secured. Baltimore Pike is our lifeline to supplies and it can't fall into enemy hands. I've got cavalry off to your right protecting that flank. Keep me informed and for god's sake, ask for more troops if you need them. I've got the Sixth Corps sitting in reserve. I'm off to inspect our lines."

Slocum looked Meade in the eye and said,"We'll re-establish our line on Culp's Hill, sir. You can count on it."

Meade nodded and led his horse to Cemetery Hill. The hill had been breached briefly last night, but Meade had sent troops from nearby to help drive out the enemy forces. The attack, initially successful, was unsupported on either flank. The rebels had to retreat or be captured as Union troops poured into the breach and helped restore the line. Meade wondered about this attack. It was not like Lee to advance brigades unsupported into a strong position. His assault on Cemetery Ridge came to a halt when one brigade was alone attacking Hancock's front. Lee's night attack on Cemetery Hill seemed a colossal mistake, unsupported as it was. If Lee were planning to attack today, Meade still had the advantage of good interior lines. He could get his reinforcements to any part of the field quicker than Lee could.

Meade conferred briefly with Howard on Cemetery Hill. Howard told him his lines were restored and his position was strong. He did not think Lee would attack on this front in daylight. His position was much too formidable. Meade looked across the landscape and tended to agree with Howard.

The entourage rode south along Cemetery Ridge. The artillery was posted behind the infantry with the numerous guns facing across the open fields to the west. Troops attempting to cross the open fields would come under a tremendous barrage of artillery shot and shell. Meade couldn't explain the feeling, but his gut told him Lee would attempt just such madness.

Meade looked at the infantry massed along the ridge. Many of them were still asleep behind walls of stone and wood. They had fought hard yesterday and deserved their brief respite. Today's work would also present great challenges.

They came upon Hancock and Gibbon riding behind their lines.

"Morning, Win," said Meade."What goes?"

"Their artillery is still posted across the valley," said Hancock."Of course they could be there to deter us from planning any attack while they retreat. I didn't see many campfires in the night, so I'm not sure if Mr. Lee is still over there with his army, or just has a force in position to keep us in place while he retires. How goes the fight on the right?"

"It's going as planned. I've been over to that sector and Slocum assures me he will restore his lines and protect Baltimore Pike," answered Meade."Our lines are strong and the artillery support is magnificent. I still think Lee will attack on your front, as crazy as it appears. His troops will face a hail of lead from our artillery before they reach Emmitsburg Road. If they get across the road and reach that stone wall, I should be able to get reinforcements to you to repel however many troops survive the heavy musketry and gunfire they will be exposed to."

"Let them come," said Hancock."We'll show them some damned Yankee stubbornness and feed them all the lead they can handle."

"Stay vigilant and keep the men alert," said Meade.

Meade continued his ride down the ridge, stopping to confer with the various brigade, division and corps commanders. He viewed the lines, inspecting for troop strength and reserve numbers. He sought Warren's input. General Warren expressed his satisfaction with the lines they had seen.

Their trip brought them to Little Round Top. Meade looked north and saw the line of his army clear to the cemetery. What he saw reinforced the notion he had while riding down the ridge. It was a damn strong position. Meade looked to the northwest. Something caught his eye and he bought it to Warren's attention.

"I see Confederate artillery being posted along the ridge in front of the tree line," said Meade."Lee is planning something and I don't think it's retreating."

Warren pointed out the numerous rebel forces in the valley at the base of Little Round Top."I'll bet those are Longstreet's boys. They are entrenched in a good defensive position. It doesn't look like they are going anywhere today."

"You could be right. Ewell's Corps is still at the base of Culp's Hill. This leaves the whereabouts of Hill's Corps and Pickett's Division as a mystery. Any thoughts?"

Warren did not answer immediately. He gazed across the battlefield. While looking off into the distance, he spoke."Longstreet's two divisions's expended much energy yesterday. They fought over rough terrain for nearly four hours. They inflicted some heavy casualties on us, but I think we gave them just as much hell. They couldn't take this flank yesterday after Sickles had advanced and these two hills were unoccupied. Today, we have troops on both round tops and a strong line with good reserves all the way up to the cemetery. I don't think this flank will be tested today. From prisoner reports, it seems only three of Hill's brigades were engaged yesterday. Lee may be planning an assault with Pickett's Division and the rested units of Hill's corps."

"Where do you think they'll hit?" asked Meade.

"Cemetery Hill," answered Warren "Last night they breached our defenses with only two brigades. They captured some artillery, but we got reserves to the area to drive them off. If they had been properly supported it might have turned out differently. We were fortunate. If Lee plans a full scale assault with many more troops, he might succeed in driving us off the hill. This would put a wedge in our line and divide our forces. Our troops on Culp's Hill would be in danger of being cut off."

Meade hadn't considered this possibility, but Warren was making some sense. The position of the troops on Cemetery Hill was a salient, and it could be assaulted from three sides. Meade may have to move his reserve troops closer to this position.

"An interesting prospect," said Meade."I still think Lee will try the center of our lines as he has failed on our flanks. He is posting his artillery to hit us in the center."

"That could be to keep our forces from moving north to aid any fighting on Cemetery Hill. He'll lob artillery shells onto the ridge pinning down the majority of our army, while he then assaults Cemetery Hill. Just conjecture, sir," said Warren.

"You're keeping me on my toes and forcing me to think of other possibilities. Don't stop. That's a direct order. Let's ride back to headquarters and get some breakfast. Who knows when we'll be able to eat again," said Meade.

☙❧

Meade was back at headquarters. He had consumed his breakfast, satisfying that empty place that had been gnawing at him. Food and sleep had been the least of his worries and he was unsure if he was more tired or hungry. Either way, the dual deprivation had not hindered his performance since he had taken command less than one week ago. It amazed him how he was able to function with such clarity. He knew he was running on pure adrenaline.

He read some dispatches and issued some orders to be sent to various commanders. He heard the fighting on Culp's Hill. Slocum had not asked for any further reinforcements. His last dispatch was that the fighting was going well. The enemy was stubbornly holding onto their gains, but they were not advancing.

Meade had a few moments to himself. He wrote a quick note to his wife:

Dearest Love,

All well and going on well with the army. We had a great fight yesterday, the enemy attacking, and we completely repulse them. Army in fine spirits and everyone is determined to do or die.

He penned a few other lines, sat back and read the letter, then signed it. His son, George Meade, Jr., was on his staff. He knew this eased the burden on his wife, for he was less apt to be in harm's way. However, anything can happen in combat. The army had lost some high ranking and valuable officers in the past two days, so he knew no person was one hundred percent safe.

He thought of the casualties. Two corps commanders were down. Reynolds was dead and Sickles was on a train to Washington, minus one leg. General Barlow and General Schimmelfennig, division commanders with the Eleventh Corps were missing after the first days fighting. The Fifth Corps reported that Colonel Vincent and General Weed, both brigade commanders, were killed defending Little Round Top. Three brigade commanders from the Second Corps, General Zook, Colonel Cross and Colonel Willard were killed on July 2, fighting on the left. Meade also knew many regimental commanders had been killed or wounded. Some had even been captured. But the Army of the Potomac had not retired from the field. Lee had not forced them to retreat. It was this reason that had Meade convinced Lee would attack today. His ego would not allow the boys in blue to hold the field.

He thought of another dispatch he had to write. This was to General Sedgwick of the Sixth Corps. This was the largest corps on the field and they had suffered few casualties the previous day as they had been held in a reserve position most of the day. Meade wanted Sedgwick to move his corps more northerly to a central position in the line. This would allow his men to be sent to any portion of the Union line that was being threatened. He confided in Sedgwick that it was his belief the enemy would attempt an attack on the center of the line. He handed the dispatch to an aide and told him to deliver it to General Sedgwick.

General Hunt entered the house, pulled up a chair and sat across the table from Meade."I could sure use some coffee," said Hunt."I've been out riding the lines all morning."

"Lieutenant, bring two cups of coffee," said Meade to an aide.

"Coming right up, sir," said the young lieutenant.

"How are the lines, Henry?" asked Meade.

"We're in a strong position. I went to Culp's Hill early and found the artillery pounding Johnny with great effectiveness. If they were asleep, they got a rude awakening. The artillery was in good shape, so I moved west and south down the lines. I made adjustments where necessary. Pieces from the reserve were ordered forward to positions that were thin. I made sure caissons were full. We're in as strong a position as I can ever remember in this war. We've got 119 guns facing west toward the enemy. If they attack there as you believe, our artillery will bring fire on them from all sectors of the line, as they attempt to cross that open field. I do not believe they can penetrate our lines if they attack the center. We have too much firepower."

"I was on Little Round Top with Warren this morning and witnessed the enemy posting many batteries in front of the tree line facing east. It appears they mean to pour down some fire on our center. They're moving a hell of a lot of guns forward. Could be they want to take our guns out with an artillery barrage of their own, before they advance their infantry," said Meade.

"Coffee, sir," said the lieutenant as he delivered the hot liquid.

Hunt took a sip."Is there anything better in combat than a fresh cup of coffee?" he asked.

"An armistice," said Meade.

The silence from that statement hung in the air. They each stared into the silence.

"I'm just tired, Henry," said Meade."We are butchering a generation of men. I am wondering what will be left when this is all over?"

"We don't have time for melancholia. Those states from the South tore apart our constitution and decided to try another course. Now they have become invaders. It is our job to defeat them and restore the young republic."

"You're preaching to the choir," said Meade. He took another sip of coffee, and then continued."You ever wonder about General Lee and his decision to turn down command of this army when the war started? He's certainly fought brilliantly with smaller forces, time and again."

"I don't agree with what he did. He made a decision to fight with those that choose to tear the Union apart. Hell, he took the same oath as we did, to defend the nation against enemies both foreign and domestic. He has chosen to abandon that oath. Has he fought well? Yes, he has, but the commanders we've had to endure has certainly helped him."

"I just hope my neck isn't the next one in the guillotine," said Meade.

"We're on good ground with deep reserves. We have short interior lines, so we can move troops quicker to the fight than Lee can. The line this army is defending today is the line you desired to occupy yesterday, before Sickles advanced and destroyed your plans. Your work yesterday saved this army, and I've heard nothing but good comments about your performance riding the lines this morning. I think your neck is safe, especially if we defeat Lee. We've got the ground to do it," said Hunt.

"I'm still concerned about Lee attacking our center. I want you to ride over there and be sure everything is in order to repulse an assault."

"Will do, sir," replied Hunt."Thanks for the coffee."

৽৵৹৻৻

The morning hadn't been quiet on Hancock's front. The troops on the skirmish lines were trading shots with their counterparts filling the air with the sound of musketry. There was a white farmhouse and barn about six hundred yards to the west. Confederate sharpshooters had captured these buildings the previous day, and were afforded great protection as they took shots at the Union line. Their fire was especially effective against the boys manning the artillery. Hancock was receiving complaints of numerous casualties suffered by the boys in the artillery from the sharpshooters in those buildings. He rode over to General Hays, his Third Division commander, whose troops were entrenched behind walls across the field from this farm.

"General, that damned white house is crawling with enemy sharpshooters," started Hancock."Those sons of bitches are picking off our artillery crews. Send some troops out there and secure that house and barn."

"With pleasure, sir. Those sharpshooters have been a pain in my ass all morning," replied Hays.

Hancock turned and rode back to the ridge near his corps headquarters. He would watch the assault on the house from there. He had delivered his orders and knew Hays would carry them out. Hancock had much respect for General Hays, a West Point graduate who had fought in the Mexican War. During this current war, he had been wounded twice, but recovered, and was back leading men into combat. Hancock didn't have to worry about Hays doing his duty.

Hancock thought how fortunate he was to have three such able division commanders, in Gibbon, Hays and Caldwell. *Hell, even though Caldwell is new to his position, he had shown his mettle in yesterday's fight. Meade thinks Lee will attack on my front today. Well, let him come and we'll introduce his boys to the gates of hell. The Second Corps is ready for a fight.*

Hancock halted his mount on the ridge. He turned and faced west to watch the planned attack on the house. Gibbon rode up to join him.

"I've ordered an attack on that damned white house and barn," said Hancock."Their sharpshooters are lodged in there, creating havoc within our lines. I want the bastards gone."

"Who are you sending out?" asked Gibbon.

"I gave the order to Hays. He'll decide who to send."

Gibbon gave a nod of agreement.

Hancock pointed to the boys in blue advancing to a knoll. This knoll afforded them protection from the sharpshooters in the barn. He counted five companies. They were being formed into a column by companies. They went over the knoll and started for the barn at the double quick. They seemed to catch the enemy by surprise and got to the barn with very few men going down. There were five stable doors facing east. He watched his boys reach the doors and enter the barn. In a few moments, Confederates were escaping out the back into an orchard or to the house. There they turned and fired at the barn. Hancock observed the enemy sending reinforcements into the fray. His troops were still in the barn and were facing numbers that were rapidly increasing.

"Damn it," he exploded."We don't have enough men to hold the barn."

৵৵৪৩৫৶৵

General Hays watched as Confederate artillery found the range of the barn his men were in. The orchards beyond the barn, and the white farmhouse were being filled with Confederate troops. Hays had not seen his men exit the barn, and it seemed they would be trapped inside under a barrage of artillery. He was pondering sending reinforcements, when he saw his men leave by the stable doors and start running back to their original lines. The retreat was disorderly, as his men ran quickly through the open fields to safety.

The enemy was re-establishing their positions in the barn. Sharpshooters resumed picking off artillery crew members. Hays wanted to obliterate the buildings with artillery, but directives from above precluded him from damaging civilian buildings, as much as possible. The invading army had no problem lobbing shells into that barn.

Hays went to see Colonel Thomas Smyth, his Second Brigade commander."Colonel," said Hays."I want you to send another regiment forward and clear both buildings of those damn sharpshooters. When you've cleared them out, I want your men to hold the buildings."

"Yes, sir. I'll send the Fourteenth Connecticut," replied Smyth.

Hays turned to an aide and said,"Ride over to Hancock and ask him if I have his permission to destroy those damn buildings."

"Yes, sir," said the aide. He kicked his horse and headed off to find General Hancock.

Hays moved higher on the ridge for a better vantage point of the advance on the buildings. He watched the boys of the Fourteenth Connecticut rush forward to the knoll. After reaching this point, they halted until all their troops arrived. They went over the knoll and ran as fast as they could to the barn. There was no order to the advance. Each man was running like hell to get to the barn unscathed. A few were felled by enemy fire, but a majority of the boys reached the barn. Clear the bastards out of there, Hays said to himself.

Like the first attack, they entered the barn through the five stable doors. Now came the waiting. Soon Confederate soldiers were leaving the back of the barn and heading for the orchards. Hays saw the balance of the regiment move forward to the knoll. From there, they rushed the house and went in the door. Confederate troops exited out the back, heading west. Hurrah for the Fourteenth Connecticut, Hays shouted to himself. They had occupied the barn and that damned white farmhouse. The question was whether they could hold onto them.

As before, Confederate artillery reigned down lead on the house and barn. Hays watched shells tear into the house. He'd seen enough. His boys didn't need to bear this shelling to keep these buildings out of enemy hands. He was going to act, with or without orders.

Just then, his aide came galloping up."Sir, General Hancock says you can burn those damned buildings."

Hays went over to the One Hundred Eleventh New York, now commanded by Colonel MacDougall, their third commander during this battle."Colonel," said Hays."I need a volunteer to carry an order over to the barn that the buildings are to be burned."

Sergeant Charles Hitchcock overheard the order and stepped forward."Sir, I'll go."

"Excellent," said Hays."Take some matches and paper and get to the barn. Order them to burn both buildings and get back here when the job is done."

"Yes, sir," replied Hitchcock.

Hays wanted to be sure the orders got through. He watched Hitchcock head off across the open field. Hays went to Colonel Smyth and asked for a mounted volunteer sent forward with the same instructions, in case Hitchcock got cut down. A captain volunteered, got on his horse and galloped across drawing heavy fire.

Hays watched and saw both men arrive unhurt at the barn. Hitchcock went into the barn, while the captain on his mount rode to the house. In a few minutes, smoke poured out of both buildings. The boys from the Fourteenth stayed outside, near the structures, until they were both fully engulfed in flames. Their work done, they returned to their line on Cemetery Ridge. Hays heard loud cheering from the boys on the lines as the buildings burned. Those two buildings would not house Confederate sharpshooters again.

Chapter 22

Midday

CHICKEN STEW AND POTATOES. It had been the best meal he had consumed since becoming commander. Meade wondered at his initial reluctance to accept Gibbon's invitation to a meal at Second Corps headquarters. The field was quiet. The fight for Culp's Hill had ceased two hours earlier, being a complete success for Slocum's men. The boys in butternut were dislodged from the Union breastworks and the Twelfth Corps line was restored to its original position. Even the skirmishing had ceased. His belly was full and he was glad he had given in to Gibbon's insistence to join them for a meal.

Newton and Pleasanton were also on hand, with Gibbon and Hancock. They were in a hollow behind Cemetery Ridge, sitting on camp stools in the noonday heat. It was hotter than the previous two days, and he could feel the humidity returning, making the heat more uncomfortable.

"Cigars," said Hancock,"but no brandy. Coffee will have to do."

Cigars were passed around. Everyone took one and fired them up. Meade puffed, held the smoke in his mouth and slowly exhaled. He watched the others enjoying their cigars. Gibbon blew some smoke rings into the air. This significance of this simple act was not lost on Meade. Gibbon seemed more relaxed, but then, he did not have the responsibility of an entire army on his shoulders.

"Wonder what old Lee is planning across those fields," said Hancock."I hope he is not waiting for us to attack!"

Newton released the smoke from his mouth."The amount of artillery placed on yonder ridge would keep me from ordering any assault against his position. My men would get eviscerated attempting to cross that field." He looked at Meade and continued."Begging your pardon, sir, but I would not attack that fortified position."

"No apologies for speaking your mind," countered Meade."Hooker would have fared better if he had listened to his subordinates. This job is too damn large for one man to think of everything and make all the decisions. Your input is appreciated."

"How goes it with Butterfield?" asked Hancock.

"It's frosty, but I haven't time to address his position now. When this battle is sorted out I'll give thought to replacing him, if I'm still in command."

"You've been in command for less than one week, but you get my vote to continue," said Hancock."This battle, like this command, was thrust upon you and you've responded to both in a damn fine manner. That bastard Hooker was marching us all around Maryland without a clue as to what to do. If he was still in charge, we'd probably be cowering on the outskirts of Baltimore, with Lee threatening to turn our flanks."

This brought chuckles from the others.

"Well, Hooker's not here and the army is under the capable hands of General George Meade," said Pleasanton.

"Hear, hear," said Hancock.

Meade put up his hand."We've done this together. Reynolds picked this ground to fight on. He gave his all so we could deploy on this ground. There's a man to toast." He puffed on his cigar."Yesterday's fight was close. They came close to turning our left. Warren secured Little Round Top just before their attack and kept it in our hands."

"I've heard Longstreet's corps attacked on that front. He's the best they've got," said Hancock."He made Third Corps pay dearly for Sickles' bloody blunder. We've got the position you wanted yesterday, with the advantage of having all seven corps present."

Meade turned to Pleasanton, his cavalry commander."Any word from your scouts?"

"The enemy is holding their position. There appear to be no flanking movements. Lee isn't retreating," replied Pleasanton.

"I still say he will attack on your front, Win," asserted Meade. The cavalry was out on both flanks and were reporting no movement by the enemy. Lee's artillery was positioned to bring its full weight on Hancock's position. Meade knew an infantry assault was preceded by an artillery barrage to soften up that sector of the line to be attacked. It seemed folly in Meade's mind to attack across those open fields, but all the signs were pointing to that probability.

"Let those bastards come," said Hancock, interrupting Meade's thoughts."We'll fill them with lead."

Meade nodded. He knew Hancock was itching for this fight. Meade took another puff from his cigar. He looked to the west and saw the smoke from the two burning buildings. He turned to Hancock and said,"I guess you had to burn those buildings?"

"I had no other option, sir. Their sharpshooters were picking off my artillery crews from the protection of those buildings. We sent troops out to secure the buildings. As soon as we cleared the barn and occupied it, the enemy started lobbing artillery shells into the structure. My men skedaddled back to our lines. Once again, their sharpshooters nested in the barn and house, and proceeded with their long-range devastation of my boys. We sent out more troops to clear those sons of bitches, and again secured the buildings. Their artillery again started firing on my boys. I ordered Hays to burn the damn buildings. Problem solved."

Meade couldn't disagree with Hancock. If he hadn't burnt the buildings, Confederate artillery would have destroyed them, and killed many of Hancock's men in the process. It was necessary. The army of succession could no longer claim the high ground of honor and defense of their homes. They were just as capable of wreaking havoc on non-combatants and upending their lives. He heard the stories of Confederate troops marching into Northern towns demanding supplies from the townsfolk. If they paid for the goods, it was in worthless Confederate money. And what of this town, he thought. After the battle there would be numerous dead bodies to bury and wounded to care for. It would be an immense task for the people of Gettysburg. Most of their crops were destroyed for this season. Meade shook his head. What would be accomplished when this war ever ended? He had no answers.

"Gentlemen, I must head back to headquarters," said Meade."Thanks for the meal and the cigars. Keep alert."

১৯৪৫৪৬১

General Stannard was proud of his boys from Vermont. They earned their stripes in yesterday's fight. They were nine-month volunteers whose enlistments would be up this month, yet none of them shirked their duty. The endless drilling they grumbled about in garrison paid dividends when they faced actual combat. He remembered the whistles and derisive taunts of pretty boys, aimed at his brigade when they arrived at the front due to their new blue uniforms that were in stark contrast to the torn and faded uniforms of the seasoned veterans of the Army of the Potomac. The Vermont boys still stood out in their dark blue colors, but they could hold their heads up, having paid their dues.

They were behind a low stone wall on Cemetery Ridge, facing west, with the Second Corps on their right. Stannard could see the enemy artillery units on the ridge to the west, aimed at his position. If it was their intent to fire on this sector of the line, they had enough firepower to kill each member of his brigade three times over. He had heard the talk of a Confederate assault across the open fields to his front. Let them come, he thought. They would pay a heavy price assaulting this position.

He looked at the bullet hole in his coat. A reminder that even generals were not immune from a sharpshooter's deadly fire. Luckily for him, the bullet only found his coat.

He had spoken with Doubleday earlier, giving his account of yesterday's fight and the condition of his men. He told Doubleday of the fighting spirit of Lieutenant Stephen Brown, the young officer with the Thirteenth Vermont who was threatened to be court-martialed for filling canteens with water on the march from Washington. It seems the provost guards had taken his sword and not returned it. Well, this would not deter Lieutenant Brown. During yesterday's fight, he went forward with his boys carrying a camp hatchet into combat. He was the talk of the regiment. These Vermont boys were a scrappy lot. They had to be admired, and Stannard was proud to be their commander.

He looked at his men lying behind the stone wall. Many seemed to be asleep. He would let them sleep. A soldier in combat had to sleep whenever the chance was afforded. The front was quiet in his sector. In fact, it was quiet all over. His senses were acutely aware of the ominous silence. This silence was screaming at him. He looked across the fields and saw a bright blue sky with white fleecy clouds drifting lazily from the west. They moved very slowly propelled by a slight wind.

A cannon boomed in the distance, shattering the silence. It came from the enemy. The screaming projectile passed overhead and exploded well behind him. What next, he thought. His answer came quickly, as one cannon after another spewed forth shot and shell in a thunderous fury.

CHAPTER 23

"SON OF A BITCH," yelled Hancock to Gibbon above the noise of bursting and screaming projectiles,"This is it. They'll batter us with artillery and then attack with infantry. Why aren't our guns firing?"

"I can't imagine why they're silent, sir," yelled back Gibbon.

"Damn it, ride with me and we'll find out," ordered Hancock.

The enemy barrage had been ceaseless for five minutes. Their batteries were covered with smoke, through which the flashes were incessant, filling the air with shells. Their sharp explosions and the hurtling of their fragments, accompanied the roar of the cannons. The Union line in Hancock's sector was getting pummeled.

Hancock rode up to the closest cannon and started barking loudly above the noise."Captain, why in hell aren't your guns firing?"

"Sir, General Hunt left explicit orders that we were to withhold our fire for fifteen minutes from the onset of any artillery barrage by the enemy."

"Captain, am I not your corps commander?" asked Hancock gruffly.

"Yes, you are, sir," replied the captain.

"Then I order you to start firing your cannons at the enemy artillery at once, or I'll bust your ass down to below private. Do I make myself clear," barked Hancock.

The captain looked at Hancock and said all he could in the situation."Yes, sir."

Hancock turned to Gibbon,"Ride back to your division and I'll ride over to General Hays. We need to get our corps guns firing. I'll not let my boys suffer an enemy barrage while our guns sit silent! If they give you the same cock and bull story about orders from Hunt, override the bastard and get them active. Hell, Hunt's got plenty of guns and ammunition in reserve close by if we should run out. I'll deal with him later."

Hancock rode north along the line until he came upon General Hays."General, I want your guns returning fire immediately. We'll not sit another minute without giving them some lead. Get your orders out to all artillery units in your command!"

"Gladly, sir," said Hays."I rode over to get them firing earlier, but was told Hunt . . ."

"I know what Hunt ordered," interrupted Hancock."I'm overriding his orders, and if you get any grief from Hunt or any of his minions, you send them to me. You are following orders from your corps commander."

This order put a smile on Hays face. He turned on his horse and rode over to his batteries, to put them into action. Hancock watched him ride up to the first gun and point to the enemy's position. The gun crew immediately went to work loading their piece.

Hancock heard his guns begin to come to life. The crescendo of cannon was increasing from the crest of the ridge. His boys would be bolstered by this sound. They would not be hugging the ground for dear life, wondering why their generals sat idly by. Hunt might wish to wait for fifteen minutes before returning fire, but Hancock would not put his men through such misery. The sound of their guns firing at the enemy would lift their spirits.

He rode over to General Gibbon. The air above was filled with bursting and screaming projectiles. The continuous thunder of the guns was his new companion. Hell itself would be a relief from this, he thought. He paused and noticed a majority of the enemy's shells were landing at the top and behind the ridge. They were cutting their fuses too long. His troops lying behind the stone wall would be spared countless destruction if this high firing continued. He could only hope. The smoke from his guns filled the air, so it would be hard for the enemy to see where their shells were landing. His artillery, on the crest of the ridge, seemed to be the target. They were receiving the bulk of the rebel fire. He was glad he ordered his boys to return fire, instead of standing at their posts and getting cut down needlessly, just to follow some fool order not to fire.

He watched them working their guns in the hot July afternoon. Many had taken their shirts off. The powder, dirt and grime covered their bodies, but they continued loading and firing, as shells burst around them, doing their duty in the face of this immense barrage. One gunner stood at the rear near the limber box. A shell exploded right under the box. When the smoke cleared, Hancock watched that gunner pull himself off the ground and start hopping to the rear on one leg. The shreds of the other leg were dangling about as he went. The ugliness of war was not for the squeamish.

He turned his horse and continued on his way. He saw General Gibbon standing out by his men, in front of the stone wall. Hancock rode over and joined Gibbon."All hell's breaking loose and you're out in front of your men with not a care in the world," said Hancock.

Gibbon replied,"I've noticed their shells are landing up top and behind the crest. This seems to be the safest place on the field at the moment. It would appear that Meade's headquarters is taking a pounding. I hope he's alright."

"He's fine. You're right about his headquarters taking a pounding, though. He sent a courier to inform me he and his staff have moved to Powers Hill. He will be conducting affairs at General Slocum's headquarters. How are the men holding up?"

"I was talking to them before you showed up. I asked the question what they thought of this cannonade. They're responses were typical of men in combat. They yelled, 'Oh, this is bully' or 'we don't mind this, in fact, we are getting to like it.' They're cracking jokes about it."

"Gallows humor," said Hancock.

"I have noticed one amazing event during this bombardment," said Gibbon."The horses belonging to the artillery units are standing perfectly still, even as shells explode around them. I've seen one horse take a direct hit and go down, yet the other members of that team stand stoically in place. They show immense discipline. I would've thought they would scatter to the wind, searching for safety."

"They are proud members of the Second Corps," said Hancock."Cowardice is not in their blood."

"Good to see you've infused your temperament into the horses," answered Gibbon.

Smoke filled the sky as the guns from both sides continued their long-range symphony. The smell of gunpowder and sulfur was heavy in the air. It seemed to encapsulate each soldier in its aroma. Hancock noticed many soldiers were now sleeping. The noise of the cannons, once frightening, was now just a normal part of their existence, lulling them to sleep.

Hancock looked west toward the enemy position. Flashes were still bellowing from their guns, hurling projectiles toward the men of his corps. He saw a caisson explode as it took a direct hit, knocking one of their guns out."Damn fine shot," he yelled above the noise."Give us enough time and we'll knock all you bastards to hell."

"It's been going on for over an hour and I detect no let up from either side," said Gibbon."I'm not sure we'll be able to knock all their guns to hell."

"Any opinions about Lee's intentions?" asked Hancock.

"When this started, I thought he was either covering a retreat or softening us up for an attack. It seems all their fire is directed at our front, so I'm thinking an infantry assault will follow. If he were covering a retreat of his forces, he would be putting fire down on every part of our line," offered Gibbon.

"I have to agree with you, John," said Hancock."Lee's sending infantry right at us."

"Funny you should say that. Last night after the meeting, Meade pulled me aside as I was leaving and told me if Lee attacked today it would be on my front. I asked him why he thought this. He said Lee had tried both flanks yesterday and failed to dislodge us, so today he would attack the center of our line."

"Let 'em come," said Hancock."We're ready. It appears their cannonade is not softening our lines of infantry, so we'll have a surprise for them when they get to the road and attempt to cross those two rail fences. Those are some damn sturdy fences, and they'll have to climb over both of them. That's when we'll rise up from behind this stone wall and fill their bellies with lead."

They looked across the smoke-filled fields. All they could hear was the continuous roar of hundreds of guns, the screaming of countless projectiles and the bursting of shells.

"Take care of yourself," said Hancock."It's sure to get hotter on your front when their cannons stop."

"We'll have a cigar tonight when this is over," replied Gibbon.

"You're on. See you then."

Hancock turned on his horse and rode down the line, so as to be seen by his men. He wished to show his men he was not afraid. He wouldn't shirk his duty and hide behind the lines. He knew this would inspire the soldiers of the Second Corps for the upcoming fight.

∽ഀഁ∾

General Hunt rode amongst the artillery units, checking their supply of ammunition. The units in the Second Corps section were down to canister. They had used all their shells and long-range projectiles. *Damn*, he thought. His plans to cut down their infantry assault with a crossfire of long-range shot and shell would now be compromised. If Lee attacked the center of the line, the artillery in this sector would not be able to fire until the enemy was within canister range. It was 2:45 and the guns had been spewing forth their destruction since 1:15.

Hunt had a plan to cease fire with all his guns, while he still had plenty of ammunition. This might fool Lee into thinking his bombardment had silenced the Union guns. He rode over to headquarters to run this plan by Meade. He was told Meade had gone to the cemetery. Hunt rode hard up to the cemetery. He found General Howard, but not Meade. Hunt explained his plan to Howard, who agreed with the plan. Rather than ride around searching for Meade, Hunt told Howard to order his guns to cease-fire. Howard ordered his aides to get this message to all artillery units under his command. Hunt then rode south along Cemetery Ridge, ordering all units to stop firing. By the time he reached Little Round Top, the guns all along the Union line were silent.

He rode back to Taneytown Road to meet with the reserve batteries he had ordered forward, from the artillery reserve. He wanted to place them in areas that had been hardest hit by the relentless Confederate bombardment. His line needed certain mending and he wanted to personally place the reserve units.

As Hunt was riding, he heard his name being called out. He stopped and turned his horse to face the direction of the voice calling his name. He recognized the person on horseback as Major Bingham, of Hancock's staff.

"Sir," started Bingham."General Meade is looking for you. He has sent his aides out with orders for you to cease fire with your artillery, immediately."

"Thank you, Major," said Hunt. He was pleased with himself. He had anticipated Meade's orders. It appeared the two were thinking along the same lines."You may return to your lines and if you run into any of Meade's aides, ask them if the order was followed quickly enough."

Meade had been in charge of this army for less than one week, but Hunt was quite impressed with his performance. Meade just might be the first general to pin a defeat on Lee. Antietam had been considered a victory for the Army of the Potomac by the press, but the generals in the ranks new it was nothing more than a stalemate. Hunt hoped Lee would attack on Hancock's front, for he had his artillery placed for maximum destruction of forces crossing the open fields to the west. Hancock's caissons were down to canister, which disturbed Hunt. He would have to investigate why all of their long-range ammunition was spent.

His mind told him to stop thinking for one moment and to listen. He listened and heard nothing. The artillery had stopped on both fronts. There was silence for the first time in two hours. It was deafening. The smoke was lifting to the sky and he could see the Confederate batteries to the west. His ploy had worked. He stared at the enemy guns and saw movement from their rear. Wave after wave of Confederate troops marched out of the woods and formed into battle formation. Regimental flags moved to the front of the ranks and unfurled in the wind. Men kept pouring out of the woods and forming lines as far as his eye could see in both directions. *By god*, he thought, *they're coming*.

Part VI
Gleaming Bayonets

CHAPTER 24

GENERAL GIBBON RODE WITH HIS AIDE Lt. Frank Haskell to Second Corps headquarters, which was on the easterly slope of Cemetery Ridge. The cannonade had ceased and all was quiet. He wanted to be at headquarters for information. If orders were issued to division commanders, he could then disperse them quickly to his brigade commanders. He sensed something big was about to transpire. A two-hour cannonade would not be wasted. It was a prelude to some attack. He thought of Meade's words last night;"If Lee attacks tomorrow it will be on your front". Gibbon still felt confident his men would repulse any assault. The ground on his front was not conducive for an assault. It was a mile of open fields, bordered by sturdy wood fences. Artillery fire would decimate ranks of any advance. If Meade thought they would come, well, let them come, for General John Gibbon and his division would be ready.

When they got to headquarters, they were informed that General Hancock was out riding the lines amongst his troops. Typical, thought Gibbon. Hancock was not one to lead from the rear. Gibbon looked down the line. The smoke was rising and the air was clearing, but the smell of gunpowder and sulfur was still strong in his nostrils. After two hours the scent would not recede.

He heard yelling from the west side of the ridge. It was coming from the position of his troops. He turned to Haskell and said,"Let's go see what's going on."

They rode to the crest of the ridge. The yelling was now taking the shape of words, which soon became sentences."Here they come.""Here come the Johnnies." Gibbon looked westerly across the fields and was stunned. Confederate infantry was stretched out to the north and south as far as he could see. He took out his field glasses and put them to his eyes. Skirmishers were advancing in front of every regiment. Behind them came their regimental battle flags, waving in the wind. These flags were followed by infantry formed in one line of battle, then a second, and then a third. Gibbon felt his heart pounding in his chest as he watched the enemy move steadily forward along his front. He estimated they were advancing with 18,000 troops.

He turned to Haskell and said,"Look at that, the sons of bitches are coming. Meade was right."

"Magnificent display," replied Haskell."Too bad we have to ruin it."

"I didn't think Lee would attempt such a foolhardy assault. It's unlike him. What the hell could he be attempting to gain?" asked Gibbon."He's attacking a well-fortified position over a mile of open ground. Any thoughts, Frank?"

Haskell thought for a moment. He shook his head."I can't think of any logical reason Lee would be making this attack, but I'm only a lieutenant."

"Let's ride down to the lines and make sure our boys stay calm. They'll need to see us today."

"Good idea, sir," said Haskell.

They rode forward to the stone wall that shielded their division. Gibbon gave orders to load all the rifles from troops that were killed during the cannonade. He watched as his men dumped cartridges on the ground beside them and slid percussion cap boxes to the front of their bodies. They were preparing to give as much lead as they could to Johnny.

A soldier on the line yelled,"Sir, should we be ready for kingdom come, or Libby prison?"

"Neither," said Gibbon."Today we give them Fredericksburg!"

A cheer went up from those that heard him.

Gibbon spoke loudly for all to hear."Men, we are fighting on our own ground and defending our homes. Now is the moment your country needs you to do your duty. Do not hurry and fire too fast. Let them come up close before you fire, and then aim low and steadily."

Another voice rose up from the line,"Look at them advance in perfect order. I'd enjoy watching this grand parade, if I didn't have to cut the bastards down."

"One hell of a sight, and we get front row seats," said another.

Hurrahs were uttered along the line.

"Save your breath for the fight, boys," said Gibbon.

Haskell sat in his saddle and looked at the advancing soldiers."Incredible, sir," he started,"wave after wave of legions advancing as an overwhelming ocean tide sweeping upon us. Their bayonets gleam in the sun. They move forward with perfect order, as with one soul. They are magnificent, grim and irresistible. We may never witness such a display again in our lives."

"Well put," said Gibbon."You've been reading Sir Walter Scott again, I see. You are correct, it is a magnificent display. You've got to admire their courage. We'll see how magnificently they respond when our artillery opens up on them and starts thinning their ranks. Ride to General Meade on Powers Hill and tell him their attack has begun."

Just then they heard a cannon erupt from the right. First one gun, then another, as the Union line came alive with artillery fire informing the enemy that their cannonade had not served its purpose of silencing Union artillery. They watched as Union shells tore huge gaps in the advancing lines. The gaps were closed just as quickly and the Confederate forces continued their march, undeterred by the death and destruction tearing into their ranks.

Haskell watched with admiration."Sir, it appears they are responding magnificently to our artillery. They may have enough troops to get across those fields and hit our lines with sufficient force to create havoc."

Gibbon kept his eyes on the approaching mass of butternut infantry. Their courage was impressive."When you get to headquarters, ask General Meade to send as much help as he can. It's going to get hot on our front in about twenty minutes," he said to Haskell."Now, go."

∽⧓∾

General Stannard was watching the advance behind his three small brigades of Vermont boys. It seemed as half the Confederate army would hit his brigade head on. His nine-month volunteers would be tested under fire today. Yesterday, the boys of the Thirteenth had helped repel one attack, and in the process had recaptured a battery of guns that had fallen into enemy hands. He knew they would stand tall, but he was not sure how the boys in the Fourteenth and Sixteenth would respond to combat. During the cannonade his regiments had moved forward for better cover. The Fourteenth were the on the left of his line, in a forward position where scattered trees and brush afforded some cover. The Thirteenth were to the right of the Fourteenth, behind a small knoll. Stannard had watched as members of the Thirteenth ran to a nearby wood fence, dismantled it and carried the rails back to their position, building a breastwork the men could use for cover. They were showing no signs of frayed nerves. The Sixteenth had been to the left of the Fourteenth, but were now deployed between the Thirteenth and Fourteenth.

Stannard watched the advancing Confederate army and wondered if they could be stopped. They were getting hit on all sides by Union shells, yet this did not slow down their advance. They moved forward with military precision, steady and firm. Their skirmishers were firing as they advanced. Their relentless progress drove the skirmishers of the Sixteenth Vermont from their forward position, back to the safety of the main line. Nothing was stopping this onslaught of gray in the sultry afternoon heat.

Stannard estimated the enemy's right would advance squarely on the position of the Fourteenth. There were no troops to the left of the Fourteenth Vermont, only artillery. The approaching lines could hit the Fourteenth head on, then wheel to the right and attack by the flank. This was a prospect that frightened him. If his boys gave way, the enemy would be able to roll up the Union flank, while simultaneously striking the center from the west. It would be a classic front and flank attack. He had to hold his line and not get turned.

On came the enemy, regardless of exploding shells hurled against them. They were approaching Emmitsburg Road, lined on both sides by post and rail fences. They would have to climb both fences and regroup on the easterly side before continuing their assault. A strategy was forming in Stannard's mind. He would send orders to all commanders. They would hold their fire until the enemy was close enough for one volley and then his boys should charge with the bayonet. He barked these orders to his aides to disperse amongst all line commanders.

That rebel yell, an effective weapon used by advancing Confederate soldiers, filled the air. That yell sounded like all the demons of hell rising from the ground. Stannard's hair on the back of his neck stood on end and he felt his spine stiffen. He could not prepare his boys for this guttural sound in drill.

The rebel infantry was across the Emmitsburg Road and advancing around both sides of the Codori farm. After they cleared the house and barn, they reformed their lines to continue their attack. Their numbers were immense and it seemed they had barely suffered casualties from the Union artillery. Stannard ordered his men to rise and prepare to fire. Orders were carried out, and all of Vermont rose as one. Just before he was to give the order to fire, he noticed the enemy move by the left flank across his front to the north. He sat on his horse in disbelief. Had the artillery from his left found the mark so often, the rebel commanders were moving to the north to get out of their range? It was the only reason he could ascertain for the rebels to change direction. His men were ready so he had them fire. Yells went up and down the lines,"make ready, take good aim, fire low." Then came the order,"Fire!" From the three regiments poured smoke from their muskets. It was a destructive fire, leaving a long line of dead and wounded as the enemy charged north across the front of the Vermont Regiments. Stannard watched as the mass of men moved across his front for some four hundred feet, while under heavy fire, before wheeling right and heading for Hancock's men behind the stone wall.

An opportunity presented itself to General Stannard. The right end of the advancing Confederates was now to his north and his men were free to maneuver. He ordered the Thirteenth to wheel to the right and the Sixteenth to deploy to the left of the Thirteenth. These two regiments would now be parallel to the charging rebels and would be able to pour an enfilading fire into their flanks. These two regiments performed these maneuvers as if on parade ground back in camp. They formed in lines of battle and proceeded to pour an enfilading fire into the unprotected flanks of the rebels charging toward the stone wall.

A few rebel regiments halted their advance and turned to face the boys from Vermont. They began firing back. Some of them took cover in a clump of bushes. The Vermont boys held their ground and fire was exchanged at a very short range. Stannard watched as casualties mounted in his ranks from enemy fire. Great sheets of flame and smoke flashed from each line. In the confusion was the sound of musketry, the roar of cannons, the exerting yells of officers issuing orders, the cheers of the boys in blue and the rebel yell. As the fight intensified, Stannard noticed his boys were holding their line. They were not wavering, even though faced with terrific, destructive fire from the enemy. His boys had slowed and in many cases stopped the advance of many Confederate soldiers. He watched as the advancing Confederates climbed over the stone wall and breached the Union line. He could do nothing about this. It was a fight another commander would have to shoulder.

He still had the Fourteenth deployed on the left and was considering moving them northerly, adding to the strength of his flank attack, when he saw two fresh Confederate brigades advancing toward the Fourteenth. These brigades were still on the far side of the Emmitsburg Road, so he had time to prepare for their attack.

Looking back to the north, he saw regiment after regiment of boys in blue pour into the breached area and masses of men converge in a sea of humanity. The advance of the enemy came to a halt and a fierce hand-to-hand struggle ensued. He looked back to his two regiments and witnessed many rebel soldiers throwing down their rifles and putting up their arms. They had had enough. They were passing through his lines and being directed to the rear as prisoners.

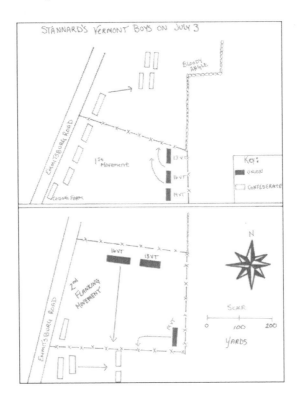

Many of those that wore gray were retreating across the open fields they had recently crossed with hopes of breaking through the Union line. Their hopes were now dashed and they were scurrying back to safety, walking through the carnage of an ill-advised attack. Their dead and wounded comrades lay all around them.

General Stannard knew the assault had been turned back. He now turned his attention to the two brigades advancing on his left. The Fourteenth was on good ground behind trees and brush that was slightly elevated, affording them a natural breastwork for protection. Stannard sent orders for the Sixteenth to do an about face and return to their original position, to aid the Fourteenth in repulsing this new attack. As the two rebel brigades entered the low ground of Plum Run, they came under fire from the Fourteenth. They were also being pounded by Union artillery. There were thickets along the banks of Plum Run that afforded some shelter for the besieged troops. From this position they began returning fire toward the Fourteenth.

Stannard watched the Sixteenth turn about and cross the field at the double quick. They reached a position to the right of the Fourteenth. There they halted momentarily, and then the whole regiment charged with bayonets at the Confederates in the thickets. This sudden charge caught the enemy by surprise and they quickly threw down their arms and surrendered. The attack was stymied. The remaining rebels started retreating across the fields towards the safety of their own lines.

Stannard looked to the west and all he saw were beaten men returning across a field of broken bodies and charred cannons. There were no more troops advancing. It appeared the attack was over. His nine-month boys had faced combat and had held firm. They had earned their battle scars and could proudly tell of this event when they returned home before the end of the month. They now had a story they could recall well into their old age. In the month that their time in service was to expire, they did not shirk their duty or ask to be placed in reserve. They stood face to face and exchanged shots with an enemy that had not been defeated since this war began, but it seemed to General Stannard that today that enemy was served the bitter taste of defeat. Vermont served her nation well. Stannard was damn proud of his brigade.

⚓

General Meade was in headquarters receiving the figures from his officers that had helped repel the charge. While waiting for all the reports, he found himself thinking of the events of the day. He had ridden earlier in the day to the assault, but had arrived as it had been completely repulsed. He looked across the fields and saw the carnage that was once Lee's mighty army. There were dead bodies strewn everywhere and he could hear moans from the wounded, moans for water and help. As hardened as he was, it tore at his insides. He was a father and a husband. Across these fields, he saw dead sons, husbands and fathers and he saw a great heartache that would soon be felt all across the South. He viewed the ground between Emmitsburg Road and the stone wall. There was no grass or wheat to see, only bodies. His heart fell at that moment.

He remembered speaking with Lt. Haskell soon after he arrived. Haskell had informed him that both Hancock and Gibbon had been severely wounded and were taken from the field. The rest of their conversation was lost to Meade. Too much death and destruction.

General Pleasanton wanted an immediate attack planned. He told Meade to advance the infantry while he rode around with his cavalry and got in the rear of Lee's army. His assertion was we could rout Lee's army within one week. He was quite certain Lee had expended all of his artillery supply. He felt Lee had rolled the dice on one grand charge and had lost. Now was a moment for Meade to attack. Meade could not agree with this assessment. He was unsure of Lee's intentions. The problem he faced was his army was set up to fight defensively and could not quickly be arranged for offensive operations. Meade had sent units from all parts of the field to help repel the rebel charge on Hancock's line. Brigades and regiments were scattered all over the battlefield. The Sixth Corps, his largest and the one having taken the least amount of casualties during the past three days had only three of its eight brigades together near Little Round Top. He would be unable to have the Sixth or any corps ready to attack before night fell.

As he had ridden south along the lines, the men rose up to cheer him. This gratified and humbled him. He wanted to cheer the men for the work they had done. Yes, he had been in command, but they faced Lee's legions and for two straight days had turned them back. The Army of the Potomac had just accomplished a victory for the first time in this war, but it had come at a tremendous price. He had stopped by one field hospital and saw the surgeons in blood soaked clothes attending to the wounded. Piles of amputated limbs spoke of their grizzly work.

Meade felt he had done enough on this day. His men were tired from the forced marches before the battle and two days of hard fighting. They needed rest, supplies and food. He could ask no more of them on this day.

An aide approached."Sir, we have the final figures from the lines. We have taken 3,200 Confederates captive and have 28 of their battle flags in our possession. Their dead are too numerous to estimate. Our corps commanders report 55,000 infantry troops available for duty."

"Thank you, Captain," said Meade."You are dismissed. I wish to be left alone for a bit."

Meade was tired. He needed to write to his wife and try to put all that he had witnessed into some perspective. His mind was beyond exhaustion and it would be cathartic to confide in her. He would let her know the army won a decisive victory, but did not annihilate the Confederate army. There was still work to be done to extricate them from northern soil. He of course would let her know her son George was well. He wanted her to know that at one point he felt he should be laid up with mental excitement from the strain of command, but it never hindered him in doing his duty during the battle. He hoped she would be proud of him.

Part VII

Chasing the Ghost

CHAPTER 25

July 4th

THE RAIN STARTED FALLING around noon. It began as a light, steady rain, soon turning into a deluge of heavy downpours. It was as if all the angels of heaven were weeping for the blood that had been spilled over these fields during the past three days. As hard as it rained, the carnage left on the fields of Gettysburg would not be washed away by one storm. The smell of death and rotting flesh lingered in the air. The rain only succeeded in making the men in the field miserable.

In the morning, General Meade had sent regiments forward to probe for the enemy's position. He discovered they had pulled their forces back, but were still heavily entrenched west and north of Gettysburg. Would Lee attack again? He did not know. He knew his men needed food and ammunition. He would order no attacks today.

The terrible task of burying the dead was being undertaken by his men after a flag of truce had been sent from the enemy so they could recover their wounded. Many trenches were dug. The bodies were separated between Union and Confederate, and then dumped into their respective trenches and covered over. They did not want Johnny buried in the same grave as their own. Body counts were sketchy, especially among the Confederate dead.

General Meade had prepared a note to be sent to his army and to Washington. His intent was to congratulate the men for their victory and to inform them there was more work to be done. One sentence in particular would be damning to him in Washington. He wrote,"Our task is not yet accomplished, and the commanding general looks to the army for greater efforts to drive from our soil every vestige of the presence of the invader."

This sentence was quite disturbing to President Lincoln. He wanted the enemy destroyed before they could cross the Potomac. This was the only way Lincoln saw of ending this war. He wasn't concerned with capturing ground; he wanted Lee's army destroyed so Richmond would be unable to continue waging war. Lincoln was vocal in his displeasure to his cabinet.

Meade at the front was unaware of Lincoln's irritation. He was busy taking care of the daily military matters necessary to sustain an army in the field. His seven corps needed to be regrouped if he intended to pursue any offensive maneuvers. The day saw regiments and brigades marching up and down Cemetery Ridge to be reunited with their respective corps. In the afternoon the marches were bogged down by mud. Nevertheless, they continued until all units were aligned within their own corps.

Unsure of what to do next, Meade called another council of war to be held that evening at headquarters. He invited his seven corps commanders, General Pleasanton and General Warren to the meeting. His chief of staff, General Butterfield would also be in attendance. With Hancock wounded,General Hays was now in charge of the Second Corps.

ஒ•கூ)(ஐ•ல

"Gentlemen," started Meade."Thank you for coming tonight. Again, we are faced with serious issues, and I desire your input. From reports all up and down the line, Lee is still in force across these fields. Whether he intends to attack again, I can't say. I do know from intelligence, he used the last of his reserves in yesterday's battle. He has no other forces available to him, and Richmond will be sending him no help. Our army has fought magnificently these past three days. It seems we have 55,000 infantry troops available for duty. You are all closer to the men than I am. I am posing four questions tonight and I will listen to your answers. Remember, we are still under orders to cover Washington and Baltimore. General Butterfield will read the questions one at a time and you will respond from junior to senior in rank as is customary. Dan, you have the floor."

Butterfield read the first question, seated at the table. Besides reading the questions, he had to record the answers."Shall the army remain here?" asked Butterfield.

There was some discussion before the vote. No one was willing to give up the field. They had earned a great victory and did not wish to leave the field for Lee to recapture.

General Warren spoke up."I believe we should remain until we see what Lee is doing."

This opinion was soon agreed by the others and became the answer to the first question.

Butterfield asked the second question."If we remain here, shall we assume the offensive?"

Many spoke against crossing the same fields Pickett had been cut down on yesterday. They felt the Confederates had a strong defensive line on Seminary Ridge. There was a resounding no to this question.

Butterfield asked the third question."Do you deem it expedient to move towards Williamsport through Emmitsburg?"

The discussion was now focused on the movement of the army to cut Lee off from crossing the Potomac. This proposed track would keep the army between Lee's army and Washington. It appeared to be the wisest choice, for it allowed Meade to attempt to cut off Lee while safeguarding Washington. The answer was a unanimous yes.

Butterfield asked the fourth question."Shall we pursue the enemy if he is retreating on his direct line of retreat?"

This was discussed, some favoring cavalry and others a mix of cavalry and infantry. General Birney voted against any direct pursuit. After the discussion, the consensus for this question became direct pursuit with cavalry only.

Meade spoke after listening to his commanders' vote."It seems to be a unanimous decision to remain on the field and not to pursue an offensive posture until we see what Lee is planning. I shall get with my staff and discuss marching orders for each corps if and when Lee pulls back. Our intent will be to get to the Potomac River before Lee. If successful, we might just trap his army against the river. Thank you for your time tonight. You're dismissed. See that your troops have food and ammunition. Keep your pickets out tonight. We don't want any surprises from the enemy. General Warren, wait here while the others leave. We need to talk."

Warren nodded in acknowledgement. Meade waited until the room was empty. Then he turned to Warren and began to speak.

"Lee must be as tired as we are. He threw everything he had against us for two days, and we held our position. The men fought as if the fate of the nation was in their hands."

"I believe it was, sir," responded Warren."There is talk amongst many in the North to seek an armistice and end this war. They are weary of the death tolls and a divided nation seems a better option than continuing this struggle. I think a victory by Lee on Northern soil may have furthered their cause."

"Only two generations from the revolution," said Meade."What would our grandfathers say of this war? Could they have foreseen of this nation tearing itself apart? And over what? Slavery." Meade shook his head, and then took a deep breath."It's an institution that has no place in the modern world. How can we live in a nation where all men are created equal, yet allow slavery to exist? The Emancipation Proclamation has made it clear this war is not only about saving the Union, but about eradicating slavery and creating a nation that will live up to the ideals of the Declaration of Independence. It's a war we have to win."

"Yes, it does seem the writers of the Constitution had to compromise on slavery to get the document signed and ratified. The problem became the new states formed after the Constitution was written. Many from the South wanted to spread slavery into these new states, which was against the spirit of the language in the Constitution."

"And this generation has to pay the price in bloodshed," said Meade. The words hung in the air. Neither general seemed able to speak. Meade walked over to the table with the map. Warren followed.

Looking at the map, Meade spoke,"I want you to make a reconnaissance in force tomorrow with General Sedgwick and his corps. They took very few casualties during the battle, being held mostly in reserve. You are to feel Lee's army out and see if there are vulnerable areas for us to attack. Don't bring on an engagement if he is still heavily entrenched. Let me know what you find."

"Which way do you wish us to move?" asked Warren.

Meade looked at the map. He pointed to the Fairfield Gap in the South Mountain range."Head toward the Fairfield Gap. It is the shortest route between Gettysburg and Hagerstown. I want to know if Lee is defending it and how heavily. If it is open, we can send one wing of our army down that road in an attempt to overtake Lee. I hope to fight the enemy before he gets into Virginia."

"We'll be on the move in the morning," said Warren.

CHAPTER 26

July 5th

GENERAL DAN BUTTERFIELD WOKE UP to the sound of rain on the canvas of his tent. It was still dark outside, so he knew it was early morning. He hadn't slept well. He had heard from a reliable source that General Meade had asked three different officers to be his Chief of Staff, but they all turned him down. He wondered why he had held his position after Meade had succeeded Hooker. Now he knew. It was hard to keep secrets in an army. People talk. Butterfield and Meade did not care for each other and Butterfield was unsure why he was retained. He had been treated with indifference by Meade and left out of many of the strategy sessions. Meade only wanted him around to write orders for his corps commanders and take notes at meetings. He was a secretary with an important title.

What made matters worse was Sickles being wounded and sent to Washington. Butterfield had no allies with which to drink and commiserate. He heard Sickles would lose a leg. Butterfield hoped the surgery would be successful and postoperative infection would not take his friend. It seemed more troops died from wounds and infection while in the hospitals than on the battlefield. He hoped he never ended up in the hospital. He was recovering from a small wound the day before, but it did not require a stay in the hospital. Physically, he would be fine.

He would stay clear of Meade, offering no opinions or suggestions. He would do his duty to the barest minimum. Besides, he rationalized, he might be replaced when this battle was over. He would do nothing to jeopardize his position, even though he would probably not hold it much longer. He would wait for the right time to get back at General George Meade.

✎∗∘∗✎

General Warren was back at headquarters late in the afternoon. He reported to Meade what he encountered at the Fairfield Gap with the Sixth Corps.

"Sir," Warren began, "we found the enemy heavily entrenched at Fairfield Gap. General Sedgwick ordered an attack to see if we could dislodge them. They put up a fierce defense. After a few hours, Sedgwick called off the attack. He pulled his corps back and is deployed on the road below the Gap. He does not wish to attack again for he feels the Gap is a very strong position that can be defended by a small force of the enemy. He awaits further orders."

"Well, it appears that route is not a viable option to take," replied Meade. He studied the map with his left arm folded across his chest and his right hand on his chin. "We'll follow Lee by a flank movement. We'll march southeast to Frederick and then move westerly to Middletown. This is the route voted on by the corps commanders last night. I thought I might attempt a direct attack at Lee's rear, but it doesn't seem prudent. This rain will hopefully slow Lee down and we'll be able to catch him before he crosses the Potomac into Virginia."

"Two days of rain have turned the roads into mud and the marching is slow," said Warren. "Perhaps it is hampering Lee as you suggest."

"The other issue confronting me is the loss of Reynolds and Hancock. I could count on them to lead an independent or wing command. I trusted their judgment. As of now, I have three experienced corps commanders, Slocum, Sedgwick and Howard. Slocum and Sedgwick will follow orders given to them, but they are not strong enough to be assertive when necessary. Howard and the Eleventh Corps have proven abysmal. If I split the army into three wings for marching, each one of these commanders will lead a wing. I'm not sure they will be aggressive enough."

"They're what you've got," said Warren. "You've got to play the hand that's dealt to you."

Meade changed the subject. "I've received some disturbing news from Washington. It seems our good friend Dan Sickles has proclaimed to everyone that he is the savior of Gettysburg. His actions on July 2 helped save the Army of Potomac from certain defeat."

Warren shook his head. "You know better than that. Hell, he disobeyed your orders and put his corps as well as the left flank of the army in jeopardy. His damn corps got its ass whipped on July 2!"

"Doesn't matter now. He's got the ear of the press, the politicians and all his cronies. He put his spin on his actions, and he'll be deemed a hero. Hell, he lost a leg leading his men. Washington has a new hero. I'll never be able to reprimand him now. Perhaps he'll be named the new commander of the army after this battle is concluded. He is certainly connected to some powerful people."

"He'd be worse in command than Hooker," blurted Warren."I don't envy your position now. You'll have to tread carefully with your after battle reports. Mustn't make a 'hero' look bad."

"As if I didn't realize this," said Meade."I'll get marching orders to Butterfield so he can write them out and dispatch them to the corps commanders. We need to cut Lee off before he slips into Virginia."

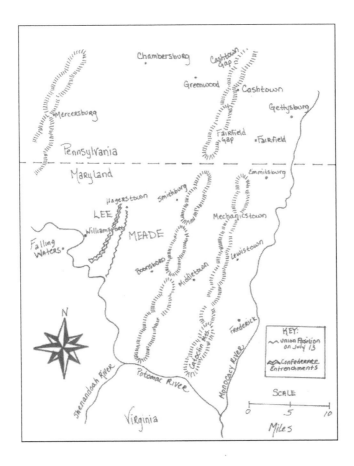

CHAPTER 27

Mid-July

THE RAINS HAD HAMPERED the marches of the Army of the Potomac. Muddy roads made for slow, miserable progress, but the rain had also swollen the Potomac River. Lee and his army were still on the north side of the river. Union cavalry had destroyed one bridge at Falling Waters and the ford at Williamsport, which had been easily crossed on foot weeks before, was now under thirteen feet of rushing water.

By July 12th, the Union Army was in front of the enemy east of Williamsport. Lee's army was heavily entrenched on high ground above Williamsport. There had been skirmishes between the two armies all day, but no major assault. From reports, Meade ascertained Lee was in a formidable position, but Meade wished to attack early on the morning of the 13th.

Meade again called a council of war with his corps commanders late in the afternoon of July 12th. He decided he would let their vote settle the issue. He proposed a reconnaissance in force all along the line in the morning, which would be converted into a full-scale assault if a weakness was discovered in the line of the enemy. He wasn't sure where the attack would be, but he was willing to take the consequences of this bold move. The corps commanders voted five to two not to attack. They said their men were tired from the marches and they would like another day to scout Lee's lines. Meade was not happy with the vote, but he would hold to his word.

On July 13th, Meade decided to act. He sent orders out for the Second, Fifth, Sixth and Twelfth Corps to conduct a reconnaissance in force at 7 a.m.

on the morning of July 14th. Meade also received a telegram from Halleck in response to Meade's telegram after the council of war and the vote not to attack:

> Yours of 5:00 p.m. is received. You are strong enough to attack and defeat the enemy before he can effect a crossing. Act upon your own judgment and make your generals execute your orders. Call no council of war. It is proverbial that councils of war never fight. Reinforcements are pushed on as rapidly as possible. Do not let the enemy escape.

It must be nice to fight the war from Washington, thought Meade. There are no natural elements to contend with like heat, rain and muddy roads. People aren't shooting at you either. He knew Halleck had come up through the ranks and had served his time in the field, but all that experience seemed to be forgotten when entering the realm of Washington. Meade had not sought this job. He did not seek glory like McClellan or Hooker. He was an engineer and he enjoyed designing and building structures that had some useful purpose. He was proud of the lighthouses he had helped build. They would stand along the coast for many years, signaling to ships at sea. This war gnawed at him. It was not only tearing the country apart, it was destroying a generation of young men.

There would be more bloodshed in the morning. If fate decided to smile on the Army of the Potomac, perhaps they would capture Lee's army that was pinned against the Potomac River. But Meade knew a trapped animal was the most deadly when attacked. It would not be an easy assault. His army would be the one attacking uphill against a well-fortified position. Some of his commanders spoke against attacking at all. They spoke of the great victory at Gettysburg and how ordering this attack on Lee's entrenched army might tarnish it. Meade had witnessed the debacle at Fredericksburg, when Burnside threw brigade after brigade against a well-fortified position on high ground. The Union army was cut to pieces on the slopes before Marye's Height, where Lee's outnumbered army held against superior numbers. This ground reminded Meade of Fredericksburg and now he was making the decision to make a similar attack. Was it the pressure from Washington that made former commanders attack when it seemed prudent not to? Meade was feeling the heat from above. He would attack and damn the consequences. If it was a miserable failure and Lee's army was not dislodged or captured, Meade would most certainly be replaced. *Damn this job*, he uttered to himself.

ॐ☃☙☩☜ॐ

Meade was sitting in headquarters when an aide handed him a telegram from Halleck. Meade was not sure he wanted to read this. It would be stinging, maybe even damning. Perhaps Meade was being replaced. The attack had stepped off at 7 a.m.this morning as planned, only to discover that Lee and his army had crossed the Potomac during the night. He had escaped into Virginia. Meade had allowed a vote by his commanders to put off the attack planned for July 13th. This did not play well with Halleck. Meade was quite sure Halleck was furious about Lee escaping. He took the telegram, opened it and read:

> I need hardly to say to you that the escape of Lee's Army without another battle has created great dissatisfaction in the mind of the president and it will require an active, energetic pursuit on your part to remove the impression that it has not been sufficiently active heretofore.

He felt his temper rise from within. There's no pleasing these bastards, he thought. I defeat Lee on the fields of Gettysburg and drive him from northern soil, but it's not enough. The President has tried and convicted me and found me guilty. Damn good thing guillotines are in France. The hell with them all, I'll send in a request to be relieved of command. I don't need this shit.

He fired off a telegram to Halleck. He would not allow himself to cool down before he wrote his reply. In it, he wrote these words:

> *The censure of the President conveyed in your dispatch of 1 p.m. this day is, in my judgment, so undeserved that I feel compelled most respectfully to ask to be immediately relieved from command of the army.*

They can find someone else to be their whipping boy. As soon as he finished writing the telegram, he gave it to an aide and told him to have it wired to Halleck immediately. He thought of his recently departed friend, John Reynolds. Reynolds had spoken of being offered the position of commander, but he would only accept if the strings were cut to Washington. This was not acceptable to the leaders in the capitol. Meade now understood why Reynolds turned down the offer to command.

General Andrew Humphries, his newly appointed Chief of Staff, entered the room. He had recently replaced Dan Butterfield, who was probably in Washington now with his old friend Dan Sickles. Meade would not miss either of these men.

"Sir," began Humphries,"we have reports from the cavalry at Falling Waters. They fought against a stubborn rear guard that kept them away from the river. This action by the enemy enabled the balance of Lee's army to get across the river. We did capture 1500 more prisoners, but it seems fair to say there will be no more fighting on this side of the Potomac."

Meade stared at Humphries. He did not wish to snap at his new Chief of Staff. He was only reporting information, but it was information Meade did not wish to hear at this moment. Meade changed the tenor of the conversation."How do you assess the outcome of the battle?" asked Meade.

Humphries thought for a moment before answering."Well, sir, I see it as a great victory for the army. We have sent a message to Lee that he is not invincible. I've heard that you are being praised in the papers for defeating Lee and chasing him back to Virginia."

"Have you heard that Sickles has proclaimed himself as the savior of Gettysburg?" asked Meade.

"Yes, I've heard that. It's a damn lie, one that only a shameless self-promoter would perpetuate, but that is Sickles to the core. Remember, I was one of his division commanders, and I will tell you, as a fellow West Pointer, what he did on July 2nd, when he advanced his corps, was to put his men in an untenable position, with both flanks hanging in the air. Longstreet obliterated the Third Corps and completely overran the advanced position. The reinforcements you sent to the southern end of the field helped to halt Longstreet's advance and restore the line. No, sir, Sickles is no savior of Gettysburg. Your commanders will testify to that."

"But Sickles has already portrayed his version to Washington and they are lauding him as a hero. How the hell do I counter that?" asked Meade.

"Just tell your version of the events, leaving out any vitriol aimed at Sickles. Your tireless efforts on July 2nd, getting units to the proper place at just the right moment, speak for themselves. You will be supported by the reports of your corps commanders. Washington cannot ignore all the voices that will commend you. Give Sickles enough rope and someday he will hang himself. It's inevitable," said Humphries.

"Not necessarily inevitable. He's a slippery bastard and has weaseled out of shady situations before. Nothing seems to stick to him." Meade walked over to the window and looked outside. He took a deep breath and then spoke."I've asked to be relieved of command. The President is disappointed in my inability to trap Lee before he escaped to Virginia. They can find someone else to whip."

"I hope you'll reconsider. You've got the backing of all the commanders and the troops will remember you as the general who defeated Lee. You can't desert them now."

"The telegram is on its way to General Halleck. He'll have it before the sun goes down. I'm tired of Washington's meddling and demanding the impossible," said Meade."I want you to gather on paper the disposition of each corps. I'll not have the new commander step into this job unaware of the condition of the army. I was faced with a similar situation a little over two weeks ago. Hard to issue orders with no information about the status of each corps. At least the army won't be spread out all over Maryland."

"I'll do as you order, but I hope I'll be putting together this information for you as my commander."

"Most unlikely," said Meade."My die is cast. Good luck in your new position. If you had more time in rank you could be replacing me."

"I'm still settling into being a Major General and a Chief of Staff. Hell, I've never even been a Corps Commander so I don't see myself being considered for command of the army. I'll start on my reports and have them ready for you as soon as possible."

"Thanks, Andrew," said Meade."We await the winds of Washington."

❧·ಌಜ·❧

The winds came later in the day in the form of another telegram from Halleck. Meade found the language in this message more offensive than the earlier telegram. He read the paragraph that irked him again:

My telegram stating the disappointment of the president at the escape of Lee's Army was not intended as a censure, but as a stimulus to an active pursuit. It is not deemed a sufficient cause for your application to be relieved.

What the hell do they think I've been doing since July 5th, sitting on my laurels in Gettysburg? They think my pursuit hasn't been active enough. Meade shook his head in disgust. He was not to be replaced, but he knew his reputation was tarnished in Washington. He would go for a ride on his horse to clear his mind. Then he would write to his wife. His future prospects seemed bleak.

EPILOGUE

BY MARCH 1864, the two armies sat across from each other, separated by the Rappahannock River, roughly in the same positions they had occupied in May of 1863. The spring campaign season would soon be underway.

Meade, who was still in command of the Army of the Potomac, had been ordered to Washington on March 3rd. There were meetings concerning the reorganization of the army. It was at these meetings he learned that General Ulysses Grant was coming east to assume command of the army. Meade was certain he would be reassigned to a new position.

On March 8th, General Grant arrived in Washington to receive his promotion to Lieutenant General. In the history of the Republic there had only been two men who had attained this rank. The first was George Washington; the other was Winfield Scott, hero of the Mexican War. With his promotion, Grant was now senior in rank to General Halleck. Grant would now be in charge of the entire Union Army. He made it clear to Lincoln, he would not command from Washington, but he would remain in the field with his army. Lincoln agreed to this condition. He wanted the conqueror of Vicksburg to come east and defeat Lee's army in Virginia. If Grant wanted to command from the field, well, Lincoln would not object.

Grant kept Meade in charge of the Army of the Potomac. Meade would remain as commander until the end of the war one year later.

Meade arrived in Washington on March 4th. While there, he was summoned to appear before the Joint Committee on the Conduct of the War. Meade was unaware that Sickles and Doubleday had already testified before the committee and bought grave charges against Meade. The most damaging charge was that Meade never intended to fight at Gettysburg, instead he wanted the army to withdraw to Pipe Creek. They used the words from the Pipe Creek Circular written in the early hours of July 1st, to portray Meade's intentions.

On March 3rd, Republican Senator Morton Wilkinson of Minnesota gave a speech before the Senate. In it were these words:

> *I am told, and I believe it can be proven, that before the fight commenced at Gettysburg the order went forth from the commander of the army to retreat; and but for the single fact that one of the corps commanders had got into a fight before the dispatch reached him, the whole army would undoubtedly have been retreating.*

Meade heard of these charges as he was circulating around Washington. When he came before the Committee, he was assured there were no charges against him. The Committee was taking evidence so they could write a history of the war. A portion of Meade's testimony is presented here to show he was aware of the subterfuge against him:

> *Early in the evening of July 1st, I received a report from General Hancock . . .giving me such an account of a position in the neighborhood of Gettysburg, which could be occupied by my army . . .Therefore, without any reference to, but entirely ignoring the preliminary order (Pipe Creek), which was a mere contingent one, and intended only to be executed under certain circumstances which had not occurred . . . the army was ordered to concentrate on the field of Gettysburg. . . I dwell particularly upon the point of this order, in consequence of its having been reported on the floor of the Senate that an order to retreat had been given by me.*

It is apparent from his testimony Meade was aware of the speech on the senate floor. He did his best before the Committee to show how the Pipe Creek line was a contingency plan. The events at Gettysburg unfolded while he was gathering his army and while he was new to command. As is in most cases, deciding what should have been done after a battle has been fought is much easier than making the decisions as a battle is in progress.

Dan Butterfield also testified before the Committee. He testified on March 25th, 1864, twenty days after Meade appeared. Butterfield also had an axe to grind with Meade and his testimony also painted Meade as a timid warrior, not wishing to fight at Gettysburg, but desiring to retreat.

Meade's thoughts on appearing before the Committee can be summed up in his own words from this letter to his wife:

> *Persons like Sickles and Doubleday can, by distorting and twisting facts, and giving a false coloring, induce the press and public for a time, and almost immediately, to take away the character of a man who up to that time had stood high in their estimation.*

Granted, Meade did not stand high in the estimation of either Sickles or Doubleday, but Meade was on target when he asserted how false or twisted testimony could damage a man's character.

The Committee took testimony from various commanders until February of 1865. The charge that Meade never intended to fight at Gettysburg was refuted by the Committee. They found there was no credible proof that Meade intended to retreat except as a contingency plan. By the time the Committee had heard all the testimony and were reporting their findings, the war was coming to an end and Lincoln's assassination dominated the news. The findings of the Committee were no longer relevant.

My attempt in this book has been to show the battle of Gettysburg through the eyes of several Union generals. They were forced to make decisions quickly as the battle unfolded before them. They not only had to fight against Lee and his army, but often had to fight against each other. In this battle they made better decisions than their opponent, bringing about the victory on the fields of Gettysburg.

AFTERWORD

The battle of Gettysburg is considered by historians as the turning point of the Civil War. Some have termed it as the beginning of the long retreat toward Appomattox. It was a long retreat, with many more casualties as the war continued until April 1865. It was at Appomattox, in April 1865, where General Robert E. Lee signed the terms of surrender for the Army of Northern Virginia, witnessed by General Ulysses Grant, head of the Union army.

The battle of Gettysburg was called the battle that neither side wanted at a place neither side chose. But once it began, neither side backed down. Men on both sides had a notion this could be the most important battle of the war. There was enough bravery on both sides to lend credit to this point. Gettysburg turned out to be the bloodiest battle fought in this country. Those three days in July saw approximately 7,700 soldiers die on both sides with casualties exceeding 53,000 men. It is not surprising that the Gettysburg Battlefield is one of the most visited National Parks each year.

This book tells the story of the battle from the perspective of several Union Generals. They were not the only generals who fought there, nor were they the only ones who performed heroically. It is not a complete history of the battle, nor does it intend to be. Battles are fought by men, and as with any human endeavor involving numerous people, there are those that work well together and those that do not.

General Joseph Hooker—After being relieved of command of the Army of the Potomac, he was transferred to the Army of the Cumberland in Tennessee. He fought well at Lookout Mountain and at Chattanooga. He was assigned to command the XX Corps during Sherman's Atlanta Campaign, but asked to be relieved when General Howard was promoted over him to command the Army of Tennessee. He was then named the commander of the Northern Department from October 1864, until the end of the war. His headquarters were in Cincinnati, Ohio. He died in October 1879, and is buried in Spring Grove Cemetery, Cincinnati, Ohio.

General Daniel Butterfield—Sickles and Butterfield were the two most damaging witnesses to testify before the Joint Committee on the Conduct of the War against General Meade. It was their testimony that Meade never intended to fight at Gettysburg and as early as July 1, Meade was preparing to retreat to Pipe Creek. They were both called to appear in front of the Committee before Meade. Butterfield went west to be reunited with Hooker, once again as Chief of Staff. He then commanded the Third Division of the XX Corps during the Atlanta Campaign. Illness prevented him from seeing the campaign through. He is recognized as the composer of"Taps", which is played at all military funerals. He died in 1901 and is buried at West Point.

General John Reynolds—His body was sent home to Lancaster, Pennsylvania, where he was buried on July 4, 1863. There are three statues of him at Gettysburg. Kate Hewitt had made an agreement with Reynolds that if he were killed in the war, she would join a convent. After his burial, she traveled to Emmitsburg, Maryland and fulfilled her pledge.

General Abner Doubleday—Doubleday had an axe to grind with Meade, due to being ousted as I Corps Commander. It was for this reason he spoke against Meade's conduct during the battle before the Joint Committee. Many historians have credited Doubleday for his fierce defensive stand northwest of Gettysburg, preventing Lee from occupying the heights on the south side of town. Reynolds had told Doubleday he intended to hold the ground as long as possible so the rest of the Union army could take possession of the heights. Doubleday carried out Reynolds intentions exceedingly well. For whatever reason, Howard reported that Doubleday's corps broke first and jeopardized the position of Howard's corps. I do not find this to be the case in all I have read concerning the battle.

Doubleday spent the rest of the war in Washington, D.C., where he was in charge of courts martial. He has been credited with the invention of baseball, but this seems to be more myth than reality. His picture does hang in the Baseball Hall of Fame in Cooperstown, New York. He died in 1893 and is buried in Arlington National Cemetery.

General Darius Couch—After his resignation from command of the Second Corps, Couch was assigned to lead the newly formed Army of the Susquehanna in Pennsylvania. He is credited with the defense of Harrisburg and not allowing it to fall into enemy hands. After the battle of Gettysburg, his army aided in the pursuit of General Lee. Couch continued his military service until the war's end. He died in 1897 and is buried in Mount Pleasant Cemetery in Taunton, Massachusetts.

General Winfield Scott Hancock—The wound he received on July 3rd made it difficult for him to ride in the saddle without pain. It became such a nuisance, that he gave up field command in November 1864. He remained in the service for the remainder of his life. He was the presidential nominee in 1880 for the Democratic Party. He lost the election to Republican James Garfield. He died in 1886, while still on active duty as commander of the Department of the East. Hancock the Superb is buried in Montgomery Cemetery located in West Norriton Township, Pennsylvania.

General Dan Sickles—One of the more controversial figures to survive the Civil War. His assertions in Washington that he was the hero and savior of Gettysburg, were probably true in his mind. In later years when people asked him why there was no monument of him at Gettysburg, he replied that the whole battlefield was his monument. Later in life he was head of the New York Monuments Commission. Strangely enough, much money had disappeared from the fund while he was in charge. He was dismissed from this position in 1912. There is one monument in the Trostle farm area that was supposed to contain his sculptured head, but after this incident, there was not enough money, so the monument stands, headless. He died in 1914. His shattered leg is in the Smithsonian.

General George Meade—Came under heavy criticism after The Confederate army crossed the Potomac and"escaped" into Virginia to fight another day. He took command of the Army of the Potomac on June 28th, two days before the battle began, not sure where his army was or what

General Hooker's plans were. He lead his army to victory riding amongst the lines and getting troops to those areas of the field, where they were most needed to stem Confederate advances. He made the crucial decisions that put the Army of the Potomac in the best position to win the battle. He remained in charge of the Army of the Potomac until the end of the war, serving under General Grant. By the time the Meade Hearings came to their findings, the war was over and the news of the Lincoln assassination dominated the country. Meade was neither condemned for his failures at Gettysburg, nor was he exonerated by the Committee. After the war he served in several departments during Reconstruction. He stayed on active duty until his death in 1872. He is buried in Laurel Hill Cemetery in Philadelphia.

General John Sedgwick—His Sixth Corps suffered few casualties during the Gettysburg campaign, due to being further east from the field than any other corps when the battle began. The Sixth Corps did not get to the field until the afternoon of July 2nd, and was put in a reserve position. When General Grant reorganized the army in the spring of 1864, Sedgwick was retained as a corps commander. On May 9, 1864, at Spotsylvania, Virginia, he was placing his artillery, when a sharpshooter's bullet hit him just under the left eye. He died instantly.

General Oliver Howard—In September 1863, Howard and his Eleventh Corps were transferred to the West and put under the command of General Sherman. Howard performed his duties so well he was named commander of the Army of Tennessee. After the war his work turned to aiding freed slaves. He was appointed first commissioner of the Freedman's Bureau. He was instrumental in establishing Howard University. He retired from the Army in 1894 and he died in 1909.

General Henry Slocum—As with the Eleventh Corps, Slocum and the Twelfth Corps were transferred to the West in September 1863. He fought under General Sherman on his"March to the Sea". He resigned his commission when the war ended and resumed his work in law and politics. He served three terms in Congress. He died in 1894.

General Gouverneur Warren—Was promoted to Major General after the battle and became commander of the II Corps, replacing the wounded General Hancock. He held this position until March 1864, when Hancock returned to command his old corps. The V Corps became Warren's next command, which he led through the Siege of Petersburg and the Appomattox campaign. In April 1865, at the Battle of Five Forks, he was relieved of command by General Phil Sheridan, for moving too slowly into an attack. After the war he requested a court of inquiry to exonerate him for Sheridan's actions, which he felt were incorrect and unjustified. President Grant refused all his requests, but his successor, President Hayes, ordered a court convened in 1879. The court heard from over 100 witnesses. The court found that Sheridan's actions were unjustified. Warren died in 1882 in Newport, Rhode Island, and was buried in civilian clothes. He is honored with a statue on Little Round Top.

Lieutenant Stephen Brown—The young lieutenant with the 13th Vermont, who was ordered to surrender his sword for disobeying orders and retrieving water for his men, survived the battle. The men of his regiment honored him in the 1880's by having his likeness adorn their statue on Cemetery Ridge, where it stands today. There he stands tall and proud with a camp hatchet at his feet, signifying the hatchet he carried into battle after surrendering his sword to the cavalry guard.

That damned white house and barn!—These buildings sat between Cemetery Ridge and Seminary Ridge. They were burned on July 3rd by Union forces to keep Confederate sharpshooters from using them as cover. The buildings and land belonged to William Bliss and his family. They lost everything during the battle. They sold the land to Nicholas Codori for $1000.00 and moved to New York to start over. They put in a claim for damages to the government in the amount of $3256.08. They never received any compensation for their losses.

About the Author

Kerry Hotaling has been a member of the Friends of Gettysburg since 2001. He has built historic fences on the battlefield with his son since 2007 during the annual volunteer workday. He has also lit candles on the graves during illumination night in November. Mr. Hotaling is also the author of *What They Endured, What They Wrought*. He enjoys curling through the winter months. "Good curling."He is married with two children and resides in western Massachusetts.

CPSIA information can be obtained at www.ICGtesting.com
Printed in the USA
BVOW03s1705310515

402466BV00002B/4/P